THE DEVIL'S CARD

THE DEVIL'S CARD

MARY MAHER

ST. MARTIN'S PRESS
NEW YORK

Library of Congress Cataloging-in-Publication Data

Maher, Mary.
   The devil's card / Mary Maher.
      p.   cm.
   ISBN 0-312-07715-7
   I. Title.
   PS3563.A358D48   1992
   813'.54—dc20   92-1268
                                                                   CIP

First published in Great Britain by Brandon Book Publishers Ltd.

10 9 8 7 6 5 4 3 2

Acknowledgements

Much of the material for this book was drawn from *The Crime of the Century* by Henry M. Hunt, published in 1889. The rest of the story was pieced together largely from the trial accounts published in the newspapers at the time, particularly those in the *Chicago Tribune*, and from the works of John Devoy. I am greatly indebted to the helpful staff of the Chicago Public Library and the National Library of Ireland, and to my niece, Patricia Maher, who is a superb researcher and second-hand bookshop sleuth.

I also relied heavily on Michael F. Funchion's excellent study, *Chicago's Irish Nationalists* (Arno Press), while other sources include *The Irish in Chicago* by Lawrence J. McCaffrey, Ellen Skerrett, Michael F. Funchion and Charles Fanning (University of Illinois Press); *Ethnic Chicago* by Melvin G. Holli and Peter d'A. Jones; *Labor's Story Untold* by Richard O. Boyer and Herbert M. Morais (United Electrical, Radio and Machine Worker's of America); *False Promises* by Stanley Aronowitz (McGraw-Hill) and, finally, many documents from the 19th-century Irish nationalist movement in Chicago which have survived in my family. The sections on Clare Abbey and on the 6,000 immigrants who died of ship fever in Grosse Island, Canada, are taken from Cecil Woodham-Smith's classic account of the Irish famine and its consequences, *The Great Hunger* (Four Square Books).

My deepest thanks to my sister Bonnie and to Maeve Binchy, for their encouragement and criticism, and to my brother Jerry, who suggested this book in the first place.

Those who know the story will see that I have trimmed some details and expanded others, but I have kept as close to the basic facts of the Cronin case as I could – that is to say, the facts that are known. The identities of Dr. Cronin's murderers have never been established beyond doubt, nor the circumstances fully explained, and many theories were put forward for years afterward. I think John Devoy was closest to the truth, and my version of how it might have been is based on his revelations in the *Gaelic American* in 1925.

To my family on both sides of the Atlantic

THE DEVIL'S CARD

Prologue
December, 1909

IT WAS DECEMBER again, twenty years to the month, perhaps the week, that he had left Chicago. Could that be? He couldn't quite remember. That in itself was something. The church he did remember, but churches didn't change. Certainly a cathedral, even one as young as this one, was built with a ponderous intimation of permanence.

He had timed his arrival very well. There was no sign of the cortège. The vestibule was empty, but there were a dozen signatures down already in the book of condolences. He went through the names rapidly, but there were none that he knew. He read the inscription at the top, "Holy Name Cathedral, Chicago, Illinois," and under it "Requiescat in Pace," the date, and "Andrew Foy." All the way up on the train he had considered whether he would sign, indicate his presence. It still seemed the only way that left the matter of a response open. He wrote "Thos. Martin" on the first vacant line and across from it his address in South Bend, Indiana. Then he slipped inside and stood well into the shadows at the back of the pews to deliberate the choice of a seat.

The cathedral smelled of candles and reminded him, as all churches did, of a tomb. For all its opulence it was clammy, and the ghost of his breath hung before him in the cold. The last time had been in May and the cathedral was so crowded people fainted in the heat and incense. There were tens of thousands then; it was impossible to get an accurate count in any of the papers. This time, he had no idea of who would come, what sort of ceremony would see Andy out. He was curious about that, too, a little. But certainly not tens of thousands, and certainly not a Solemn High Requiem with a choir

1

and five priests on the altar.

He stood still and waited, watching as people began to arrive. Most of them filed into the front pews before one of the side altars. When Tom was certain they were mourners, and not just the passing pious trade, he found a back pew in the same section and sat as nearly behind a pillar as he could. It would be foolish to expect that anyone would recognize him, but if he recognized any of them he couldn't be sure what his face would show.

Before he saw them he heard the shuffle and stamp of their feet in the vestibule. Up in the loft the organ sounded a few tentative notes and then the priest appeared on the side altar in his black stole and surplice. He was young, as fresh-faced as the altar boys who carried candles on either side of him, and he swept them along with him swiftly down the aisle. Tom turned and saw the bereaved like black wraiths at the door, shielding their coffin and waiting.

At the foot of the coffin the priest stopped and lifted his hand, sprinkling holy water. His voice rang like a new bell right through the hollow nave of the church: "Si iniquitates observaveris, Domine; Domine, quis sustinebat?" The organ began the funeral march, and the pallbearers lifted the coffin to their shoulders and moved forward a bit unsteadily.

Six pallbearers. One or two looked familiar, but that was no doubt fanciful. There was a gap, and then, unmistakably, there was Liz in the centre of the group that was her family. It had to be her, though he couldn't see her face under the veil and her hair was a thatch of gray. She was much smaller than he remembered, or perhaps it was only that she was dwarfed by the men all around her – the sons, for sure, Robert and Henry. Named for the 18th century Irish patriots, Robert Emmet and Henry Grattan. There was a George – George Washington Foy. Tom caught himself smiling slightly. He could almost hear Andy announcing them, rolling the names of his sons forward in his just faintly ironic declamatory style.

He scanned the women; they could be either wives of the sons or her own daughters. There was one with a large black hat and a veil not quite covering her red hair Tom thought could be Kate. She would be in her thirties now. And Liz, Liz would be fifty-four. They passed by his pew. Tom studied the impassive dark coffin, willing himself to imagine the corpse. If Thou, O Lord, wilt mark iniquities; Lord, who shall sustain it?

The mass began. I will go unto the altar of God.

Had he expected to be affected, deeply moved? Tom shifted with the faithful, from his knees to his feet to his seat. He counted as best he could the congregation in the pews behind the family. Nearly a hundred, anyway, and perhaps more. At the epistle the organist was joined by a tenor, an excellent tenor, too. Andy would be gratified. He sang a hymn of Christmas for the dead of December, "Veni, Veni Emmanuel." Gregorian chant. It would be "Panis Angelicus" at the communion. Tom, as always sourly relishing the Latin, listened closely to the young priest trying out his confident cathedral voice. Et gratia tua illis succurrente, mereantur evadere judicium ultionis; and by the help of Thy grace may they be enabled to escape the judgment of vengeance.

Amen to that. His hands were unbearably cold. He'd forgotten gloves, rushing for the early train. There had been frost during the night. Everything he could see from the train window was touched with it, the first silvery film that gave no hint of the fury that would follow in a few weeks, when the blizzards thundered down on the midwestern plains. Calvary Cemetery would be under a thin white crust with the bare trees along the main avenue scratching at heaven. He remembered it as he had seen it, May, twenty years ago, a magnificent lawn bellying out into Lake Michigan. The Irish who put in short, hard lives in ugly city tenements went there to lie in pastoral splendor for eternity. Andy would be consigned to the same earth as Patrick Henry Cronin and Tom would not witness it, because he'd be conspicuous at a graveside. But his presence was now recorded in the book. If Liz wrote to him, he could reply. If not, that was just as well. He was here to pay – well, respects couldn't be the word. He was here to bury the dead, to perform a Corporal Work of Mercy as urged by the Church; to bury the dead and put his name to the deed.

The organist bore down on the warning notes of "Panis

Angelicus" and the tenor came in on cue as the priest gave the altar boys communion. He could see nothing, really, back this far. Perhaps his sight was faltering. He'd often thought before that one of the real disadvantages of growing up without parents was that it left an orphan with no useful benchmarks, no way of knowing what to expect, for instance, of aging. But he had not been orphaned quite early enough to escape the common inheritances of his tribe, the legacies in the line of either holy grail or unholy grievance, useless and sometimes dangerous talismans.

How well he had learned that lesson! And now he put in his days trying to teach it, under the guise of history. But he grew more doubtful every year about whether that was possible. In the fall when the boys streamed into South Bend, all those long-limbed and freckle-faced great-grandsons of emigrants, their faces seemed innocent enough to him. It seemed reasonable to believe that they could all learn something that would change their lives and change the world. They ran over the campus under the golden dome and they cheered at games and absorbed enough information to be examined and nodded on four years later; then they went forth to create as much chaos and pain as every generation before them.

All right, not completely true. Tom closed his eyes and gave up thinking.

Eventually there was a rustling change of pace on the altar. The mass had ended, and the young priest was hurrying down the steps with the boys behind him. He circled the coffin, sprinkling, then returned for the censer and circled again, chanting rapidly. Sed libero nos a malo, a porta inferi; deliver us from evil, from the gate of hell. Oremus; let us pray. We humbly beseech Thee for the soul of Thy servant; deliver it not into the hands of the enemy, but command it to be received by Thy holy angels and conducted into paradise.

He'd intended to be a bit bolder about scanning faces when they returned down the aisle, since he was sure now that they wouldn't look, not to either side. But he couldn't do it. He shrank back as far out of sight behind the pillar as he could manage, but just the same he saw that the little widow behind her veil was weeping as though her heart would burst.

For a long time Tom sat there, until the cathedral had emptied and there was no sound except a stray cough here and there from some devout petitioner who had no connection with the funeral. The tiny red vigil light on the altar flickered knowingly at him and he stared back at it, unflinching. He gave them time, as much as it would take and then half of that again, to marshal the hired hacks and the private rigs and point them north towards the cemetery. Finally he rose noiselessly, turned his back on the vigil light and pushed the door out to the vestibule.

The woman with the red hair was there. She had lifted back the veil and he knew immediately by the thin sharp profile that he'd been right, it was young Kate grown up. When she looked around at the creak of the door, he knew by her face that she had been waiting for him.

I

May, 1889

IN THE FIRST months of the year he worked on the *Chicago Tribune*, Tom came home at dawn and fell asleep with his ears still quivering from the waterfall roar of the press room. He rose at noon and washed from the jug and bowl on the wash-stand, and while he shaved he recited his prayers in Latin silently.

The words retained not a residue of religion, and by long-standing arrangement with himself they were directed no-where. But he found the ritual necessary, the means by which he aligned to the day, and it was all he had salvaged from five years of seminary training. Once, talking to Liz of good and evil, eternity, damnation and redemption, he had said as much. But Liz, dry and impudent, replied that she said her prayers on the grounds that even if they did her no good, they did her no harm either.

When he'd finished shaving he lifted the window-sash and disposed of the dirty water into a drainpipe outside, set the jug in the bowl outside the door for Mrs. Delaney to refill, and then dressed and went out to buy a morning paper from the newsboy on the corner of Washington Square. Usually he didn't look at much on the morning walks. They were poor streets behind the square, where frame boarding houses and working-men's cottages leaned together in shared wretchedness. Tom picked his way along the sidewalks, a few paved with rotting wooden planks, most no more than dirt-paths pockmarked with gullies and holes that froze in winter and flooded in summer. The newsboy on the corner of the square came to recognize him after a while and flourished the range of Chicago papers before him: what there were of weeklies, skimpy foldovers in foreign languages, and the substantial dailies, mornings and evenings, the *Daily News*, the *Herald*, the *Mail*, the *Inter Ocean*. He selected one, never the *Tribune* because that came free with the job, and then he turned back to Locust Street, rifling through the pages to see what trapped his attention.

When he passed Foy's, going or returning, he checked their window; he did it every time, without thinking. Then he went back into Mrs. Delaney's boarding house and down the narrow passage to the kitchen where his plate and mug were set out for him, with bread, butter and preserves. In deference to his peculiar working hours Mrs. Delaney had agreed to make his coffee at midday, but he ate in the kitchen rather than in the room she called the parlor, where the other boarders were fed in the morning. Tom knew that Mrs. Delaney had rather hoped this concession would result in a dividend of conversation, an extra slice to her daily portion. But he had firmly and politely set the terms from the start. Once they had exchanged a few conventional wisdoms on the prevailing conditions of climate, Tom rattled the newspaper sheets studiously and began reading as he ate.

He read closely, pondering why those who knew the trade chose to publish what they did. That was what he needed to know. What he knew was the language, the matching of tense and mood, syntax and grammar, the ordering of phrases. But it had become clear to him that this was nowhere near enough if he wanted to become a newspaper man.

A week after his twenty-first birthday, he had finally admitted that he did not want to become a priest, and Father Farrell had reflected on his options. "You may as well try journalism," he'd said. "You're not bad at writing." Father Farrell thought it would be better to leave Baltimore, go west.

He gave him a letter of recommendation to an influential monsignor in Chicago. Tom never saw the monsignor. He left the letter in the monsignor's rectory and two days later a note arrived in the tenement house where he was staying in Goose Island, near the river. The note directed him to see a Mr. John Percy at the *Tribune*.

Percy was the city editor, the most powerful man in the paper. Somewhere in the building there was a publisher in whom ultimate might resided, but it was Percy and Percy's judgment that ruled the lives of the staff. It was Percy who had assigned Tom to the copy-editing table on December 1st, and six months later, on the first week-end in May, it was Percy who had beckoned him away from the galley-proofs and announced that the moment of his trial as a reporter had come.

That was not the way Percy had put it. He'd said, "You're Irish, that right?"

"Yes, sir."

Tom's surprise must have shown because Percy smiled briefly. "Don't worry, nothing personal. Huntley said you were Irish. He thinks you maybe can help him out. Ever hear of a Patrick Cronin?"

"Cronin?"

"Yeah. Big name in the Irish societies in town; know anything about him?"

"Yes, sir. Well, I know who he is, that is. I heard him sing once."

"That's the one. Supposed to have a nice tenor. 'Had' might be the more accurate word; looks like he's disappeared. His landlady thinks he's in big trouble."

Tom waited uncertainly. "Didn't hear anything about that, I guess?" Percy added.

"No, sir."

"No. Well, story is he went out on a call last night, some emergency, never came back. His landlady, this Mrs. Conklin, she's been on to the cops and papers, sure as hell he's been knocked off or something. She says he's got enemies, somebody out to get him. Huntley's done an interview with her for tomorrow, you can read the galley. He wants you to meet him in the morning, help him out on whatever comes up. Okay?"

Percy handed him the galley and walked away, and Tom followed him hurriedly. "Mr. Percy, sir?"

"Yeah?"

"Did Mr. Huntley say what he'd like me to do?"

"I dunno. He needs a Mick to give some background, that kind of thing." Percy turned away again. "No offense," he called back. Tom nodded.

9

What Tom read in the galley was much the same story that he found the next morning in the *Herald*. He had planned to be up earlier than usual because he was to meet Huntley at noon, but in fact he was awake and alert from first light, and rushed through his rituals to get his paper. He chose the *Herald* for the blunt headline – "Is P.H. Cronin Dead?"

"Dr. Patrick H. Cronin, prominent physician with office and residence at 470 North Clark Street, is missing. His landlady, a Mrs. Conklin, has told this reporter that he was called out shortly after seven on Saturday evening to attend to an injured worker in O'Sullivan's ice-house, and he has not been seen since. Contact has been made with Mr. Patrick O'Sullivan, proprietor of the ice-house in Lakeview, and we are in a position to report that he claims to have no knowledge of a summons to Dr. Cronin or of an accident affecting any of his men . . ."

There was quite a lot of detail from Mrs. Conklin on Dr. Cronin's usually punctual habits, but very little about the stranger who'd arrived with the urgent message. She hadn't managed to get a good look at him because she'd been in the front room attending to the doctor's books. All she was sure of was that the buggy that took him off was drawn by a white horse. Dr. Cronin had said to tell anyone who asked that he'd be back as soon as possible.

"That was the last I saw of him," Mrs. Conklin ended.

Tom read down carefully twice, and when he had finished he folded the paper into a jacket pocket. He thanked Mrs. Delaney and ran swiftly up the two flights to his own room to spend five minutes tidying. There were benefits to seminary discipline he'd learned to appreciate, as Father Farrell had promised they all would. Five minutes of covering over and putting away emptied the room of his existence; it was as anonymous as the day he had moved into it – one bed, a dressing-case, two chairs, a table, the wash-stand with the jug and bowl neatly centered and the towel at the side. Tom did not intend to live this way forever. He was unsure what he did intend, but he had a number of reveries to rely on, and somewhere in the future he believed there was a room where he would put his feet to his own stove on winter nights, and perhaps read a book for pleasure rather than a newspaper for training. There would be others there as peaceful as himself, indistinct faces and shapes. A wife, family, something like that. But he had time.

When that was done he got his hat and ran lightly down the stairs and out again. On Locust Street he began to whistle softly. He saw that it was nearing summer. In the May sun filtering timidly through the permanent pall of smoke, the clapboard houses looked worse than usual, showing bald patches like sores where the paint had rubbed away. But there were weeds fighting through the cracks in the boarded walk. They'd survived the vicious midwest winter, and so had he, a fragile southeastern transplant.

It was a victory worthy of announcement. He crossed the road to Foy's and knocked softly and rapidly, then opened the door very slightly and called, "Hello? It's myself." It was a compromise entrance line, intimate enough to assume a welcome, but not more than that.

"Hello, yourself," Liz replied promptly.

He pushed the door wider and saw her in the small square front room, framed in the rectangle of light from the doorway, smiling at him. She had a small face – Tom could have spanned it with his hand – a slightly crooked dimple and a way of gesturing imprecisely when she talked that was distracting but pleasant to watch. He saw immediately that she looked drawn though she was feeding the babies briskly, one tucked up at either end of the baby buggy. Her sleeves were rolled back and she worked away methodically from a pot of oatmeal balanced on her knees, spooning up, to each mouth in turn. At another time Tom might have lapsed into one of his reveries, the kind he was quite capable of maintaining even while he visited sociably. This morning, though, he was a participant in life's riches rather than an aspirant to them, and he waited to arrest her attention.

"Come inside and close the door, that's an evil draught," she said. "Are you well?"

But Tom was reluctant to move. "I'm grand. It's a fine day, really. It'll be summer soon." The babies turned together when he spoke and stared at him, round-eyed.

11

"Ah, I want to take care with this lassie. I'm afraid of my life she'll catch a chill," Liz said. "Sit down a minute."

He closed the door behind him and came in to stand beside her. She turned back to her task, and the babies forgot him and turned back, too. The bigger one had a rosy face and curls, and hummed and babbled. The little one was frail, though, and often ill. Her skin was like winter milk, blue under a membrane of white. Tom looked away, at a pitcher of flowers, a bit wilted, on the table, and his eye fell on an envelope near it, lavishly inscribed with his own name. "What's this?" he asked, picking it up.

Liz glanced without turning her head. "I don't know. It's been there a few days now," she said. "I suppose it's something of Andy's – he must have wanted you to read it."

"I'll take it with me to read on the car downtown," Tom said, stuffing it into his pocket. "Has she been all right, the little one?"

"Not too bad, thank God." With her free hand Liz stroked the baby's cheek. "My little flower, aren't you, Marie?" But the lamp had been on late a few nights recently, Tom knew, when he passed the house coming home.

"The summer will help the croup," he said heartily, hoping it was the right few words.

Liz half-turned; he could see the dimple again. "Is it the summer that has you in such flying form, then?"

"No, it's not," he grinned. "I'm going off reporting today, Liz, my first try. This Cronin, Liz – the fellow who sang at the Emmet commemoration concert. He's gone missing. Did you read anything yet?"

"Cronin? I did not."

"Here, look. Seems he was called out to a patient on Saturday night and never came back, and his landlady thinks something's happened to him."

Liz set the pot on the floor to take the paper from him. "And what are you to do, did you say?" she asked after a moment, looking up.

"I've been asked to go with the reporter, fellow named Dick Huntley. He's very good, too. It's a good chance for me." Tom paused. He could tell the whole truth, which was that his selection had to do with his ethnic origins and not his ability. But there was no need to spoil the moment, either. "So. I guess I'm in a state," he concluded lamely. "I only stopped by to tell you."

"Well," Liz said, "I'm glad you did." The paper still in her hand, she lifted the big baby out of the buggy and slid her to the floor, and then went to the window to finish reading. In the light Tom saw that she really was tired, her eyes smudged with gray shadows. He looked at her, twirling his hat, a little discomfited. Perhaps he had been boasting. But she smiled at him again, reassuringly. "I'm glad you did," she repeated.

He insisted that she keep the paper, and realized as he spoke that for the first time since he'd been diligently buying one every morning, he had failed to read anything other than the single story he was interested in.

They talked at the door for a minute or two, admiring the weather together. Liz kept one hand on the big baby, who was determined to stagger out into the world. "You must come by and tell us how you get on," she said. "Come for supper tomorrow, why don't you?"

"I'm not sure what time I'll get off."

"Yerra, 'tis all right, come when you can. We'll be here and I'll have your name in the pot." She watched him from the doorway as he set off, and at the corner he turned and waved.

She was a friend to him in a way that Andy could not have been, Tom knew that. Liz thought of things he needed that he didn't know himself, the room in Mrs. Delaney's, for instance, cleaner and just as cheap as Goose Island. But it was Andy he felt the glow of gratitude to, just the same. If it weren't for Andy, he might have slunk back to Baltimore like a defeated cur long ago. No one at the copy-editing table had spoken to him in those first painful weeks in Chicago, except to give orders or put questions – not, as Tom gradually saw, because they were particularly hostile. They were genial enough on the rare occasions when work was slack, but a close-knit group, cynical and tough; and when they worked it was in solitary, pressurised silence. He felt his isolation terribly after the intense companionship of the seminary, where he'd lived as one of a pack for years, in study, recreation, in prayer, even in sleep.

When he wasn't working Tom walked for hours in the shocking cold, shoulders hunched, past the waist-high snow-drifts that walled in the streets for weeks at a time, and thought of the briskly agreeable chill of Baltimore winters. Then he returned to the tenement which was damp and smelled of the river. It was at just the point when he might have fled that Andy had befriended him.

He noticed how high the sun was suddenly, and hurried. It must be nearing midday; he should be concentrating on his approach to Huntley. Tom had studied him often, and once or twice nodded a bashful greeting when they'd passed each other. Behind his frameless spectacles, Huntley was bland and unremarkable, a balding, rather short man, easily forgotten. There were jokes in the paper at how frequently he was taken for anything but a reporter – a salesman, a clergyman, a city hall clerk. The chameleon quality was said to be quite useful to him. His reputation was the kind other reporters longed for: the best in the business, they told each other approvingly, with envy. Fast and accurate and nerveless.

Tom adjusted the hat more securely. The hat was a touch of vanity, a good wool slouch brim that had cost far too much. But it set him off clearly from the thousands on the streets around him in cheaper versions or ordinary caps. If he did well he could get a good increase, afford to move nearer downtown, a better room, an apartment of rooms, a new life. He pinched the notion quickly. Locust Street was home for a while yet.

In the street-car he remembered the envelope. Inside it there were three foolscap pages, the final draft of a ballad, every letter scrupulously sculpted and shaded in good ink.

There are some in our land who are ever despairing,
Whose minds trace no glory except in the past,
Whose eyes flash no fire, and whose souls know no
    daring
Who tell us the Saxon has triumphed at last.
But, ah! These are few. We have those who are
    stronger . . .

14

Tom looked at the title. "The Men of Today." Andy was the principal composer of essays and ballads for the Columbia Club's literary evenings, and he had enthusiastically recruited Tom's services as consultant and critic. "Every poet laureate should have one," he said. Tom read another verse and then folded the pages and returned them to the envelope. He settled back into the seat, feeling the precise way the car ground along its path. It would take him all the way to the *Tribune* on Dearborn and Madison. The hat was not much use against the wind.

II

THE EDITORIAL ROOM of the *Chicago Tribune* was four stories over Dearborn Street and seemed to Tom to be in constant motion. Even early in the day there was always some corner that was busy, someone drumming on a typewriter and someone tearing back and forth with sheaves of galley-proofs, long strips of newsprint awaiting correction; a wire machine in a corner chanting insanely, ignored and unattended. By evening it was a hive of motion and the entire row of machines rattled like gunfire.

Tom's usual table was peripherally placed. The copy-editors there dealt mostly with literary and theatre notices, social events, nothing too late or too urgent or too important. They sat at a narrow table facing the chief copy-editor, who was hedged in by baskets – baskets for stories coming in, going down to be set; for proofs coming back, then going out again, corrected. But today Tom turned tentatively toward the City Desk in the center of the amphitheater, the very heart of the fearsome enterprise. The copy-editing table there was long and flanked by the tables where the reporters sat, littered now with the evidence of last night's efforts, crumpled copy paper scattered between upended, exhausted typewriters.

Huntley was there, with Percy, and he ambled forward as soon as he saw Tom, smiling genially. "Howdy, Martin!" he said.

Percy gave Tom a curt nod and strolled away without comment.

Huntley put a hand on Tom's shoulder and turned toward the door he'd just come in. "I'm mighty grateful to you for joinin' me. Looks like there's a nasty murder shapin' up."

"Murder?"

"Could be," Huntley said cheerfully. "Cops found a trunk up in Lakeview, drenched in blood, pretty battered. Somebody ain't seen a happy night in it, anyway."

"But do they think it was Dr. Cronin was murdered?"

"Well, that they ain't sayin', not yet. Know anythin' about Cronin?"

"Not very much." Tom hesitated. "I don't know that I'll be much help to you, Mr. Huntley, though I'm awfully happy to be asked, sir."

Huntley shrugged. "Fact a' the matter, we're a bit stuck. No one's too familiar with this scene. No 'misters' or 'sirs', by the way; call me Dick and I'll call you whatever you like. What do you like?"

"Tom, I guess."

"Right, Tom. Let's get a hack out to Lakeview, have a look at this trunk."

All the way down Michigan Avenue, hurtling along in the hired rig, Huntley kept up a constant flow of polite chat, on the nice way the day was turning out, the traffic, the quality of the horses on the road. When they got to Lake Shore Drive the buggy picked up speed, and he pulled open the side window and breathed in deeply.

"Beautiful," he called to Tom over the wind. "Beautiful. Don't you think so yourself? I been in a lot a' cities and there ain't one I like as much as this one. Damned few cities in the world can spread themselves right along a great lake, end to end, free ventilation and all the water you could ever want, wash in it, drink it. No salt. Swim in it. Done much swimmin', Tom?"

"No," Tom cried back. "I haven't been here just six months." He looked at the great gray waves crashing along the beach with as much interest as he could muster.

"Swim much in Ireland?"

"I've never been in Ireland," Tom raised his voice above the wind. "It's my parents were born there."

"That so? Got a face like the map a' Ireland. Heard that expression?"

18

"Yes." Tom thought it was an exceptionally silly one. As far as he could see, Irish faces showed the impressions of every tribe that ever crossed the European continent and ended up leaving members on the farthest island.

"Truth is, I heard somebody say you were Catholic," Huntley went on, closing the window. "Catholic in the *Trib*, probably Irish. Germans, Poles, they have enough trouble speakin' English let alone try earnin' a livelihood writin' it. But your name ain't too Irish, I notice. How's that?"

"Martin? Martin's an Irish name," Tom said.

Huntley said "I see" agreeably and smiled again, at nothing in particular. He was more like a man heading for a sociable business meeting than a murder investigation. Tom wondered who could have said he was Catholic. He hadn't discussed religion with anyone. He didn't know anyone that well, for one thing, and apart from that, religion wasn't something he'd heard much talk about from his colleagues. Race, yes. They talked about krauts and hunkies and the newcomers, the waps, dagoes. Micks or turkeys, red-necked turkeys. And niggers, of course. Tom tried not to hear the talk.

He looked away from Huntley to view the parade of mansions across from the lake, huge brick and stone houses. They were tricked out in porches and turrets as if whoever built them had had new inspiration at every corner, and they were all well back from the road, behind high wrought-iron gates. Tom knew them from his long walks last winter. He used to amuse himself miserably, wondering about the lives inside, the servants, food, the grandeur, then turn and go back into the city past the banking and merchant houses and the long gray blocks of wooden factories that generated it all. He hadn't been as far north as Lakeview before, though. Eventually the mansions grew farther and farther apart and gave way to marsh grass. The driver turned inward, and the buggy lurched more severely as they continued west. Here the houses were small and cheap, the same dingy frame houses that lined Locust Street; but they were clustered together, three or four or six in a clump, and spreading between them, empty lots, with weeds grown high and wild.

This was like country, and yet not like country. Here and there they passed through a dusty road with a few shops huddled around a tavern. The police station was in one of these roads and there was a small crowd at the door, men with no work to go to, their hands in their pockets, and women straddling babies at their hips. They were kept back by one uniformed policeman, and they watched him idly since they could see nothing else. Huntley told the driver to wait and greeted the policeman, who immediately moved aside for them.

It was bedlam inside. The sergeant's desk was high on a block in the centre of the bare room, with two great round glass lamps on either side. A dozen men, maybe more, were pressed against it, arguing with the sergeant who growled back at them. There were a couple of photographers hovering protectively over their tripods along the wall. Huntley edged his way around the crowd, greeting one after another with a nod. Tom followed, close behind. When Huntley had finally positioned himself in a far corner he leaned back casually and said to Tom, "In a few minutes now that door behind the sarge will open and there'll be a rush like cattle, so step nimbly, Tom, will you?"

Huntley seemed uninterested in the crowd or their arguments. He kept his eye on the door and talked softly. "Thing is now, Cap'n Villiers will want good press out a' this, so he'll be anxious to show us everythin' there is to see, lots a' guff about his boys in blue, Chicago's best, detectives the sharpest and so on. But from what I hear this here trunk was practically dropped off personal delivery on their doorstep. What we want to know is whether the Doc was in it or not, that's all. 'Course if he wasn't, it would be interestin' to know who was." Tom nodded.

In another minute the door opened and the crowd surged as predicted. They were pushed into a long angular hall, with a narrow table at one end and chairs against the walls. On the table was a trunk, an ordinary black trunk, a large one, with the lid flung back at a lopsided angle. A half-dozen policemen stood at the table, the captain in his tall hat in the center. The reporters pushed forward, pulling notebooks from their jackets.

"If we could have order, gentlemen," the captain said

severely. They fell silent, waiting, and he gave a short nod of satisfaction. "I am Captain Villiers. If the photographers would like to assemble their equipment to my left, I will take questions while they are doing so." Tom listened as closely as he could, but the questions were fast and in no particular order. The trunk had been found at seven-thirty Sunday morning, on Evanston Avenue. The lid had been forced open and the interior was spattered with blood. There were chunks of absorbent cotton in it, also saturated with blood.

Every answer bought another clamor of questions. Who found it? Was there evidence of a body? Any connection with Cronin? Why hadn't the papers been told yesterday? Huntley was making notes in what looked like hen scratches. In fact it wasn't the police who'd found it, Captain Villiers said; some local men found it and raised the alarm. "A detachment of officers went in a patrol wagon to the scene and removed the trunk to the station house. I have made a thorough investigation and I have found enough evidence to satisfy me that a person had been murdered, stuffed into this trunk and then removed before the trunk was dumped."

The reporters scribbled in their books and Huntley spoke. "You say a person, that right, Cap'n?"

"A man six foot tall could be crammed into this trunk quite easily by determined murderers."

"Could ain't was," Huntley said. "Couldn't 'a been a dog, now, I suppose?"

"You can take it that there was a human in this trunk, Mr. Huntley," Villiers said evenly. "The blood has been examined and ascertained as human blood." He paused a moment and then picked a layer of paper from the trunk and laid it on the table. There was the wad of absorbent cotton, stained with something thick and dull, more brown than red.

The reporters pushed forward; all but Tom, who stepped back, and Huntley, who never moved. "Cap'n, you got any other irrefutable evidence you want to tell us about right away?" he asked.

Villiers was annoyed. "As you're in a hurry perhaps you'd like to step up to the front, Mr. Huntley?"

21

"I'll take your word for what's in there, Cap'n. I just want to hear it all in a piece."

Several of the reporters had turned to look at Huntley, grinning.

"Certainly," Villiers said. "We must oblige the *Tribune*. We have, in fact, a sample of hair, clearly from an adult head, dark brown, severed from the head but not pulled by the roots."

He produced another sheet of paper, with a thin hank of dark hair on it. After a moment someone asked whether it could belong to a woman. Villiers said it wasn't possible to tell. The din resumed, and he lifted his voice above it and went on quickly, reciting his statement from memory: examination by microscope showed the hair was clotted with blood and absorbent cotton. All the evidence suggested that a brutal murder had taken place, probably within the last two days, that the body had been jammed in the trunk and that the murderers had disposed of it hurriedly, breaking the lock in their haste and forcing the lid back so that one hinge had broken.

He swung the lid back and forth, demonstrating the point, and then added, "There are still pools of blood in the trunk and the inside of the lid, as you can see for yourselves."

Everyone but Tom and Huntley stepped forward again. Huntley had been writing carefully as Villiers spoke and without lifting his eyes from his notes he asked what the Lakeview police had done in the time that had elapsed since the trunk was found. "Seven-thirty yesterday mornin', Cap'n, was it?" Huntley asked. "Searches in the area produce any clues about who done in whoever got done in?"

Villiers gave him a hard look. A patrol wagon full of officers had been out all day, he said, searching all the brush, prairie and vacant houses for two or three miles around. Evanston Avenue was paved and there was no way of finding tracks there. The grass has been too badly trampled elsewhere.

"Nothin' else to suggest a corpse?" Huntley asked. Villiers looked away from him, watching the reporters as they wrote, and waited a full moment before he spoke again.

"And now, gentlemen, that concludes the evidence we have to present as to the trunk itself. The central question on your minds, as you have indicated, is whether or not the trunk is connected with the disappearance of Dr. Cronin."

The room fell silent again. "We had no evidence to suggest this until late last night when Officers Smith and Hayden reported for duty. Officer Smith has given us a statement positively identifying this trunk as the one he saw on the back of a carpenter's wagon, at Clark and Diversey at two o'clock on Sunday morning – some seven hours after Dr. Cronin was suddenly called away from his office. The wagon was proceeding rapidly northward at the time. What is more to the point is that Officers Smith and Hayden saw the same wagon returning, again at Clark and Diversey, an hour and a half later. But, this time, there was no trunk on it. Officer Smith is here now, if you'd like to put your questions to him."

The silence broke into a babble again. Villiers looked at Huntley and gave a thin smile. But Huntley only smiled back and turned to Tom. "Guess we'll hear these gentlemen out and then go pay a visit to the ice-house man, don't you think?"

III

THE ICE-HOUSE was a two-story frame building at the corner of Bosworth and Roscoe, on an isolated lot with two other houses, the three huddled together. There was a sign on the gate announcing "Patrick O'Sullivan," and a picture of a workman with an exuberant smile bent under an enormous cube of ice strapped to his back.

O'Sullivan was a small man, wiry and watchful, and he tugged at his mustache when Huntley questioned him. His answers were adamant: there'd been no one injured on Saturday night, and he had never sent for Dr. Cronin. "I know nothing about this," he said.

"You have an arrangement with Dr. Cronin, ain't that right?" Huntley asked.

"That's right."

"Had it long?

"Not too long ... pretty recent, matter a' fact. I hear he's a good doctor. I wanted someone I could get any time I had trouble. We get accidents. Ice-hooks slip, the men get hurt bad sometimes."

"I can see that'd happen. Ain't Doc Cronin's a long way away from you?"

"He's a good doctor, I hear."

"And he's Irish like yourself, and your men would be Irish, too, I suppose? That might be a consideration."

"I'm from downstate," O'Sullivan said. "Born in Galena."

"A hick like myself," Huntley smiled. O'Sullivan did not respond. He stopped tugging his mustache and pushed back his hat to scratch his head.

"Not many neighbors around you out here," Huntley said. "I could see you'd worry about accidents."

"Yep."

"Think the neighbors might know anythin' about Doc Cronin comin' out here on Saturday night?"

"Couldn't say about that. Wouldn't think so."

"You think maybe somethin' did happen to him, though?"

"Couldn't say, mister."

Huntley thanked him, and O'Sullivan nodded in silence. "It seems Mrs. Conklin might be right, doesn't it?" Tom said when they'd climbed back in the rig.

"It's worryin', all right," Huntley replied. "I gotta admit that."

The rig took them back into the city, but Huntley turned the driver away from Michigan Avenue, over to Dearborn, where he called quickly to the driver to turn again. One block further on they stopped in the office district, respectable quarters for enterprising businessmen.

"Well, there it is," he said. "470 North Clark. Windsor Theater, and over it the residence and offices a' Doc Cronin. Suppose we might as well have a few words with this Mrs. Conklin, what do you say?"

The building was ten stories of solid, dignified brick, with a deep lobby and a carpeted stairway. A woman sweeping down the carpet directed them to the fifth floor. There were twenty or thirty people milling in and out of the entrance of 501, where Dr. Cronin's name was printed on the door.

Tom stepped in, on to a floor covered in overlapping Oriental rugs, and looked around him, disconcerted. He realized that he hadn't seen anything like this yet in Chicago. Not that it was extravagant – not what he dimly envisaged in the Lake Shore Drive mansions – but it was expensive and comfortable, like the visitor's parlor in the seminary. It was clearly the doctor's waiting-room, densely furnished with big armchairs of leather or tufted upholstery, ornate tables at their arms and ashtrays on stands. And paintings, lined up along the walls; Huntley looked at them carefully in turn, snow scenes and mountain ranges under orange sunsets, as if they yielded vital clues. Then he asked for Mrs. Conklin. She was in a far corner, sitting with two other women who were speaking in low mur-

murs. It was like a wake, Tom thought, already like a wake.

"More reporters?" Mrs. Conklin, who was thin and erect, shook Huntley's hand briefly. "Yes, come inside; we can talk there."

The room where the doctor saw patients, with its couch and screen and corner sink, was almost as large as the waiting-room. Huntley stopped at the fireplace and looked at the framed papers above it, and Tom dutifully followed him. Documents of medical certification, honorary commendations.

"Dr. Cronin has a busy practice?" Huntley asked.

"Very," Mrs. Conklin replied. "He was an excellent doctor. The best in the city." Her voice was dull and tired, but still firm.

"You seem pretty sure somethin's happened to him," Huntley said.

"I'm quite certain of it. Now there's a trunk been found, hasn't there? Captain Villiers sent his men around to tell me. A trunk used for a murder. And the police saw that wagon, and the trunk. It's so, isn't it?" She put her handkerchief to her eyes, but withdrew it again almost immediately.

"Why'd you think Dr. Cronin was murdered, Mrs. Conklin?"

"I've said everything I know to the newspapers, and to the police, for that matter. He had enemies. He told my husband and myself that more than once."

"Did he name any names?"

"Alexander Sullivan he named." Mrs. Conklin looked straight at Huntley, clutching her handkerchief in her folded hands. "But will you print that in your newspaper? I've already said that, too. I told that to the man from the *Herald,* but it seems Peggy Sullivan can put into that paper and out of it what she likes."

Huntley nodded. He had his notebook opened but had written nothing. "Well, Ma'am, the newspapers like to think they print facts, and the only facts we know so far is that Dr. Cronin's vanished. 'Course there may be some fact you could tell me that'd show why Alex Sullivan was an enemy a' Dr. Cronin's, and then I could print that."

Mrs. Conklin shook her head. "I only know what he said. And now he's vanished. He's never done anything like that in the seven years he's lodged here. And he was a good man," she added, a touch of anger in her tone. "A good man."

"Dr. Cronin had a fixed arrangement with this O'Sullivan to tend to his men; that right, Mrs. Conklin?"

"Yes, that's right. He was on a retainer. It was arranged only four weeks ago. I keep his books for him, so I recall that. O'Sullivan paid him twenty-five dollars for the first six months."

"I see. And can you tell me why O'Sullivan'd choose Dr. Cronin to look after his men when his ice-house is what, maybe six miles away?"

"I don't know that. Doctor said he'd been recommended to him by a mutual friend. I don't think he knew him."

"Don't know who the mutual friend was?"

She shook her head.

"I guess the doctor had a lot a' friends?"

"Dozens of them. Hundreds of them. Since Sunday they've been coming, like this." She gestured toward the closed door to the waiting-room. "He was well-liked. Loved, really, since the day he came here. He made so many friends, gave so much of himself. Never too busy."

"But enemies too, you say. Alex Sullivan, maybe."

Mrs. Conklin looked directly at Huntley again. "I've said what the doctor said, and I've named who he named. I think he'd want me to do that."

Huntley went over the details of the disappearance again, and Mrs. Conklin answered each point, nodding, "Yes, that's right. That's what happened." When he had finished she brought them through the waiting-room and to the door, and stood there while they descended the stairs.

On the sidewalk outside Huntley commented, "Now there is a woman devoted to a man. Doctors do have that effect. What do you make a' her, Tom?"

Tom cleared his throat. "I'm not sure." He could not in fact make much at all out of what had happened. "She certainly seems to suspect this Alexander Sullivan, anyway."

"Common sort a' name in Chicago; Sullivan, O'Sullivan," Huntley said. "Common in Ireland, I guess?"

28

"I think it's a Cork name. I guess a lot of people from Cork ended up here," Tom said.

"Must be."

They walked slowly down Clark Street to the river. Huntley seemed in no hurry. "This ice-house fellow, Patrick O'Sullivan," he said. "He'd be no relation to the others – Alex Sullivan, Peg Sullivan. They're connected all right. You must know who they are?"

"I've heard of Alex Sullivan. I heard his name, anyway," Tom said. "He's a politician." Huntley nodded but didn't reply. "Peg Sullivan; is she the woman that writes in the *Herald*?" Tom asked.

"Peg Sullivan," Huntley said, "is some lady. She's his wife, and she is some lady. She's a woman a' malignant hatreds. And, a' course, invidious charm. You wouldn't get the freedom to vent the first without the second. Editor a' the *Herald* is an Irish American name a' Walsh. Seems to think Peg Sullivan's the most gifted writer in the English language, though some'd say that's largely 'cause he wants to keep in good with Alex. Gives her free range, a column to write what she likes. Great favorite with your Archbishop Feehan. Know much about Feehan? Peg suits his style, tough and in control. Rails a lot about proper order; shreds anyone she doesn't like."

"Yes," Tom said. "I've read what she writes, sometimes." He didn't add that since he didn't know the people she wrote about, her views had slipped past him without impression. "Is she able to say what goes in and out of the paper, like Mrs. Conklin says?"

"She'd have a lot a' say with Walsh. If she didn't want it known that Alex Sullivan and Doc Cronin were enemies, why, I imagine she could persuade Walsh not to let it slip into print. On the other hand . . ." Huntley stopped.

"What?" Tom prompted.

"On the other hand, ain't no good reason why that should get in the paper, is there? Not yet, anyhow. Thing about Alex and Peg Sullivan, somethin' about the pair of 'em, you either love 'em like Feehan or hate 'em like Mrs. Conklin there. Think at the last count it was more love 'n hate, but then nothing's so lovable as clout. Peg's got Walsh's ear, and that's useful, but Alex's got clout at City Hall and that, Tom boy, is Mount Olympus."

Huntley had raised his voice as they walked. They had turned east along the riverfront and were suddenly dodging by delivery wagons, engulfed in shouts from the dockworkers and the rumble and screech of wheels on the cobblestone paving. The river was overpowering this close, a smell of gas and rot, and Tom put his hand over his nose and glanced at the sweating men who pushed their carts by, wondering how long it took to get used to it, how long before you'd stop noticing. Huntley didn't seem to notice either. He looked around with the preoccupied gaze of a tourist, as if it were a fresh and invigorating sight, while he talked. "Alex is one a' the wealthiest lawyers in this city. Specialty is handlin' boodle for City Hall, but he can turn his hand to anythin'."

"Boodle? What's that?"

"Boodle. Boodlin'. Sellin' off the city piece by piece in franchises. Sort a' good government and good business goin' hand in hand."

"And that makes him very wealthy?"

"That's just frostin'. The man's been involved in every shady operation you can name for years, includin' murder, and no jury could bring itself to convict him. Nobody's ever proved jury bribin' either, though some tried," Huntley answered.

"Murder," Tom echoed.

"You'll get it all in the Morgue cuttin's. I can tell you, though, he's somethin' to reckon with in this town. Kind a' man other men fear by instinct. Don't know do you know the type, but they make powerful politicians."

They crossed the river and headed up Dearborn and, at the corner of Randolph, Huntley stopped abruptly before the polished double doors of a saloon and said "Come on, boy, let's get some lunch."

It was a fashionable place, with a long marble counter studded with heavy brass lamps along one wall and tables set to the rear. A rumpled waiter led them to the back and took

Huntley's order for beef, potatoes, and a pitcher of beer. Most of the lunch customers had gone, and there were only a few men left at the nearby tables, loitering over whiskeys and coffee.

"All right now," Huntley was back on track. "Let's have a look at what we got. We got one missin' Irish doctor, one bloody trunk, two cops who saw a wagon with, and then without a trunk, at an hour when a wagon ain't usually got no particular business. We got one landlady makin' dark hints. Right so far?"

"Yes," Tom said. He thought of the battered trunk, and the thick brownish clots on the bits of cotton. He'd seen, even though he'd hung back.

"'Course, May is movin' month. Lots a' families shiftin' from one place to another, gettin' their stuff carted around the city any hour a' the day or night on the back a' wagons."

"I hadn't thought of that."

"If I was a man doin' in somebody I'd think a' that. But then I'd 'a figured better than to leave a trunk in a ditch, shoutin' to be found. Could 'a been somebody else entirely in that trunk, a' course. This is Chicago." The waiter brought the beer and Huntley poured out two glasses with lingering care. "This is Chicago," he repeated. "Anyone can have a fight and decide to dispose a' the defeated party in a trunk. What we need to think about is why somebody'd want to tuck up the doctor in a trunk. He's a pretty important fellow in the Irish societies; suppose there'd be somebody in one a' 'em had a grudge against him?"

"I don't really know anything about the Irish societies," Tom said.

"Might be the case if you did know, you couldn't tell me?" Huntley asked.

Tom looked up blankly and Huntley smiled as he went on. "I know one or two a' these societies are secret affairs, members bound by oath not to say anythin', that sort a' thing."

The waiter appeared again and bent over them slapping the hot plates down swiftly. Tom waited until he'd sauntered away, and Huntley pinioned a potato on his fork. "I don't

31

belong to anything," Tom said. He was bewildered and a little hurt, though he wasn't sure why. "I've been to concerts and that, with friends, but there wasn't anything secret about them."

Huntley glanced up as soon as he spoke, still smiling. "Hope I ain't offended you, didn't mean to. Just thought I'd better bring it up early on. Point is, an awful lot of Irishmen in Chicago do belong to somethin'. What are there – fifty societies for Ireland, somethin' like that?"

"I don't know. Are there that many?"

"About that. Well, that's a lot a' goin's-on; there'd be bound to be differences and arguments on one thing or another. Even if it's only about who gets to sing at what concert and so forth. From what I know, and it ain't much, that seems to be mainly what all these fifty societies spend their time at, organizin' concerts and meetin's." Tom didn't answer and after a minute Huntley continued, "There's a big one there every fall, commemoratin' some poor devils got killed in Manchester, twenty years ago or so. You know about that?"

"Allen, Larkin and O'Brien? Yes, I know about that," Tom said. "There was a skirmish in Manchester, England, and a policeman was killed. Those three were hung for doing it."

"As I remember the feelin' was that it was a frame-up. That so?"

"It's what's generally believed, I think," Tom said.

"Even the *New York Times* said it wasn't a fair trial. I was in New York at the time. I guess that's the kind a' thing keeps these Irish societies tickin' away, ain't it?"

Tom shrugged. "Well, I guess it's understandable."

"Sure is," Huntley said. "Grievance is powerful glue for keepin' people together. Mostly fund-raisin' they get up to, these societies? Crowd passin' the hat not too long ago to buy some burial plot for their members, Clan na Gael. Heard a' them?"

Tom nodded.

Huntley lapsed into rumination, busy with his potatoes. "Before that a memorial to some Irish poet name a' Kickham. He a famous man?"

32

"I have a friend who's talked about him — he was a sort of patriotic writer, a novelist, I think."

There was a burst of laughter from the table nearest them, where three men were sitting at ease, legs stretched. Tom looked over, distracted, and Huntley followed his gaze. "Know 'em?" he asked.

"Me?" Tom said. "God, no."

"Well," Huntley said. He selected a toothpick from the little glass jar on the table and set to work with it. "Burial plots and memorials. Don't want to be givin' offense, now, as I say, but am I wrong in thinkin' the Irish get pretty preoccupied with graveside matters?"

Tom smiled reluctantly. "I guess it's been said about us, all right."

"Anybody in the paper ask you do you read the Irish sports pages?"

"Irish sports pages?"

"Newspaper joke. Means the death notices." This time Tom laughed, and Huntley watched him, pleased. "Good you ain't too sensitive," he said. "Finish up there and we'll get back to work."

IV

AFTER TWO DAYS at his new reporting duties, Tom began to worry whether there was something he should be doing that he had not grasped, something other reporters knew by grace or intuition. He hadn't taken a note or spoken a word to anyone but Huntley, who let him off early on Tuesday with the laconic observation that there was nothing much to do. Tom couldn't see that there was more or less than there had been. He had plenty of time before he was due at Foy's for supper, and he roamed along the lakefront, aimlessly watching the waves lick the sand.

He wanted to succeed. He even recited it to himself self-consciously: I want to succeed. But he was not yet certain at what. The ambition was new and furtive and most easily defined in the negative: he did not want to make choices that would leave him, at the far end of life's long tunnel, wretched or morose or bitter. Or poor. He was determined to avoid poverty, because even at twenty-one he had learned that poverty was the cruelest enemy of hope. He did not understand how others could be less conscious of this bare fact. It was certainly one of the things about Andy that puzzled him, and once in a while surprised a little envy in him. As far as was humanly possible, Andy concerned himself with matters of the mind and spirit and, at nearly forty, he was a free man in a way Tom felt he never could be. Once in a while, Tom thought it might have been nice if experience had shaped him less pragmatically.

Most of the time, Tom was simply grateful that he had slipped loose from the various traps behind him to the point where he was now, ready for his destiny. He kept himself prepared for its arrival. But he was also careful about avoiding complacency; it was best to know your own weaknesses. Tom had a weakness for human affinity. Even as a new small pulse of excitement now alerted him to the possibility that his moment had come, he watched himself wistfully needing to share it, and was profoundly thankful that within a month of starting at the *Tribune* he had, literally, fallen across Andy.

Three nights before Christmas Andy had pushed out the door of Gleason's saloon as Tom was trudging past. Tom didn't notice, because he was blind to everything but his own loneliness, so large and numbing that he had begun to see it could become unbearable, beyond endurance. They collided, and slid along the wet sidewalk clutching each other until they fell. While Tom apologized frantically and repeatedly, Andy remained sprawled, staring up at him with his strange pale eyes. "Clarence McFadden, will ye teach me to dance?" he said eventually. "Where you from, boy?" In an exchange of four or five sentences Andy established Tom's birthplace and that of his parents, and then he pulled himself up with an exuberant whoop of laughter. "Mayo! A Mayo man abroad in evil Chicago!"

"No, my father . . ."

"Technicality!" Andy grabbed Tom's arm and turned them both into the saloon. "I'd given up praying for the excuse I wanted, and you've been sent to me like a gift," he cried. "Far from the land you are, and come to think of it, I'll sing it."

He did, too, and then someone else sang, and then eight or ten more men sang, Irish songs, mournful ballads or rapturous melodies of war. None of them sang as well as Andy, though. He had a marvelous voice. The saloon was so crowded Tom could scarcely move but Andy gripped his shoulder with one hand, called for more whiskey and introduced him around, shouting names: "Dan Madden, Jack Gallagher, Pat Cooney, Martin Burke, Packy Ryan . . ."

Afterward, when Tom began to sway unsteadily, Andy steered him out of Gleason's and got him into his jacket and cap, muttering, "Isn't it the mercy of Jesus we're not fond of the stuff just the same." Then he brought him back to Locust Street. Tom was too drunk to remember much about that night except the way the snow crunched under their stumbling boots and the way it settled into every window-frame in an identical curve, brushed into perfect symmetry by the wind.

And so he was befriended. January lapsed into February, February into March and April, and the dirty snowbanks streaked with yellow by the dogs dwindled and disappeared. On most Saturday nights Tom stood in Gleason's with Andy and the others, a part of the circle though he said little. They spoke at length to each other with all the jibes and arguments that marked them as a close and self-contained group. The only other newcomer was Burke, who was younger than the rest, like himself, but a greenhorn, not long in the country, and a quiet type. Tom's mind often wandered when they talked of union problems and ward politics. But it didn't matter. He was accepted, and he was easy there. More important, he was accepted into Andy's home. With no effort on his part, he had secured a family to draw around himself when he needed it, without hindering his independent status.

Now he would have liked not just to warm himself at the family but perhaps shine a little in it, if he knew how. When he heard the cathedral bells he turned away from the lake and strolled through the streets named almost as an afterthought for the other Great Lakes, the ones Chicago hadn't appropriated – Ontario, Erie, Huron, Superior. The houses were grander here, stone and gravel, with full basements below and wide porches and bay windows above. At Chicago Avenue he passed Gleason's, glancing in the open door to the cool darkness, and crossed over to the wooden sidewalk on Sedgwick Street where the houses were clapboard and more familiar, shabby and small. From the corner of Locust Street he could see young Kate in front of the Foys' cottage, hopping on one foot with the other gripped behind her, her face tight with concentration. When she saw Tom she returned quickly to both feet and came toward him, skipping.

"Mama said you might be coming for supper. Are you?"

"Yep. If I'm still welcome."

"And will you sit next to me?"

"My pleasure," Tom answered solemnly.

"And not Robert?"

"Ah," he said. She was eleven or twelve years old and too thin, with gingery hair like her father and the same eyes, long and pale blue. But the coloring that served him well had somehow failed her.

The kitchen was steamy and boisterous with noise from the small boys who were under the table wrestling with each other. Andy ignored them, absorbed in the evening paper, but he threw it aside when he saw Tom. "Ah, the hard man," he said, pulling out a chair. "So you're reporting on this story about Pat Cronin, I hear. A true gentleman of the press at last."

"Not exactly. I haven't done much yet but look and listen, to tell the truth," Tom said, determined to do that. "It's a strange way to earn a living."

"Are you boasting, now, or complaining?" Lizzie called from the stove.

Andy grinned. "Yerra, don't mind her," he said. "Is there much in the way of news?"

"They've found this trunk. Yesterday."

"Aye, I saw the papers. A grim thing."

But Liz looked around warningly at him, nodding at the children, and then summoned them all to sit down. Tom looked up and down the table as he ate, enjoying it all: the children arguing and Lizzie reaching across them to spoon out more, chiding and coaxing in turn, urging them through the meal. There was a pitcher of beer on the table and one of lemonade to rinse down the ham, generally estimated tender enough though salty. Andy cut the meat into pieces on each plate and passed it down to one child after another. The window was open, and Tom could see a scraggly little tree that he'd never noticed before, a tough little city tree. Andy talked energetically of work. He'd been signed on for four weeks on the city tunnel. "Not much skill in it, Mr. Darwin's orangoutang could do it. But if we don't get a blast of wet weather it'll be steady for a good bit of the summer."

"And I'll be working this year, when I finish school," Kate said. "Won't I, Papa?"

"Why, you most certainly will!" he answered. "You'll be up

to that factory sewing rings around it. I'll be expecting a fine lawn shirt with hand-stitched embroidery down the front, to wear it when I run on the ticket."

"Oh, Papa," Kate groaned. But her eyes were shining.

"Oh, this is the serious business now," he protested. "I'm counting on you." He winked at her and edged a bit of ham from his plate on to hers so adroitly that her brothers didn't notice.

When they were finished the children slithered away from the table. Liz called after them as she poured the last of the beer into Tom's glass. "Mind you don't go near that vacant lot again, there's rats there." She sat down with a sigh of finality, pushing the apron over her head. "They never listen to a word I say. I could be talking to the coffee-pot."

Tom turned to her to comment, to joke, but Andy cut in suddenly, tapping his arm. "So. Tell us what's been happening." He fished a slightly battered cigar from his pocket and scratched a match off the edge of the table to light it.

"Just what you've read, I guess. I'm sort of assisting the reporter who's on the story, Dick Huntley. I'm not much use to him, but I suppose I should learn what I can while I have the chance."

"I know him, you know," Andy said. "Cronin."

"Do you?"

"Well enough. A cunning rat he is, too."

"Really?" Tom looked at him, shocked. "This landlady of his, she talks about him as if he were a hero."

"That doesn't say much," Andy said. There was a jeer in his voice. He held the cigar away from him. It had gone out, and he reached for another match and scratched it in a wider arc under the table.

"I wish you wouldn't do that," Liz interrupted. She sat gazing down, arms folded on the table.

"It does no harm." Andy lit the cigar again and inhaled tentatively.

"And there's no need to be nasty about Mrs. Conklin either," she said.

"All I'm saying is I wouldn't take her great admiration for

her lodger too seriously. Or any histrionics about his disappearance, either."

"And I say there's no need to mock her," Liz said sharply. "I've never heard anything to say she isn't a decent and generous soul, and you've no call to blacken her name."

"Blacken! Ah, Liz, give over now." Andy put his hand on her arm. She was still staring down, and she didn't move or answer.

"You don't think anything's happened to him then?" Tom asked after a moment. "But what about this trunk?"

"Well, that's a strange one, all right. But it's only all conjecture so far, and Cronin could be anywhere."

"I suppose he could," Tom said. "Why don't you like him?"

Andy took a moment to reply. "He's a particular kind of charm-boy, that's all. Even the Yanks think he's a lovely man. In fact he's particularly well got with the Yanks. A respectable Mickey."

"Still," Tom said hesitantly. That didn't mean he couldn't be in some kind of trouble, he thought. But Andy dismissed the subject, tipping the cigar ash on to his plate. "I'd be inclined to wait and see, myself. Now, what about a beer or two in Gleason's? I want to see some of the lads about a project I've in mind, and I'd like to get your thoughts on it."

"Your ballad!" Tom slapped his jacket pocket. It was still there in the envelope, unread and forgotten, and, watching him, Andy laughed.

"Sure, I didn't expect you to look at it given the day that was in it. Don't be worrying."

"But I did," Tom protested. "A quick look. It scans very well, I thought."

"Good," Andy nodded casually. But he was gratified. Andy regarded Tom's credentials as beyond dispute: a seminary education plus employment in the professional world of words. Sometimes Tom tried to point out that Andy's own breadth of knowledge was extraordinary, but Andy was matter-of-fact about his disadvantages. His formal education had ended at fifteen, and had been heavily influenced by the clandestine tradition of hedge-schools of his father's generation. He'd gone to Glasgow and been lucky enough to get an apprenticeship in an Irish building yard, where half the workers were like himself, he said, lightly spattered with Latin and Greek and the better-known classics. "A little learning, Mr. Pope failed to remark," Andy told him, "is an insecure thing."

Tom admired him for acknowledging insecurity. It was more than he could do himself. Nor could he, yet anyway, rise to the task of writing, sitting down to it and facing the limits of his own ability. But Andy did, regularly. He wrote whenever he had an hour, laboring over drafts with a pencil and then copying them on clean foolscap with a fine-nibbed pen. Some of his verses had been printed in the bulletin of the Columbia Club, which most of the group in Gleason's seemed to belong to as well. Once in a while he sent a verse or an essay off to a newspaper but nothing had ever come of his efforts. He didn't seem to mind.

Andy went into the front room to gather his papers from the wooden letterbox on the table, and Tom helped Liz to collect the last of the dishes. He stood beside her as she clattered them into the sink. "You're very good to me," he said suddenly. "It was a lovely supper, thanks."

"You're always welcome, you know that." She didn't look up.

Tom stood, twirling the hat as he had done just yesterday morning. He would as soon have stayed, that was the truth, drinking coffee with her at the kitchen table while the dark fell. As if she'd heard his thoughts Liz turned, smiling, and said, "Go on away off now, the pair of you. I've plenty to do. Andy, you won't be late?" Andy called back that he would not, and was out the door, his folder of papers under his arm.

When Tom had joined him he withdrew one and passed it over, saying, "See can you have a glance at that while we're walking; it's a letter to Ford at the *Irish World*. I've an idea for a production, but we'd need a bit of financial backing."

"A production? A play?"

"That's it. I've knocked out a draft of a play about the 1798 rebellion. We could get it off the ground in the Club, and if it was anyway good we could work on a bigger theme for the centenary."

41

"But that's years off."

"Ah sure, it'd take a few years to build it into something. But I need to persuade Ford to use his influence. I just want to get the tone of the letter right – not too pleading, you know, or boastful. Polite but confident. Here, have a quick read."

Tom looked at the paper in the fading light. "Friend Ford," it began. Andy's usual salutation in letters. The direct translation of the customary Gaelic salutation, he'd explained to Tom, who had tried to suggest that it wasn't a suitable form of address in America. But Andy was stubborn about it. He said he liked an egalitarian greeting that deferred to no rank. That was the sort of obstinacy he enjoyed, even when it was self-defeating.

The text of the letter was deferential in the extreme. That wasn't out of character either, Tom thought, half-smiling.

"Friend Ford; I hope you will pardon this intrusion on your time but I have been an almost constant reader of the *Irish World* for fourteen or fifteen years and this itself I hope is a sufficient apology to ask your aid. I hope you will carefully read the enclosed and if you see anything meritorious in it – as I think you will, since you are the father of a good many of the thoughts expressed in it – I know you will do all that you can to help me to place it in the hands of a good manager. It is only another way to spread the Light that costs you so much time and trouble to spread in your own way . . ."

He scanned down the rest of the page quickly. "It's fine, Andy."

"But will he bite the bait? Would you, say, if you were Ford?" Andy winked at Tom as if he were Kate. "Do you think it'll rouse his good green blood?"

"It's ringing stuff, if that's what you mean," Andy said, handing it back. "I don't know whether you should leave in that part at the end where you say it's hard for you to write because you have so many little kiddies."

"Do you think not?" Andy studied the page. "No, it sounds as if I'm looking for pity, you're right. I'll take it out."

"Would there be much of an audience, do you think, for a play about the '98 rebellion?" Tom asked. A failed rebellion, almost one hundred years past.

"I do, if it were given the right push. We don't forget our history." He gave Tom a good-humored nudge with his elbow. "Even a narrowback like you should know that." Tom smiled dutifully.

There were a dozen customers in Gleason's when they arrived, not bad at all for a Tuesday night, Andy observed. "Seems like every Mick in Chicago must be working this week," he said. He greeted a few of them and ordered while Tom waited, looking around him slowly. On Saturday nights, filled to capacity with men in a Saturday mood, the saloon always gave him a lift. But he saw it now as what Huntley had described yesterday, passing a similar place in Lakeview; a plank-between-two-barrels rough-house, nothing more than a low-ceilinged room lit by a single hanging-lamp over the counter. The walls were bare and browned with smoke and the layer of sawdust on the floor had been kicked by restless boots into a grubby carpet of whorls and ridges. The air was musty despite the open door, permanently stale with beer and sweat. Tom took his glass absently, seeing with Huntley's eyes. "Andy, do you know this man Alex Sullivan?" he asked.

"I do. Not well, of course, but I know him. Why?"

"Dr. Cronin's landlady, this Mrs. Conklin, she said – well, she said she thought anyway – that he was a great enemy of Dr. Cronin's."

"Did she now? She doesn't leave herself short of a dramatic line, does she? Alex Sullivan has done more good turns than any man in this town, and he's a man who never turned his back on his own. He's the living opposite of Cronin and if he dislikes him, you can take it there's a good reason. Here, will you try a chaser with that?"

"Not for me, you go ahead. Just what is it that's so admirable about him? From what I hear . . ."

But Andy interrupted, calling out to the man who had just come in the door, "Jack Gallagher, the very man; tell Tom what's admirable about Alexander Sullivan – and you and Packy have a whiskey." He turned to order and Jack joined them with one of his cronies, little Packy Ryan.

43

"Alex Sullivan is the man," Jack said. "You can't but admire him."

"But I've been told . . ."

"I won't hear a word against him," Jack insisted. He was one of Andy's workmates, a big, jovial man, but he looked warningly at Tom now and shook his head. "He's a friend to the working man, and that's what counts in my book. Damned few rich lawyers will stand out in the rain with the laborers, but during the Eight Hour Campaign Alex Sullivan was there every night, speaking his heart out."

"And the nig-ra civil rights," Packy put in. "Spoke for the nig-ras, too, and Jesus knows there's no joy to be had in that. Can't say I'd do it myself, now, but you have to admit the man's got honor. Are you distilling that yourself, Andy, or what?"

"It's coming, coming," Andy answered. "Jack, I've got something to show you before we get too scuttered."

"I've no intention of getting scuttered. Not that I'm not happy you're back on the payroll, of course. Your '98 play, is it?" Jack grinned at him. "I told you, I'm having nothing to do with this one. Unless I get to be Emmet."

"Oh mother of Jesus, is he at it again?" Paddy took his whiskey from Andy. "The bard of Kilgubbin. Plenty of ballads in the script now, I suppose?"

"You're a shower of begrudgers," Andy said. "Two ballads, possibly three . . ."

"Original compositions . . ."

"To by sung by Andy only . . ."

"I have Tom here in mind for Emmet, as a matter of fact."

"Me?"

"Ah, your moment is come, Tom. The bard has spoke: you'll be on the stage of the Lyceum before the year's out."

"I can't act, Andy. You're not serious."

"Hold your whisht," Andy said, and winked again at Tom. "Let's go to the back." He spoke briefly to the bartender who took keys from behind the counter and unlocked the back room. Tom had been in there before with them. It was darker, smaller and smelled even more sourly than the main saloon, but

44

it was private. The bartender lit the lamp in a wall bracket and took Packy's order for another pitcher of beer before he left them.

Andy spread his script out on the table, full of scribbled notes on the margins of the pages, and urged them to stop joking and listen. He was genuinely enthusiastic, anyone could see that, Tom thought; but Jack and Packy were equal to him and he couldn't get more than two sentences out without interruptions of rising hilarity. At last Andy forgot the script, and they were all laughing and on a fourth pitcher of beer. Jack's intentions had also been put aside, and he bought a half-pint of whiskey to supply chasers. "Here's to the best of Yankee initiative," Andy toasted, flushed. "Sour mash bourbon."

The talk turned to the job, then, and the three men began to argue with heat about a foreman with a Boston accent. Tom had trouble following them. He concentrated on pretending to sip whiskey and sheltered his glass from the pitcher, thinking prudently about the morning. Andy borrowed his hat and strutted around the table, mimicking: "O'Connah, what's the big idear taking a break? What ah yah, a smaht guy? Pick up that hawd and move."

It was past midnight when they got back to Locust Street.

"I'm done for with Liz now," Andy said. "Sure, I'll blame you." When he saw Tom's look, he burst into laughter and slapped him affectionately on the back. "Jesus, don't look so outraged: I'm joking. She won't mind. She knows I need a long leash now and then. A good night, wasn't it?"

"Yes. A good night." But Tom was a little outraged. Sometimes Andy went too far, too far, and it wasn't fair to Liz. Andy stared ahead into the street, lit only by moonlight. "The moon hath raised her lamp above," he whispered, and then sang the line, his voice echoing between the still houses.

"Hush, man, you'll wake the dead," Tom said.

"No fear of that," Andy said, his strange eyes drunkenly vacant but brilliant. "It's 'The Lily of Killarney'. That song always reminds me of my mother." He waved Tom off and went in, fumbling only slightly with his latchkey, and as swift and graceful as a cat as he sidled in the door.

45

V

THERE WAS A copy boy waiting for Tom when he arrived in the newsroom on Wednesday. "Mr. Percy wants to see you in his office, Mr. Martin," he declared shrilly. So much for that short-lived trial, Tom thought; no surprise really. Still, the "Mr. Martin" was nice. His stock might have gone up a fraction of an inch even in just two days.

Percy's office was a dim little room in the far corner of the editorial floor, furnished with a few chairs, a table with a badly scratched top, and shelves overflowing with papers and ancient almanacs. It was usually used only to hire, fire and occasionally berate. Tom had gone through his own interview in there, battling off convulsions of sneezing from the dust.

But Percy was not alone, as Tom had expected. Huntley was there, and Percy sat across from him, hunched over a thick manila folder of cuttings. An assistant city editor named Winslow Elliott was on Percy's right, but a respectful foot or so back. Elliott was a cadaverous young man with pale hair and eyebrows and a fixed expression which signified that life was earnest. He was next in line to Percy, and the rest of the staff, who called him "the Dauphin," claimed Percy had appointed him to discourage any uprising against his own stewardship.

Huntley greeted him with this usual "Howdy" when Tom pushed the door open, but Percy merely looked up, preoccupied. "Martin," he said without preamble, "I want us to get our thoughts together on this Cronin story, figure out what way we're going with this. You know Mr. Elliott? Sit down there. Winslow, what are you, taking a few notes?" Tom nodded to Winslow who, intent on his notebook didn't notice. "Okay, Dick, you think Alex Sullivan's probably implicated?

How, where, why – the usual."

"Still ain't certain there's anythin' to be implicated in, John, but if there is, Sullivan's name is the one bein' whispered," Huntley answered.

"Sonavabitch." Percy growled into the folder. "Sullivan. Look at this bum's record: '68, arrested on arson and fraud charges, setting fire to his own shoe-store. Released. '70, Internal Revenue . . ."

"Released on an alibi," Huntley interjected. "Supplied by none other than Peg, ain't that right? Said they was at church when the fire broke out?"

"Yeah, yeah, that's right. Miss Margaret Buchanan, later to become Mrs. Alex. At church saying their prayers together. Goddam sonavabitch. '70, Internal Revenue collector, Santa Fe, New Mexico; fired after financial irregularities discovered. '71, postmaster, Santa Fe. Fired, financial irregularities discovered. What a Little Boy Blue we got here."

"Any trials there you'd like me to take a note on, John?" Winslow asked, his pencil poised. Percy looked around at him distantly and then turned back to the file. "No. No trials. How the hell does he do it?"

"With money," Huntley said. "Bought up the Santa Fe *Post* the same year, that in the file?"

"Yeah, yeah," Percy sighed now, and turned another loose page in the folder. "Came to Chicago in '72 and worked as a reporter. Christ Almighty, I'd almost forgotten that. On the *Post*. Then he got into politics. '76, murders Francis Hanford and pleads self-defense. Acquitted. Fixed the jury; am I right, Dick?"

"They say the sheriff did that for him," Huntley replied.

"Whosit, Frankie Agnew?" Percy asked.

"Frankie Agnew." Huntley shifted in his chair and stared at the ceiling. "On account a' Alex was too big a name to risk gettin' convicted a' jury bribin'. Let alone convicted a' murderin' a man in cold blood just because he said Alex's wife was a whore." Huntley snorted once, grinning, and then said: "I reckon that's how Alex impinges on this here story, 'cause it appears Cronin is pretty big, too, in the Irish societies."

"Or was . . ." Winslow prompted. "Or was pretty big."

They all looked around, and Huntley said, "Yes a' course, Winslow; or was. I'm forgettin' myself. And Cronin and Alex are, or were, not too friendly."

Percy slammed the folder shut. "Is or was, Cronin's no Alexander Sullivan. Sullivan controls more patronage than any man in Chicago, dogs in the street'd tell you that, right? Who's Cronin in Chicago? Something in the Irish societies maybe, but he's no big man in this town. What are we talking here, Dick? We're talking some Clan feud, right?"

"I dunno," Huntley said simply. "Not yet. Think it's a bit early for this kind a' meetin', as I said before Tom here come in."

"Okay. All right." Percy turned for the first time to Tom, who felt alarm prickle his skin. He cleared his throat to reply to whatever Percy would ask, but Percy stood up and handed the folder to a startled Winslow. "I say we got to get some line on what's going on inside the Clan, these societies, and, Tom, any way you can help Huntley would be good. We'll drop it for now."

"Will I schedule another conference, John?" Winslow asked. His pencil hovered edgily over his notebook.

"Not yet," Percy grunted, walking out, "couple of days."

Winslow stood and shut his notebook. "I imagine we'd want to be awfully careful with this one," he said to Huntley.

"We sure would," Huntley agreed.

"Well, if there's anything more comes up you can get in touch with me and I'll see that John's informed," Winslow said and followed Percy out, nodding solemnly at Tom as he passed.

"I'll keep that in mind," Huntley said when the door closed.

Tom smiled uneasily at him, and Huntley rose. "Let's go," he said cheerfully.

They walked along Madison to State Street and caught a street-car headed south. It was crowded with shoppers, women clutching children and bundles, and Tom grabbed an overhead strap and swayed next to Huntley. Ahead of them the traffic thickened in a kind of chaotic battle, the pedestrians crossing haphazardly, the cars bearing down against horse-drawn hacks.

When the cable line above sparked and fizzed, the horses shied. Tom could hear their frantic whinnying and see cab-drivers leaning out to curse the cars, but their voices were lost under the jubilant clanging racket of grip-wheels and gongs.

Two small boys, barefoot and filthy, darted in front of their car to put pennies in the grooved tracks, and a half-dozen of the women near Tom leaned out to scream at them. As the car churned steadily ahead Tom turned back to watch the little boys retrieve their flattened coins and dance back to the sidewalk. One of them stuck his tongue out, and then turned his bottom to the passengers and ceremoniously stuck that out, too.

They whirred on, past huge stores, and new stone office buildings next to drabber, humbler shopfronts. Adams, Jackson, Van Buren. Straight on south were the bawdy houses, gambling parlors open all night, well-kept brownstones that housed expensive prostitutes. Tom thought of them shuttered against the daylight and of Mrs. Sullivan, accused of being a whore. At Harrison, Huntley nodded to him and Tom realized they must be headed for Harrison Street station. But Huntley stopped on the sidewalk and looked around him, and then his face brightened. "Now, that's just what I'd like to start my day," he said, and pointed ahead to a barber's striped pole. "Like a shave, Tom?"

"I've shaved already," Tom said.

"You can sit and watch me," Huntley said. "Won't be too long. A good class a' barber this end a' town. Them riverboat gambling types don't care to be caught lookin' seedy."

The shop was as hushed as a saloon after the street noise. It smelled of clean aromatic tonics. The tiled floor was shining, the huge oval mirrors before the chairs were polished and flawless. There were occupants in every chair, apparently comatose, eyes closed, swathed in towels. A few customers were waiting, in vast leather armchairs that looked as if they came from a gentleman's club, some of them talking in a restrained but convivial way, one or two deep into their newspapers. Gamblers, men of high income dubiously acquired? Men whose income didn't require their afternoon input, anyway. Business magnates and bankers and brokers, maybe. Or indolent reporters. He and Huntley settled into two chairs at the end of the row, and Tom sat back to survey the scene covertly through half-closed eyes. But Huntley leaned toward him and remarked, "You're lookin' a bit weary a' all this, Tom. Not bored, I hope?"

"God, no. No, not at all. I'm just – ah, you know, thinking."

"What about?"

"Well," Tom said, "Oh, about Peg Sullivan accused of being a whore, for instance." He looked around carefully, but they were some distance from the others, whoever they were.

"Not exactly a whore," Huntley said. "Near enough. This fella Hanford, a teacher, said she was tryin' to influence patronage in the school system by dispensin' her feminine favors to a certain politician. Alex went around to Hanford and there was a bit of a flare up; Sullivan shoots him. He was tried for murder, but the first time around trial ended in a hung jury. Just couldn't make up their minds. Next trial Alex got off."

"That was when the jury was bribed?"

"Never proved. Seems likely to most people. But it did Alex some harm – they say it's why he's never run for office himself. Too many people think he should have swung from a rope for Hanford if for nothin' else."

"But he's still very powerful in politics?"

"Ain't nobody to touch him." Huntley's voice was casual, but he looked at Tom closely as he spoke. "It's said he's top man in this here Clan na Gael, though bein' a secret society, it ain't down in black-and-white that I can find. But you heard Percy. And the Clan's got the power in City Hall, that's known too. Do you follow me?"

Tom thought of how frequently he'd heard the Clan mentioned in Gleason's. Toasts, usually, after a few beers: "Here's to the Clan," someone might cry, or "Up the Clan" or "Thank God for the Clan." But it was hard to believe that the men there – Andy and his friends, out of work much of the time – had connections with the city's powerful. "I'm not sure," he said. "I can see that you're back to the business of secret Irish societies, though."

Huntley laughed, a bit ruefully. "All right, that's so. I am. But it connects with this Doc Cronin disappearin', don't you

51

see? That's why I bring it up. When things like that start happenin', and a gory trunk gets found, people start thinkin' about secret societies like this Clan, and Alexander Sullivan and his pretty dirty past, and it works on their minds. I'm tellin' you so's you'll be prepared for hearin' remarks about the Irish and what they're up to."

"Clan na Gael," Tom said reflectively, "is an organization that supports Irish independence. That much I do know. Lots of Irishmen will tell you they support that, there's no secret about it. I don't see why anyone should care what the Irish are up to about Ireland's independence."

"You ain't listenin' to me. No one's bothered about Irish independence — not here, anyway — but they're bothered that the Irish run the city, and what with so many Irish in the Clan, that the Clan runs the city. And it's all done in secret, which is what's bothersome."

"That's an exaggeration," Tom said. "That the Irish run the city."

"Not much." Huntley leaned toward him. "Look at this now for a fact, Tom. Irish don't make up anythin' like a third a' the population a' this city, but there's Irishmen sittin' tight in one-third a' the city council seats. Most of 'em Democrats — now and then you get fellas switchin' over for one reason or another, but it don't matter none. One ward boss does a deal with another ward boss and the whole show keeps runnin'. Chicago ain't New York. We ain't got one big machine working here, we got a whole lot a' small ones workin' together. Mike McDonald and Chesterfield Joe Mackin out in front, and Alex Sullivan in the back room, all dealin' out the jobs and whippin' up the vote and shakin' hands with the priest on Sunday. So the Irish in this Clan have the say. They get to pick who gets the jobs in the police, and the fire department, and the sewers and lightin' and city maintenance."

"And the rest of Chicago?" Tom demanded. His voice was a little more annoyed than he'd expected. "What about them? They don't mind?"

"What rest? Eighty per cent a' the city's foreign, or children a' foreigners, and who they gonna depend on but the Irish?

Germans and the Poles, they ain't got the experience to run a political machine. Ain't got the English language to begin with. The Irish got that. And they seemed to have some practice at the politics, too, so they run things. Get first crack at the jobs and give the Germans and the Poles and such whatever's left over. That's a lot a' power, and power frightens people. Eighty per cent a' the city, that's a lot a' foreigners to be frightened. There's my chair ready. Got anythin' to read?"

Huntley stood up as he spoke, nodding to the barber in the last chair who shook out a fresh towel and smiled at him. "Be right with you, Ray," Huntley called to him, and leaned once more toward Tom. "Ray here's a good source a' mine, don't say I told you. Never know what I might pick up."

"It doesn't seem like that in the *Tribune*," Tom said. "Eighty per cent foreign, I mean."

Huntley laughed and straightened up. "No, the *Trib* is the other twenty per cent. They aim to keep it that way, too," he said. "That's another kind a' secret society."

VI

THERE WAS A telephone message waiting for Huntley when he and Tom came back to the newsroom late that afternoon. A Miss Annie Murphy, employee in the City Recorder's office, had a statement to make on the Cronin case. Annie had been making her statement all day to reporters but she delivered it to Huntley and Tom when they arrived as if it were the first time, speaking in a low and thrilling voice. She had seen Dr. Cronin on the night he disappeared.

"I had been paying a visit to friends on Garfield Avenue and left at nine o'clock, taking a Garfield Avenue car. At the corner of Clark Street this was attached to a cable-train. When we reached Division Street I looked into the cable-car and I am positive that I saw Dr. Cronin sitting in it, his arms folded and his head bowed as if in deep thought. He had an oblong bundle of some kind resting on his knees. I am as certain of his identity as I am of my own." She knew him well to see, Annie explained, looking gravely from Tom to Huntley. Elocution was her first love, and she had shared numerous platforms with the doctor at Irish entertainment evenings.

Later that afternoon the street-car conductor corroborated the story. He spoke to the reporters gathered in the car barns when he came off duty. He was self-conscious but very definite. The car that left at 9.18pm had picked up a passenger at Frederick Street who fitted Miss Murphy's description. "I took particular notice of him because he was a striking looking man, tall and good-looking sort of fellow. Well dressed. He was carrying a black case and a long kind of bundle. Didn't look at it too close." The car was nearly empty and he watched the passenger, having not much else to do. "I noticed that he seemed caught up in his own thoughts, and didn't look out the window much, but he looked up when we passed the Windsor Theater. He asked which stop was nearest Union Station and that's where he got off." That drew a scatter of exclamations from the reporters and one surprised whistle. Even Huntley had no questions.

By Thursday the papers were reflecting the theory that was beginning to gain currency in the police stations, that Cronin had engineered his own departure from the city in peculiar circumstances for reasons unknown. The story was big, front page and at length in every daily. The city was as intrigued with a doctor who'd devised his own theatrical exit as one who'd been kidnapped by villains of his landlady's imagination.

But Huntley wanted reasons, at least possible reasons. When Tom came in that afternoon he was sent to the basement room known as 'the Morgue', where clippings from all the papers were filed on wooden shelves reaching to the ceilings. The envelope on "Cronin, Dr. P.H." was respectably hefty – short items from the major papers, wordier articles from the *Celtic American*, the *Irish Nation*.

Tom unfolded each column of print in turn and held it down flat with one hand while he took notes. "Born 1845 in Mallow, County Cork. Emigrated with family as a child to Ontario, served in Canadian army. Moved to St. Louis, 1867, studied pharmacy and medicine. Traveled abroad, arrived Chicago 1882. Appointed to Cook County Hospital."

The refolded clippings piled up beside him, layers of testimony to Dr. Cronin's cultural and educational achievements, his involvement with the arts. Reviews of public meetings quoted his speeches; he seemed to have been a regular invited speaker at the Manchester Martyrs commemoration every October. He also sang frequently at concerts. Tom found the review of one he had gone to with Liz and Andy in March. "The 111th anniversary of the birth of Robert Emmet, given under the auspices of the Irish Nationalists of Chicago, at Central Music Hall . . . a fine tenor rendition of 'The Last Rose of Summer' from the esteemed Dr. Patrick Henry Cronin." He was president of the Celto-American Club of Chicago and active in the Ancient Order of Hibernians as well as more societies than Tom had heard of: the Royal League, the Legion of Honor, Ancient Order of Foresters, the Royal Arcanum, the Knights of Pythias.

"Nothing but praise and honors," Tom told Huntley.

"Any personal background – never married? Could 'a been a lady somewhere."

"No sign of her, anyway. Seems he's lived with the Conklins over the Windsor Theater since he came here."

"Nice place, big suite of room. Solicitous landlady. I guess it'd suit some. No debts? No previous mysterious disappearances?"

"No."

"Nothin' about any secret societies, I guess?"

Tom shook his head. "No. Nothing."

"There wouldn't be, though, would there?" Huntley said affably. But he agreed now with the general opinion that Mrs. Conklin's forebodings had begun to look a little silly.

They went on working, in the pattern they'd maintained since Monday, Tom trailing after Huntley, as silent as an Indian scout but considerably less useful, he thought. He had no sense of what Huntley could need him for. Each day they'd meet in the newsroom about midday, Huntley greeting him every time with a genial "Howdy" as if they were the neighbors passing time at the back fence. Then they went out to talk to people: cops, shopkeepers, bartenders, city officials, Huntley's contacts. Tom could see no efficiency or planning in Huntley's method. Three times they had gone out to Lakeview to watch the police searching for clues. There were dozens of them crawling over the sand-dunes and scuffing up the dirt-road with their boots, bored and irritated. Tom was in some sympathy with them.

Huntley talked to everyone. After one or two studied efforts, Tom gave up trying to pluck up conversations and kept to answering when he was addressed, which was seldom. He gave up, too, cudgeling his wits with the conundrum of Cronin's disappearance, though he maintained an absorbed expression during the endless conversations – a small frown, the occasional nod. Much of the time he kept a sideways watch on the girls hurrying past them on the streets, brisk in their white office shirtwaists, fresh as the ice-creams in the drug-stores where he and Huntley sometimes stopped for coffee. He tried them out mentally, inventing situations in which he might meet them and stroll with them in the evenings, discarding one and promoting another. His face showed nothing, though. He had acquired a certain expertise in this sort of thing in the seminary. He knew any imagined scenes had to remain fairly tepid.

Every day they had returned to the newspaper in the late afternoon, and while Huntley wrote his reports Tom read the opposition papers, tearing out the items related to Cronin for Huntley's attention. Huntley wove it all into a long narrative of facts and descriptions and rumors. When he'd finished his holding story for the first edition, they went back out to the night, two tiny figures in the deserted canyon of office blocks, toiling forward into the yellow pools spilled by the gas-lamps. Sometimes, drawn by music from pianos and hurdy-gurdys, they wandered along State Street, a bright carnival after dark with all its shabby edges in the shadows. They strolled from the music hall and theater district, where the crowds who poured along the pavement smelled of perfume and good cigars, down to south downtown, where country boys gawked at chippies who stood under streetlights and blew kisses. They flowed into the night crowds of drifters, vagrants, hobos, part of the carnival, with the uniformed black men outside casinos and the barkers luring the lonely into shows for only a nickel.

They went to City Hall, dark except for the press room, and then to a police station or two. Before the paper finally went to bed they returned to the newsroom. Huntley usually changed a paragraph or two for the morning edition, adding fresh speculation or re-assigning the importance of old information, and Tom went through the later editions of the other papers.

If Huntley expected something more of him Tom saw no hint of it, and when they were alone they talked, trading information little by little as they moved through the city. Huntley talked most, about Indiana, where he'd grown up, and the east – New York, Boston, Washington – where he'd gone to college. His father was the kind of man America loved, Huntley said.

He'd started with a horse and cart traveling farm to farm, selling bolts of cloth and pots and pans, and ended with a dry-goods emporium that multiplied its own profits effortlessly.

Huntley had expected that he'd follow into the business, and spend his life chatting to customers and fishing in country streams and reading on a country front porch. But his father, in the way of fathers, wanted more for him and hoped that the years in an eastern college would set him on course to becoming a congressman or a lawyer. All it did, he said, was give him an insatiable wanderlust and so he pursued the rising sun across the Atlantic to the European capitals, London and Paris and Vienna. He started working as a journalist there for the international agencies and the dispatches directed to America finally stole over him in a wave of homesickness. "Realized I missed the place. Took me a long time to get back and now that I am I don't aim to go no further away again. Might even end up back in Indiana someday, just fishin' and readin'."

Huntley had no clear memory of his mother. She died when he was very young. That was the one bond of experience they shared, though in fact Tom remembered his own mother's death well. Tom told Huntley about the orphanage in Baltimore. He gave facts, which Huntley liked: the number of orphans, the different duties of the nuns, the schedule of their day. He thought, while he talked, of the rows of white beds tidied in the morning before early mass and the smell of the nuns' serge habits when they bent over him to help with lessons, the nuns who had taught him sums and geography and English grammar and then placed him in the seminary.

But when Huntley asked him about Ireland, Tom had to struggle to summon up anything worth saying. "My mother never talked much about Ireland, nor my father either," he told Huntley. "Not that I remember. I know there was terrible poverty and fear of trouble, and people believed America was salvation, a sort of heaven."

"And yet when you hear these Mickeys here singin' about Ireland, they seem to think they're singin' about heaven," Huntley said.

"Yes, I know. It's what exile does to you, I suppose."

"Exile," Huntley said. "That how you think a' it?"

"Not me. Others, I mean."

It was Friday night when they had that conversation, heading along Chicago Avenue to the police station on the corner of Clark Street. Something about the night, exceptionally still for Chicago, stirred Tom's memory deeper. It had been warm all week now, and each day the trees were a little greener. Even the wind had given up and died away. But dark had fallen without warning, though it was barely seven o'clock, and what Tom remembered suddenly was the way his mother had talked of the long evening light in Ireland in the summers. She had hated the way that day dropped into night in America. Rude, graceless, like America itself. He smiled and immediately thought of Liz. It was the sort of fancy she enjoyed.

But the thought of her tweaked another worry that had nagged him since Tuesday. He had meant to call in on Liz and Andy again, to find out more if he could about Cronin and Alex Sullivan. He had seen himself telling them – with some enhancement, he suspected – of his part in the reports so far. Well, he had been busy. But with every turn the story took he had also felt unhappier about the entire way it turned on things related to Ireland. Supposing Cronin's disappearance had nothing to do with Ireland? Wouldn't they all look fools then? But no one gave any consideration to that; not Huntley, not Percy, not any of the other papers, either. There was a general conviction that some Irish feud, as Percy said, was behind it all, possibly something quite ridiculous. Yes, there was a touch of contempt in the public curiosity. More than contempt – derision. Once or twice it had struck Tom that perhaps the others, the other reporters, thought of him with derision, too, an ignorant young Mickey roped in to trot tamely at Huntley's heels. He wished that his chance, whatever it was amounting to, had come about some other way.

He was examining the problem, pondering, when he caught Huntley smiling placidly at him.

"Penny for 'em."

"Ah, nothing. They're not worth that much."

"Dunno – we were talkin' about songs and Ireland and

heaven and you go into a trance. Must be somethin' on your mind."

Tom was working on an answer when they were interrupted.

"That you, Huntley? I been looking for you." They were in front of the police station, the entrance lit by a single lamp, and the man who leaned heavily against the doorway stretched lazily and approached them. He was big and heavy and even in the dark Tom recognized him by his walk, slouched but alert. A street animal.

"Why, Detective Dan, friend of the free press," Huntley said. "You recall Detective Inspector Coughlan, Tom?"

Tom mumbled good evening, but Coughlan ignored him. He loomed over Huntley, who smiled at him cordially and said, "Give up scuttlin' around sand-dunes for the night, I see."

"Got something better inside here, Huntley. We're keeping him just for you, a special for the breakfast readers."

"Mighty kind a' you. What might it be, I wonder?"

"Horse-thief, name of Frankie Woodruff. Picked him up on his usual charge this afternoon and he decides to make a perfect act of contrition, starting with the trunk that held the missing body."

"That right?"

"Seems he carted it around last Saturday night and waited while some gents dumped the body in it, then he ran right off and got rid of the trunk for them."

"Most obligin'," Huntley remarked. "Don't suppose the body was Doc Cronin's?"

"Nope," Coughlan cocked his head slightly. Tom could see him grinning. "Appears Doc Cronin was one of the gents."

Woodruff was a little ferret of a man, jumpy and wild-eyed. He spoke so rapidly Coughlan had to stop him several times and make him repeat his words slowly enough for Huntley to get them down. He said he'd been in Sol Van Praag's gambling house on South Street on the Wednesday before Dr. Cronin disappeared and had lost a lot of money. "Guy come up to me, never saw him before, says he'll put me in the way of a few bucks if I can get a horse and light rig for a job." They hit on a price of $25 and Woodruff agreed. The job was set for late Saturday night. Woodruff lifted a rig from a livery stable on Webster Avenue and drove to a barn at the rear of 528 North State Street where three men were waiting. One of them was called Doc.

Woodruff helped them haul a trunk out of the barn and load it on to the wagon, with the one they called Doc urging them to hurry. "He was rattling," Woodruff said. "Kept telling us to hurry, get a move on." The other two got into the wagon with Woodruff, who drove up the lake shore to the north end of Lincoln Park and turned there for another quarter of a mile. "These two guys tell me to stop and keep my eyes on the road and I hear one of them say, 'Here's where we drop Alice.' I look around quick and see they'd dumped a body outta this trunk, it smelled terrible. I didn't see nothing else. They paid me off and said to leave them there and get moving and get rid of the trunk somewhere."

Huntley wrote steadily in his hen scratches. Woodruff said he'd dumped the trunk about fifteen minutes later, where it had been found the next day. He remembered the hinge breaking when the trunk crashed to the ground. He knew it wasn't a good hiding place but he was too scared to look further. "I didn't know it was nothing like this or I wouldn't 'uv said I'd do it."

He said it twice and Coughlan cut him off. "Okay, Woodruff, that's enough. A decent ordinary thief like you, why, it's shocking to see you dragged into this kind of thing. Huntley here knows that. He'll give you a nice write-up." Huntley asked some questions and Woodruff went over the story again, watching Coughlan, who stared indifferently out the barred window of the interrogation room.

"That enough for you, Huntley?" Coughlan said finally. He signalled the policeman outside to take charge of Woodruff and walked with Huntley and Tom through the station house. "Got it all to yourself for tomorrow morning's paper," he said to Huntley as they stood at the door. "Can't say I'm not thinking of you." Huntley didn't answer. He was looking at the line of men beginning to form on the sidewalk at the bottom of the steps.

"Ever strike you, Dan," Huntley said, "what a barbaric thing it is that there's so many people in this city with nowhere to go, they gotta spend the night with the cops?"

"Strikes me if it weren't for the cops there'd be a lot more dead on the streets," Coughlan said, following his gaze. "Half of them'd be better off dead, maybe."

There weren't many tonight, half a dozen men too tired to keep moving and determined not to lose their place on the station-house floor when the doors were opened at midnight to the city's wretched and homeless. Tom had seen it much worse last winter, hundreds of men in thin, dirty clothes, elbowing each other for first places.

Huntley looked at Coughlan. "Well, what are you boys goin' to do with your horse-thief?" he asked.

"Book him. And start looking for Alice's body instead of Doc Cronin's. Suppose we might be looking for a live Cronin now."

"Seems logical. Botched criminal abortion, that ain't a nice thing and the Doc might want to stay missin' a while. Seems like abortion, don't it?"

"Most likely. Even an experienced hand like Doc Cronin could go wrong."

"And this fellow approached Woodruff, he'd 'a known on Wednesday night that there'd be some terrified woman who was gonna get her innards ripped away and be ready for dumpin' by Sunday mornin'?"

"That had us at first, too. Then I realized that'd be why the corpse would smell so bad."

"Sure." Huntley nodded. "So. Cronin's hand slips, say, Tuesday maybe, and he hides the body in a barn for four, five days while he arranges to get rid a' it. Risky, ain't it?"

Coughlan shrugged. "Safer to make careful plans. Cronin was shrewd enough."

"Guess so," Huntley said. "Well, we better take off. Mighty grateful to you." He started down the steps, Tom behind him. They skirted the line of waiting men, who looked after them sullenly.

"Don't mention it," Coughlan called.

Huntley took off his glasses and polished them on his handkerchief as they walked and then paused under the streetlamp to hold them up for inspection. "What do you make a' that?" he asked Tom.

Tom was not ready, though he'd been thinking about what his response should be to the inevitable question the whole time Woodruff was hurtling through his story. "It seems crazy for anyone to hide a body so long, but his description of the man called Doc sounded exactly like Mrs. Conklin's description of Dr. Cronin, anyway," he ventured.

"Perfect. But he'd 'a read that in any paper this week."

Tom, defeated again, watched Huntley adjust his glasses on his nose. "S'pose Coughlan thought a' that, a' course," Huntley went on. "Think Doc Cronin was the local abortionist?"

Tom fell into step beside him and turned over several replies before he said, "It doesn't seem like it, after everything everybody says about him."

"No," Huntley said. "It don't. Though Coughlan's suggestin' it, ain't he? Wanted me to fall for that one, but I wasn't bitin'." His face showed a brief flash of grim satisfaction, the nearest Tom had seen to malice. "Then again," he added, "there's always the possibility this would 'a been a special exception. Most people will allow themselves any crime you care to name if it's a special exception. What I can't see is, even if he needed to get out a' town for a while, why he'd do it such a way as to be sure that everybody'd be talkin' about him."

"So you don't think it's true?"

"Well, it could be – happens sometimes with murders, the mysterious ones – you get a fellow begins to imagine he was there. Could be Woodruff's plain off his chump."

But Huntley put every detail of what Woodruff had said into his report, typing steadily while Tom finished reading through the other papers and went on to the "missing persons" file. There was no mention of an Alice, no mention of a woman reported missing in the last two weeks. But that didn't mean anything. Alice could have been a woman no one had missed yet. An out-of-town visitor known only to Dr. Cronin. Or a country girl he'd never heard of but took pity on, someone who'd traveled up from a dusty Southern Illinois town to

64

prowl Chicago in a frantic search for a solution to her problem. Or a streetwalker no one noticed wasn't on her beat.

Percy came up to them. His face was as benign as Tom had yet seen it, glowering with approval

"This should blow up a storm," he said.

"More so if there were only an Alice," Huntley answered, yawning.

"You think it's palaver?"

"More'n likely. But you never know."

"Well, it's a good lively yarn anyhow. We'll let it run." Percy frowned and considered Huntley for a minute as if he'd just noticed something different about him. "Better take tomorrow off. Things'll be busy Sunday." He turned to Tom. "You, too."

When he'd done, Huntley let his fingers rest on the typewriter keys and to Tom's amazement began to sing, in a shrill schoolboy's voice.

"We want to feel the sunshine,
We want to smell the flowers,
We're sure that God has willed it
And we mean to have eight hours."

He broke off. "Don't suppose you heard much a' the Eight Hour Movement in the seminary?"

"Not much," Tom laughed.

"Eight hours for work, eight hours for rest, eight hours for what we will," Huntley recited. "Not in this game. Better take off now and I'll see you Sunday."

VII

L YING IN BED on Saturday morning, Tom laid drowsy plans for the day, beginning with his usual routine with the papers and proceeding to another explorative foray into Chicago. On his last venture he had wandered into the Jewish community at Milwaukee and Division, and picked his way behind the peddlers with handcarts, examining posters printed in the tight, upside down figures of Yiddish. But there would be no life there on a Saturday, of course. His ultimate afternoon destination was Clark and Kinzie, where he had established on several previous visits a nodding acquaintance with a startlingly pretty girl in the Chakonas grocery shop. He did the nodding, to be honest, and she studied the floor and smiled. But he knew her name now, an absolutely wonderful name, Nanda; exotic but vivacious. And pronounceable.

Mrs. Delaney dragged him from his meditations. She had a habit of summoning her boarders with a hammering of knuckles on the door interspersed with a few words at a time. "Mr. Martin?" Knock, knock. "Are yez awake?" Knock, knock. "Message for you." Knock, knock, knock, knock. The effect was galvanizing. Tom leaped from the bed, yanked on his trousers and staggered to the door crying "Yes! Coming!"

"Young Kate Foy to see you," Mrs. Delaney announced.

"Thanks," Tom said. "Thanks, I'll be right there."

Kate was practising her one-legged balancing trick on the doorstep. "Papa says will you be in Gleason's tonight, he's a message for you."

"Well. A message." Tom yawned. "Tell him unless I can find an heiress to take me off this afternoon, I'll probably be there."

"A what?"

67

"A wealthy wife."

"Oh, you." She stuck her tongue out, turned and hopped away.

Tom watched her go up the street, a puff of dust rising behind every hop. It was warm, the warmest day since he'd come to the city. He would not really need his hat, but he had no intention of not wearing it.

He went though all the morning papers before he went out, satisfied that the *Tribune* had the Woodruff story to itself. Coughlan had kept his word. The afternoon papers would pick it up and be full of speculation on the sinister journey and the identity of Alice.

Then he dressed and set off to the corner where Clark Street crossed Kinzie Street. It was the center of the Italian district, but lately more and more Greek immigrant families had begun to settle there. On Saturday afternoon the corner was jammed with hucksters' carts heaped with fruit and vegetables, where the women jostled each other with their shopping baskets. There were dozens of stalls up and down Kinzie selling sausages, or bread dipped in olive oil and tomato sauce, and restaurants no bigger than the Foy's kitchen where the men sat together and viewed the street benevolently. Part of Tom's enchantment with the place was that it smelled of nothing he knew, dark and overwhelming coffees and tobaccos, strange and indolent spices and herbs.

But the real pleasure was the flood of strange language. If he averted his eyes from the crooked tenement buildings behind him, it was as if he were not in America at all, but in some Mediterranean village. He continued to marvel at the fact that they all understood each other, the shouters and jokers and the voluble conversationalists who waved their hands while they spoke, and he understood not a word.

The Chakonas grocery was a little way down a side street. Tom had deduced from his earlier expeditions that when Mr. Chakonas was on the premises, he dealt with all customer communications. Both Nanda and the wispy little woman he assumed must be Mrs. Chakonas were confined to the parceling counter, backs to the world, as silent as if they had taken vows. When Mr. Chakonas was out – and he did apparently while away some of his Saturday afternoon with the other men over their miniature coffee-cups – he had seen that it was quite different, but he hadn't managed to work up a chat with either of them himself.

Tom passed the shop twice, glancing in. When he was reasonably sure Mr. Chakonas was not lurking in a back room ready to sabotage his offensive, he pushed open the door, which had a jolly little bell to announce arrivals. The two women were behind the counter, Nanda holding a vast bowl while the old woman poured a basin of black olives into it. She was really quite beautiful, Tom decided. There was a lovely sheen to her skin and her eyes were enormous, large and lustrous, like the very olives tumbling into the bowl clasped in her arms.

"Well, I'm just in time, I see," Tom said. He smiled from one to the other, starting shrewdly with Mrs. Chakonas. "That's exactly what I've come for."

"Eh, you like olives, they like you; they're verra good for you," the woman said. She grinned back at him and Nanda looked at the floor.

Immediately, just as before, Tom felt elated with himself, bold and easy-going, a man with a captivating way of speaking. "They're wonderful," he said. "Last time I was in I bought a quarter." A regular customer, a steady young man with income and taste. He smiled again directly at the old woman. "I had them eaten before I was down the street. I suppose I'd better get more this time?"

The woman dumped the last of the olives out, shrugging and smiling. "Nanda, you give the man as many olives he likes. What, five pounds, fifty?" They all had permission to laugh immoderately together, and then the woman gave Tom a blessing of an opening. "You gotta big family to feed, or what?"

"No family at all," he answered resonantly. "I'm new to Chicago." He allowed himself to look at Nanda then, who was waiting, scoop in hand, to fill a bag with olives for him.

"Let's see now," Tom said, brooding over the olive bowl, but the woman crossed her arms on the counter and asked, "So where you are from then?"

He had thought about the best answer, should the question come up. Immigrants never wanted to be reminded of their greenhorn status by someone who was native born, even a first-generation narrowback. "Ireland," Tom said easily. "The little island of Ireland, the land of the greenest hills and bluest lakes in the world."

"Ah," the woman nodded. "And there are no olives in Ireland?"

"Not one," Tom said. "And I've fallen in love with your olives." He was glad Huntley couldn't hear him.

At this the woman threw back her head and laughed again, and slapped the counter with one skinny hand. "And that's what they are for, the olives, did you know that? They're good for love."

"Really?" Tom was slightly disconcerted. He hadn't anticipated any boldness being lobbed at him from the other side of the counter. "Well!" The old woman laughed again and picked up her basin, turning into the back room.

He and Nanda were left face to face. "How much I will give you?" she asked finally. Her voice was every bit as nice as her face. Tom looked straight into her eyes and thought of replying, "How many do you think I need?" but he felt somehow that he had lost the initiative.

"A pound? Yes, a pound," he said.

"Is a lot," she answered doubtfully. But she wasn't looking at the floor anymore.

"Not at all," Tom said firmly. "They're beautiful. Don't you think so?"

She smiled at him and his heart or something very near it lurched ever so slightly. "I like all right, but I like sweet things better."

A whole sentence! And a sentence suggesting at least ten possible rejoinders a man of captivating speech could supply. But Tom's nerve had collapsed completely. "Really?" he said again feebly. "What kind of sweet things?"

She ladled the olives into the bag, glancing up at him so artfully Tom was certain for a moment she would wink. "Greek sweets," she said. "You come again sometime, we might have Greek sweets you can try. Maybe you fall in love with them too, eh?"

If she'd leaned over and kissed him Tom would not have been more stunned. He left the shop, nodding and laughing vacantly, and turned north in a state of exhilaration mixed with a new wariness. It was always possible he wasn't in the control he thought he was here.

By eight o'clock that night, when he arrived in Gleason's, he'd only managed to make a small inroad into the bag of olives, now damp and squashed in his pocket. "Here," he said to Andy. "I'm sorry they got a bit battered, but the kids might like them."

"My Jesus," Andy said mildly, sniffing. "They're not black-berries, anyway. Do you cook them or what?"

"You don't buy them by the pound, if you've any sense," Tom said.

Andy picked one out and nibbled it, made a face, swallowed, and took a sip of beer before he stuffed the bag in his pocket. "Well, thanks for that. Sure, my divils would eat anything. What exotic business are you up to, and you on your day off?"

"I like wandering around and trying out strange things," Tom said vaguely. He thought of Huntley and veered neatly away. "Do you know what Dick Huntley told me, Andy?"

"Jesus, it's easily seen this fellow's made an impression on you. No, what did he tell you?"

"Ah, nothing really," Tom smiled. "Just that he said eighty per cent of the people in Chicago were foreigners, immigrants or children of immigrants. It seemed an awful lot, that's all."

"I could believe that. They're mostly Germans now, you can see it in the number of bakeshops and breweries around. The trouble with us is the only trade we know is the pick and shovel. Not much choice of work if all you can do is hack rock and dig dirt. Did this Huntley tell you it was all foreigners on public assistance, too?"

"No. I guess I could see that would be true, though."

"Yes, and ten, twenty years ago every other person on assistance was an Irish immigrant. And there weren't that many Irish in Chicago even then, not compared to, say, Germans or

Poles – well, maybe not that far back, Poles are more recent. But the Mickeys were the bottom of the pile for a long time. When Liz and I came first we stayed out near the stockyards. One room in a cottage like a shed, you wouldn't keep a pig in it. George was born there. A living hell, the stockyards; people scrabbling and begging and taking dog's abuse for any kind of work. Kiddies with no shoes all winter tying their feet up in rags. Have you been out to the stockyards?"

"No. I've been near enough to smell it, all right."

Andy snorted. "Not hard to do that. Everything south of downtown as far as Indiana stinks like the inside of a cow. It's the hole of hell for human beings condemned there, Tommy, the hole of hell. You need to pay it a visit sometime." Oh no, Tom thought, I don't need that. But he said nothing and Andy changed the subject abruptly. "Listen to me, the evening papers are full of strange stuff about the almighty Cronin."

"Picked it up from the *Tribune*," Tom said. He had almost forgotten. "I was at the interview with this Woodruff, with Dick Huntley."

"And this story about a woman named Alice, that's what he told you?"

Tom nodded. "It's been an odd week." He tried to order the facts in sequence while Andy listened, arranging all the varied accounts of Cronin's movements, and as he talked he pictured Cronin for the first time: obsessed, fearful on the street-car with his case, springing off to rush toward Union Station. Or half-crouched in the shadows of the alleyway at three in the morning, begging hired accomplices to hurry loading the trunk with its butchered burden on to the wagon. Terrified, turning sharply at every noise, thinking of how he had killed the woman: with a knife, perhaps, scraping the pulp away inside her.

He put Huntley's question to Andy. "But if he had to go away for some mysterious reason very suddenly, why would you think he'd do it in a way that everybody would be talking about him?"

Andy leaned back against the bar counter. "Maybe he had no choice. A medical emergency might have been the only ruse that would fool people who might have been watching to see if he intended to slip away." Andy took another drink, ran one hand through his hair, and leaned over to Tom. "That's what I wanted to talk to you about."

"I don't understand what you mean."

"Here's the picture I'm going to paint for you, Tom," Andy dropped his voice. "There's Cronin, planning to leave town for reasons that are, to be blunt, as nefarious as can be. He discovers that he's been found out. He has to find a way to slip off that won't arouse suspicions. Of course! He's a doctor! A medical emergency, no questions asked, and he's gone."

"Gone where? Why?"

"I've been talking to some people, and there's reason to believe he may turn up in London shortly. Answering the beck and call of the British government, as a sorry number of Irishmen do."

Tom looked at him blankly, and Andy took his elbow, bringing him closer still. "Isn't there a British government commission sitting right now in London trying to get evidence to hang Charles Stewart Parnell? There's supposed to be some letter, something Parnell wrote that connects him with the executions in Dublin a few years back, you know?"

"What executions?"

"Ah, man dear, Cavendish and Burke, representatives of the Crown, killed by this crowd the Invincibles – we were talking about it not long ago at all, you remember!"

Tom didn't. "Oh. Yes, vaguely, I think," he said.

"Wasn't there a Henri Le Caron of this city went over to give evidence on what the Irish revolutionaries in Chicago were doing?" Andy was jiggling Tom's elbow in his impatience. "Tom Beach, his real name turned out to be. Passed himself off here as a Frenchman sympathetic to Ireland's cause. One of your crowd, a journalist. Well," he said, whispering, "and isn't Cronin the mortal enemy of the leading Irishman in Chicago, Alexander Sullivan? Is there any creature on God's earth lower than a spy?"

Tom shook his head. "A spy? For the English? But what about this woman? What about the trunk?"

"What about an elaborate dodge that would keep everyone

tearing around in circles while the bold boyo gets away safely?"

"But how do you know this is true, Andy?"

Andy straightened up again, releasing Tom's elbow, but he kept his voice low. "I have it on good authority from some very senior men in the Clan, that's how. Cronin's been named and he appears to have found out, and that forced him to move fast. And if this Huntley wants to write the truth about Cronin, that's what I'd tell him."

"I should tell Dick Huntley this?"

Andy considered a moment, and then nodded. "You should tell him, yes. Tell him you have information from someone who's in a position to know. Not me," he said, shaking his head firmly. "I'm only an ordinary two-by-four. But there are men whose word I trust. It's going to come out in the end anyway, and it would put a stop to the rumors. So you can tell your friend Huntley. "

"All right," Tom said. "I'll tell him. He guessed it might have something to do with the Clan, you know."

"Did he?" Andy said. "Well, you can tell him as well that Cronin is no friend to the Clan, anyway." He retrieved the bag from his pocket and selected another olive. "I can see what the appeal is in these little fellows; they grow on you, don't they? Also give you a fierce thirst."

"My round," Tom said. He stood up to order.

VIII

ONCE AGAIN IT was Mrs. Delaney who wakened him, rattling the door with a tattoo of knocks. "Someone to see you. A visitor," she stressed when he opened the door, her moon face sly. "Could be one of them debt collectors. Will I say you're out?"

Huntley was on the sidewalk, pacing slowly, examining his surroundings. "Reckon you're mighty safe with your landlady," he said by way of greeting. "I'd say Cronin slipped out easy compared to what your chances'd be."

"Is something wrong? Am I late?" Tom could hear church bells; it was Sunday; the light was still early morning.

"No, you ain't late. Percy was around to my rooms routin' me out at sun-up, and I thought I'd do the same for you. He wants to see us, and I thought we should have some breakfast before the bear pit."

"Then there is something wrong."

"Looks like we failed in our mission. Didn't find out what the hell happened to Cronin or why. Dispatch from Toronto this morning says the Doc is there, fully alive, and that he left town under cover to avoid gettin' killed by his political cronies."

"Killed? Listen, Dick – I heard something last night."

"Wait till we're somewhere comfortable. Go on, get your clothes on. I'll go up to the corner there, see can I hail a cabby. Think we should eat fancy, don't you? Been to the Palmer House yet?"

Huntley was back by the time Tom was dressed. Mrs. Delaney had abandoned all pretence at propriety and watched them from the window as the rig pulled away. Huntley nodded to her, smiling, and then nodded at the women coming up the street, in twos and threes, carrying their prayer-books with fingers expertly crooked in the pages they'd need to turn to.

"You need to go to church before we eat or anythin'?" he asked Tom.

"No," Tom said. "The truth is, I don't go much. But no one knows that."

"Is that a fact, now; thought it was obligatory?"

"It is. I'm not what you call a practicing Catholic."

"I see." Huntley was surprised. Tom was pleased that he'd said something that surprised him. "That's unusual, ain't it?" Huntley asked.

"Oh, yes. Very. I was in the seminary . . . you know, training to be a priest." Tom looked out at the women hurrying to mass, eyes down, pretending they didn't see Huntley smiling at them. "I got doubts," he said. He was still stunned with the fresh round of news, and not completely awake.

"Doubts about what?"

Tom shrugged. He wished Huntley would stop peering at the passersby. "Doubts," he said flatly. "That's what they call it; they say 'you've got doubts,' like you've got spots, the symptoms of a disease."

It made Huntley laugh and look away from the window at Tom, who also laughed, slightly scandalized with himself. He had not discussed this with anyone since Father Farrell, and he certainly hadn't laughed about it. But he could see that Huntley was freshly curious about him, which was flattering. "I learned doubt, in fact," he said. "The more they taught me about why I should believe, the more I learned about why I should doubt."

"Did you want to be a priest?"

"The nuns put me there. They wanted me to be a priest and I thought they would know – I don't know. I thought they were sane."

"Sane?"

Tom nodded, and Huntley said "I see" again. "Well, then," he added, leaning forward to the driver, "straight to the Palmer House."

The Palmer House. They said it was the most spectacular hotel in America now, beating anything even in New York. No one in Chicago really believed that, of course. It occupied a solid block on State Street, and porters in uniforms like army officers swarmed in front of the huge golden doors, hurrying to ease guests from their carriages. Tom scrambled out, avoiding assistance. The lobby was as high and wide as a cathedral, and the carpet was deep red, red as a cardinal's robe, and so thick their steps made no sound. Huntley's voice was thin and lost when he called Tom to the double glass doors of the barber shop.

"Have a look at the floor," he ordered. "Paved with silver dollars."

Tom looked. It was true. "My God," he said, hushed.

"Has a cruel shine, don't it?" Huntley said. They passed on, almost gliding, into the Grand Dining Room. It was long, and lined with Roman pillars down the center. Tom looked up at the carved ceiling, at the chandeliers drooping with crystal glass, and then around him at the tables, shrouded in white linen that shimmered in the sunlight, caught between a wall of windows and a wall of mirrors opposite. It was almost empty, except for the waiters, who were black and lined up along the wall opposite the door as if facing a firing squad, sombre men in formal evening suits, each with a white napkin folded over one arm.

Huntley addressed the first waiter he came to with "Howdy" and asked for breakfast — "Pancakes, I think; sausages, anythin' else you got to put us in shape for the day." The waiter nodded gravely and seated them near a window. Tom, still blinking, sat with his hands on his knees studying the cutlery laid out before him but Huntley immediately tucked the napkin over his collar and said, "So. What's this news you got last night?"

Tom told him, careful to eliminate any specific reference to Andy. Their breakfasts arrived, hidden under silver covers.

"What's this make it, theory number five or six?" Huntley said. "Do you believe this fellow, your source?"

"Oh, yes. He's been told this by people he trusts, that's what he said."

"Mightn't mean it's true. Lot a' rumors goin' around. Unless your fellow would be in the know about these things, would know people who did know?"

Tom hesitated. He somehow didn't want to admit Andy's weak points, even anonymously, to Huntley. He barely admitted them to himself. Neither, he was aware, did he want to cast doubts immediately on the only contribution he'd yet been able to make toward the story. "I don't think he's the sort of man who'd be very knowledgeable about things like this," he said finally. "I mean . . . he's hard to explain. He's clever, and funny, and he writes a lot and he's idealistic, but he's not very practical or anything. He has a lot of friends, though, he drinks with and that. And I guess he'd know – oh, people in the know, as you say." But would such people, whoever they were, bother telling Andy anything? Who would take Andy that seriously? Tom queried himself in silence, discomfited. He didn't, not really. Not even Liz did.

Huntley chewed reflectively for a while before he said, "Well, it makes as much sense as what Charley Long's sayin', anyway, I guess. No more sense, but just as much. But you're gonna have to tell it to Percy, who's gonna be in what you might call sceptical humor."

"Who's Charley Long?"

Huntley grunted. "Well, in my book, he's a bum. Worked here, on a few different papers, a few years back, then took off for Canada. Less competition. Wouldn't know the truth if it stood up and socked him. Don't matter, though. He's hit a winner this time; every paper in the city will want somethin' from him."

According to Long's dispatch from Toronto, Cronin was there, but refused to answer questions about what he was doing in Canada. Long had come across him by accident in the street, and only got a limited interview after pursuing him. "Long says all Cronin would tell him is that people are out to get him in Chicago, that he had to devise a way of escapin' without tellin' anyone," Huntley went on. "Named Alex Sullivan and a few others – Long thinks Cronin seems to be a bit deranged. Can't really say that, but he hints it okay. Anyhow, Charley's gonna keep after him, and he'll squeeze a few more twists into the yarn before he's done."

Tom listened, struggling over the food. He hoisted the fork as if it were a heavy primitive weapon, aware of the waiter submissively at his elbow, of the chandelier above which seemed it must collapse of its own weight, cascading crystal droplets over the vast white table.

"Nothing really pieces together, does it?" he said. Woodruff's story, Andy's opinion, Charley Long's report. Three accounts at variance with each other, except in the view that Cronin was alive. "And this meeting – with Mr. Percy – what's this about?"

"I think what he wants from you is an Irish history lesson."

Tom fitted his cup, light as an eggshell, into the snug circle of the saucer. It was lovely if frightening to touch. He couldn't remember ever drinking from anything like it before. "I'm not too bad on history," he said.

"I think what he has in mind is history in the makin'; that ain't quite the same thing."

"Like?"

"Why Cronin's skulkin' in some Toronto hotel in fear a' his enemies. Or, if your source has got it right, why he's about to turn-coat on those who thought they were his pals. To be blunt, what's goin' on in this Clan business."

"But I don't know. You know that."

"Turns out you do know somebody – or bodies – who do know, though." Huntley stopped eating long enough to look at him. The sun on his spectacles gleamed blindly at Tom; he looked like an elderly turtle.

Tom was silent a long time, watching him skewer the last bits of sausage and bacon. "I guess this was what I was asked to work with you for all along, then," he said.

"That's it, and don't sound bitter about it."

"I'm not bitter."

"You are, and maybe I'd be too. But don't sound that way. Percy has perfect hearin', and it ain't worth it to give him anythin' on you. Anyway, it hasn't been so bad, has it? Lots a' fresh air, meet new people, see the city. Plenty of my cheerful company."

"No," Tom said, smiling. "It hasn't been bad at all. But I still don't think I'll be much help."

When they arrived in the newsroom Percy was in his customary seat at the copy-editor's desk, sorting through the wire machine dispatches. He rose instantly, pointed toward his office, and walked ahead of them inside. They sat around the scruffy table again, and Percy folded his arms and looked sharply from one to the other before he spoke. His face was slack with loose flesh, Tom noticed for the first time, heavy jowled.

"Listen, do either of you got the faintest goddam idea what's going on with this story? You been ploughing up and down this town for a week now and all we got are fairy tales. What's the deal with this sonovabitch?"

"Copy's been pretty entertaining, though," Huntley said thoughtfully, tipping back in his chair. "Abortion, manslaughter, dumped bodies a' butchered ladies – that's livelier stuff 'n what Charley Long sends up."

"You're an insolent bastard, Huntley," Percy sighed morosely. "Butchered lady's bodies are real easy copy when they're invisible."

"A foul-smellin' decayed butchered lady's body."

"Yeah, the whole goddam story smells. I hear now this Woodruff's changed his yarn two or three times since Friday, different line for different people, depending on who asks the questions."

"Well, I'm real sorry to hear that," Huntley said. "Can't say I'm surprised, though. Anyway, Tom here's got another tale to add to the anthology. This one's pretty good, too – he's got a source says Cronin was a spy."

Percy switched his sullen glare to Tom. "Go on," he ordered.

Tom repeated what Andy had said again. Huntley was right, it made just as much sense as anything else that had been said all week. Another theory. And if Cronin was alive, as every story now suggested, did it matter which one was the right one?

When he'd finished, Percy sighed again. "Okay, you say you trust your source, Martin – well, that's just fine. I'm not going to ask you about it, either, because this whole goddam crazy thing is beginning to bore my behind off. Say Cronin is kidnapped. Well, that's interesting, I could care about that.

Say he does abortions and kills his patients, well, that's even more interesting. I could care about that. But I don't care if Cronin is some kind of a turkey spy and I don't care if he's got a lot of other turkeys annoyed with him. Yeah, I remember Hen-ree Lee Care-on — goddam ridiculous man. So he turned out to be a British spy, so what? So Cronin's a spy. I should care? Should I? Is there something important going on here I should know about? Or anybody else? Or are we all wasting time about some Irish brawl that'd bore the behind off you? That's what I want you to tell me about, Martin. Okay?"

"Yes. Okay. I can try, sir, I mean."

"Fine." Percy sat back and stretched his legs under the table. "Now, let's begin with the Clan na Gael. What do you know about them, Martin?"

"Well," Tom said, "not a lot." He'd thought about it all the way down State Street, walking over to the office; where to begin. "It has links with the Irish freedom movement in Ireland, the Irish Republican Brotherhood."

"Irish freedom. A revolution against England, that what they want?"

"That's it, really. Yes." Tom felt dull and slow, and his breakfast was beginning to trouble him. He wished he had the courage to ask about opening the window in Percy's airtight little office, but he didn't.

"So now we have this movement," Percy said, still staring at him. "That could mean anything. A secret society, an army, what is it?"

"Not an army. I think they mostly raise funds and that."

"Funds for the revolution? Say, for trying to blow up London there a few years back?"

"I've heard that, of course."

"Let's see, there were maybe a half-dozen or more bombs put all over London — Tower of London, Westminster, House of Commons," Percy said. His bulldog jowls quivered slightly when he spoke. "*Times* office they tried; didn't work. London underground railway, Victoria Station, Scotland Yard."

"I remember hearing about it."

Percy nodded. "Fellow from Chicago was killed trying to

blow up London Bridge, ever hear about that? Lomasney, made some news here. Blew himself to kingdom come. Now you tell me this Parnell – what's he? – is being investigated by some big British commission for encouraging murder, and Cronin's got information here he's got to rush over and present against him, that it?"

"Not murder, John," Huntley interrupted. "Conspirin' with whoever done in this British official, Lord Cavendish."

"Cavendish. That was it." Percy nodded. "Gang called themselves 'Invincibles' that did him. What a name."

"Chopped him down on his front lawn or something, very darin' stuff," Huntley added in a conversational tone. "Tom here would hardly know much about that, he weren't more 'n a schoolboy."

"Wouldn't know whether this Parnell did have anything to do with it, Martin?" Percy asked. "What would they say in Ireland about that?"

Tom drew his breath in. There'd been a massive misunderstanding, that much was clear. "Mr. Percy, I'm not Irish, I'm an American. I was born here, in Pennsylvania. I don't know what they say about anything in Ireland, Mr. Percy, and that's a fact," he said earnestly.

But Percy lurched forward to come close to him. "You got friends here who keep in touch, that right?" Tom thought immediately of the police he'd watched all week, and how they must pounce questioning their prisoners. "This source, now," Percy went on, "who gave you the information that Cronin is a spy, and alive and well and on his way to England? He'd keep in touch, no doubt."

"I suppose he must, sir, but I don't know. He's just a friend. We don't talk much about, you know, political things."

"No? But he just ups and tells you, all of a sudden, that this sonovabitch Cronin's a spy and is hotfooting it over to England to tell what's going on in Chicago. Don't suppose your friend told you anything about what Cronin might know that would be worth telling?"

Tom kept his eyes on Percy's face, and shook his head. It was like the seminary in Baltimore, and before that the orphanage, sitting in a small chair enduring a berating. The important thing, when you could think of nothing to say, was not to move or look away, or in any way suggest that you were keeping anything secret. But in fact he had nothing to say. Percy's question had not, he realized, even occurred to him when he and Andy were talking. A spy was a bad thing in itself, surely?

As if he shared the thought, Huntley interrupted again. "Seems to me if you're the one being spied on you wouldn't take kindly to the spy even if he hadn't much to say."

Percy turned to him quickly. "I see," he said, "I see. Well now, Huntley, maybe you'd like to share your thoughts on all this with us, instead of just tossing in your two cents' worth here and there."

"Certainly." Huntley pulled his chair forward, level to Tom. "Way I see it, this Mr. Parnell is just a politician lookin' out for his country's interests. The London *Times* prints some letters, sayin' he's involved in murder conspiracies, and he ignores 'em. But when someone else finally sues for libel don't the British government let their Attorney General act as legal counsel for the *Times*? Can't see a government doin' something like that unless there's something big at stake in it for 'em."

"Glad to see one goddamned reporter on this paper reads the wire service," Percy said. He sat back. He sounded suddenly weary. "Well, I gotta admit I can't make head or tail out of the whole goddamned thing, and what in Christ we're worrying about it for – Cronin's a spy or an abortionist or who the hell knows what." Percy stood up, and gave another lugubrious sigh. "Martin, maybe you'd better go back to the copy desk for the time being. Huntley, you keep your eye on the thing but don't give it too much time, right? That's enough for now. I gotta newspaper to look after."

IX

THE CRONIN STORY trailed on, relegated to the lower reaches of the inside pages. The front page was preoccupied with fresher topics, or fresher versions of constant topics, strikes and fires and political skirmishes. As a gesture toward his somewhat improved stock, Tom was moved up the table, "to handle hard news," the chief said. He inscribed three-line headlines on the nightly column of shorts from the wire machines: "A Farmer Who Wanted a New Spouse is Charged with Using Poison," on the unsavory deeds of Mr. Wiggins of Pickens County, South Carolina, and "Heavy Damages for Woman Who Was Scalded in a Turkish Bath," on amends made to an injured Mrs. Gurick of New York City.

Almost nightly, he processed the dispatches from Charley Long in Toronto, pencilling off paragraphs and underlining capital letters. There was an interview with Cronin, which Long reported he had managed to get only after great difficulty, in which Cronin would only say about his departure from town that it was "a long story and the telling of it would implicate a great number of my friends who are in no way responsible for any of my actions. I trust you will not press me on that point." Long didn't. In another dispatch Cronin was reported as adamantly refusing to say whether he had arranged the summons to a false emergency at the ice-house. One night Tom read that Cronin was waiting to board the next steamer for France, and, another, that he had vanished and was believed to be in New York City, headed for London.

Finally there was a short dispatch from London from a freelance correspondent, not attached to any of the international agencies: "Le Caron, the man who acted as a spy for the British government on the movements of Irish leaders in America, and who testified for the *Times* before the Parnell Commission, declares that he and Dr. Cronin were the closest of friends. Le Caron believes that Dr. Cronin has been killed and that his own friendship with the doctor may account for his murder."

Tom brought the long scroll of copy paper to Percy and waited for the words acknowledging his vindication. But Percy only read it through quickly and then wondered testily whether it was safe to use it. "What's on the agencies tonight about Cronin?" he asked brusquely.

"Nothing, sir."

"Anything else this week on these lines?"

"No, sir. Only Long's dispatches from Canada."

"Well, the others are likely to use it, we gotta cover our behinds. Make sure you get 'alleged' in, will you? Le Caron sounds as cracked as Mrs. What's-her-name."

"Conklin," Tom said, but Percy had turned his back and didn't hear him. Tom put a four-line head on the copy – "British Spy on Irish American Leaders Says Dr. Cronin Was Killed Because He Was a Friend" – and the story appeared in a top inside column, but there was no response from the readers.

Listening to the copy-editors up the table in the early hours of the morning, gossiping while they read the first edition, Tom realized that they no longer thought Dr. Cronin was either dead, or particularly interesting. On the whole, people preferred the tale of the abortionist who had fled justice, which Tom pointed out in some irritation to Huntley at lunch one afternoon.

Percy might have dismissed him but Tom was grateful to find that Huntley had not. He turned up at the copy-editing table at some point nearly every day, chatting in his laconic way and peering over Tom's shoulder at the dispatches. When he asked Tom to come out with him for lunch, the chief only nodded assent without comment; Huntley's status in the paper was very high. They ate in a stand-up saloon frequented by the printers, taking the cheese and pickles on offer at the free lunch-counter with their beer, hemmed in by men hustling quick meals between shifts. Huntley was still curious about

Cronin, and he laughed when Tom asked, exasperated, why Cronin as an abortionist seemed so plausible a notion when it was the least suited to such facts as had emerged.

"Why, Tom, my friend, it's because there's a lot a' them around. Lot a' demand for doctors who can get a woman out a' that fix, compared, now, to the demand for spies. Anyhow, a spy ain't an American thing at all."

"How do you mean?"

"Spies are a European sort a' things — kings, emperors up to intrigues and suchlike, uncoverin' conspiracies and oppressin' peasants. Your average Yank'd think spies and conspiracies were like elves and wizardry."

"People think there's no spies in the United States?"

"Prevailin' myth here is that we live in a good, clean democracy, one man as good as the next, no one oppressed and no one oppressin'."

"What do you think?"

Huntley laughed again, his glasses glinting. "I think all sorts a' things, and I don't much like myths — any kind."

On the sidewalk outside Huntley put a hand on Tom's arm. "See that pair ahead a' us? Peg Sullivan. And that old fool Walsh. Must be on their way over to the *Herald*."

Tom watched them turn at the corner, waiting to cross. Walsh was portly, and leaned on a walking stick. He couldn't see the face of the woman with him, but her hair was golden and thick, wound up in the fashion of the year, and her costume even at thirty paces was distinctly expensive.

"She looks an attractive sort of woman, doesn't she?" Tom said.

"Elegant as a snake," Huntley said. "Wonder what she knows about our friend Cronin? Been talkin' to your pal about it at all lately?"

"My source?" Tom smiled. "I'm going around to see him, my first night off."

He called two nights later, in the early evening. Liz saw him from the open front window and leaned out, pushing the lace curtain aside, to call that the door was on the latch. He gave it a jiggle and a push, as she directed, and went in. She was sitting at the table, littered with foolscap pages, idly shuffling a pack of cards. The house was quiet. "Andy will be back soon," she said. Her voice was subdued. "Will you wait? I'll put on some coffee."

"I'll wait, but don't bother about coffee," Tom said, sitting opposite her. "How's everyone?"

"Ah, not too well, I'm sorry to say. Andy's been laid off again."

"Oh, God. That's terrible news," Tom said.

"It's bad luck, all right. Every time you think you might just get even again something knocks you back. He's gone off to see a fellow about a job and I'm sitting here keeping my mind off my troubles, foostering with cards."

"Where are the children?"

"Kate's taken the babies for a walk up the street to her friend. The boys are playing till the lamps are lit. Can't you hear them?" She tilted her head to the window, smiling slightly. The shouts were faint in the distance, measured by the steady tick of the clock on the shelf. "I love that sound. It's like something eternal; it must have been the same all places and all times, do you think?" Tom, listening, heard what Kate called her mother's "serious" voice, the measured, almost formal way Liz spoke when she was in that mood. He didn't really want her to be serious with him, and, as if she guessed that, Liz began to lay the cards out on the table, face down in a row. "Will I tell your fortune for you, while you're waiting?" she asked.

"I didn't know you held with false gods," Tom said, leaning back in his chair. "You're giving scandal."

She laughed, turning a fifth and a sixth card up. "I hold with diversion," she answered. "And as well as that, it's a very effective way of getting information out of children."

"Aren't you a devious woman, though," Tom said. "And do they beg to have their fortunes told?"

"Ah, the boys have no patience for it, but Kate asks sometimes. She's coming to an age for secrets. My mother used to tell my fortune with the cards, and hers before her, and I see now what a useful trick it was. And times like this, now, to tell you the truth, I think it may be as useful as going through these oul' sheets of sums." She pointed to the pages of writing nearest Tom. "Andy's accounts. Look at them, columns of figures going back over months. As if writing it down would make it go further."

Tom glanced down. The pages were neatly ruled off, with "Income" inscribed on one side in Andy's stylish handwriting. Total pay in January, $24.62. February, $35.53. March, two weeks idle, started with Board of Trade to Easter Monday, $22.75. On the other side, under "Expenditures", the list began with $90 for the grocer, $22.75 for the coalman, $30 for the rent and went on to smaller items: $1.25 for working shoes, 30 cents for baby's medicine, and then names – Moriarty, Brennan, Gallagher – with one and two dollars recorded after them. Debts repaid? Tom pushed the pages back from the edge of the table. "I wouldn't have thought Andy would much like bookkeeping," he said.

"It's a side of him that always surprises people," Liz responded without looking up from the cards. "Andy's the kind of man who wants to put order on the world, for all his romance." She went on slapping one card into place after another, face up, face down. They were forming a pattern now, squared off across the oilcloth.

"I'd have thought that was the definition of a romantic," Tom said, watching her hands. "Someone who has a view of how things should be and wants to set what's wrong right."

"Is it? Well, then maybe the trouble is that romantics start off with the answers and try to make the sums fit them. Like those accounts," she said, tapping the pages with a card. "That's not how the world gets ordered." She turned the card around and placed it carefully, and then sat back, folding the rest of her cards in her hands. "Not that I always saw it like that myself, I'd be bound to confess. I was going to marry Andy's brother once. Did I ever tell you that? Tom, his name was, too." She looked at him directly. "Isn't that a strange thing, now?" Tom looked down, not quite sure that he was meant to respond.

"I was betrothed to be married to him," Liz went on. "Andy

was off in America the first time. And when he came back, Tom introduced us and said I was to be his wife. And Andy said, "Twill never be.' And he was right. Mind you, there's things in my life I'm prouder of than the way I left off with Tom. But there you are, I took Andy's answer straight away, and never mind how the sums were."

"Yes," Tom said. "That was romantic, all right." He was disconcerted to hear the touch of envy in his voice.

"Wasn't it, just. Then we were married, and we had children; and he went back to America and finally I followed him. And the babies died. All but Kate."

Tom sat still and kept his eyes on her fingers. They were so small and slender, curved lightly over the cards, and he could so easily reach over and cover them with with one hand. "I didn't know that – it must have been terrible for you," he said finally.

"Terrible, yes. Charley and Joe and John. Three little graves I left behind. And I landed in Ellis Island with Kate in my arms and we went to find Andy, and when I did, we started all over again, hoping that this time the world would be put in order for us." She pulled her shawl tighter around her. "There isn't a night of my life I don't think of those little graves, just the same."

Tom felt his way silently through a series of possible phrases, then abandoned them, but Liz continued in the same monotone. "And through all that's happened since, I've changed," she said. "But Andy's the same. He sees things the same as he did then, sixteen years ago. The same things are important to him. And he has the same answers, too." She began to shuffle the cards again, delicately and expertly. She bent over them and bit her lip and Tom studied her little even teeth and slight mouth, imagining himself reaching over now and touching her cheek, exactly where the dimple should be. He shifted in his chair, aware once more of the clock, and said finally, "Isn't that what you call having principles?"

But Liz shook her head doubtfully. "Is it? Or is it just sticking to your answers because you can't bear asking new questions? And as I sit here, I can't tell you whether I admire him or whether I think he's full of terrible foolishness. Terrible dangerous foolishness."

"Ah, Liz."

She looked up at him, still shuffling the cards. "I shouldn't be burdening you with my meanderings," she said.

"It's not that."

"Ah, I know it isn't. I don't mean to be disloyal, either. That's the worst of all sins, isn't it? No, don't answer me, I'm only downhearted. I feel like I've no strength. You're a good friend, Tom."

"You and Andy have been the best of friends to me," Tom answered with a rush of feeling. "The best. And I want to help you out now, Liz, if Andy's down on his luck. Please let me."

She stood up, and swept the cards on the table into an untidy heap. "If we need it, Tom, and I appreciate the offer. But please God something will turn up soon. And – oh merciful hour, look at the time! I must see where these youngsters are."

She went to the door and opening it began to call them through her cupped hands, pitching a litany of names into the night: Kate, Robert, Henry, George. Tom stood, too, and stacked the cards, and then the foolscap pages of accounts. He could hear the sounds of the street through the open door, children calling their final shouts and a baby buggy bumping over the dirt path. "I don't know why you can't remember to get back before dark, you worry the life out of me," Liz cried at the door as the boys tumbled breathlessly past her. He heard the despairing cry of a baby and followed Liz down the steps. She extracted the squalling smallest one from one end of the buggy while Kate tugged the drowsy large baby from the other end. "Look, Papa's coming just now, I can see him," Kate said. "I want to go meet him."

"No, come inside now, Kate, I need you. Tom here will walk up to meet him, won't you, Tom?" Kate, wailing of injustice, followed into the house and Tom started down the steps. He could make Andy out at the end of the street, trudging with his head down, his shadow looming ahead as he approached the streetlamp. When he was within hailing distance Tom called out and Andy looked up and gave a short wave, and moved faster to meet him.

"So," he said, flinging one arm around Tom's shoulder. "I've had a touch of bad luck. Liz told you?"

"She did, and I'm damned sorry to hear it, Andy."

"Ah, it'll be only temporary, I'm told. It's just the worry to Liz. And I thought I had a lead on a job tonight but it turned to dust."

"I want to do something to help, Andy," Tom began, but Andy squeezed his shoulder with one hand and cut him short. "You're a good man, Tom. I'll hope it won't be necessary, but I thank you all the same. Tell me anyhow – about your story. It's all coming to pass as I predicted with Doc Cronin. The sneaking toad went to Canada and has disappeared again."

"Yes. It sounds pretty odd now, doesn't it?" Tom replied.

"Why odd? It's exactly what I was told was the situation. To the letter. You told that to your reporter friend?"

Tom told him, while they walked to the house, of the interview with Percy, the queries on the Clan, and Andy laughed. "You did well, you're a credit to your country," he said, amused.

"I doubt that, but thanks anyway," Tom said. "Did you read that this Le Caron says he and Cronin were friends but he thinks that Cronin's been killed?"

"I did, and it sounds like a blind to me. Cronin got out of Chicago safe and he'll turn up in London any day now, and Tom Beach probably knows better than anybody. Tom Beach. Lee Care-on," he said, just as Percy had, mocking. "Lee Care-on and Cronin. A pair of evil bastards. Anyway, to hell with them; I've trouble enough on my own plate. Come inside for a cup of coffee, and we'll have a natter."

They sat while the cottage grew dark. Tom talked as much as he could, trying to invent accounts of his life at the copy-editing table that were more entertaining than the reality. All the time he listened to Liz as she put the children to bed, her footsteps crossing above him in the attic. He wished that he had brought beer with him, but he couldn't think of a way to get a pitcher now that wouldn't be a show of charity. While he talked Andy moved about the little room, closing the window, searching his papers. When Liz came in she sat behind them, sinking into the rocker without speaking. Andy never looked at her. He began to light the hanging lamp, twitching the wick restlessly and cursing softly. Tom went on talking foolishly, and wondered again whether he hoped for more from marriage than most people.

X

THEY FOUND CRONIN'S body jammed in a sewer basin out in Lakeview, not far from the place where the broken trunk had been found three weeks earlier. "Would 'a found it a week ago if Failmerzger weren't such a lazy bum," Huntley said. "Turns out complaints about the stench been comin' in for the last ten days, pilin' up on his desk. But Otto's no man for movin' too quick."

When the complaints about a blocked basin at Evanston Avenue and North 59th Street began hitting his desk, Otto finally filled in an inspection order form, under the heading "Otto Failmerzger, chief clerk, Board of Public Works," and hung it on the hook for the foreman of the gang working northside gutter and sewer maintenance. It was a three-man gang – Nick Rosch, John Finegan and Billy Michaels. Their names were in all the papers the next day, with their own accounts of the discovery in paragraphs of quotes, inches deep. It was the next best thing to a photograph of the discovery, which the Chief of Police put an absolute veto on as soon as he saw the corpse. He wouldn't have an artist's impression, either. "Nice thing about Hubbard," Huntley said. "Sense of delicacy, very befittin' a police chief."

Rosch, Finegan and Michaels had no similar inhibitions and they gave as much detail as they could on the state of the body; Rosch, mostly, as he was the foreman.

They knew from the start that whatever was causing the trouble must have been alive once and was rapidly rotting now. They had to stop and go back for fresh air a few times. It was also obvious that the obstruction was pretty large, Rosch said, because the ditch for twenty feet along the east side of

Evanston Avenue was choked with sewer water that had backed up from the basin. But there was no paving in Lakeview, so the sand had sifted down and dammed up the opening of the basin. It took them a long time to dig it out, and it was nearly four in the afternoon when Rosch got down on his knees to peer into the catch-basin.

"I thought it was a cow when I seen it first," Rosch said. "Or maybe one of them really big old dogs, I dunno; all you could see was something white like a big swollen belly floating down there. Finegan here says it couldn't be a cow, how the hell would a cow get down there, and then he presses up against the bars and says, 'Oh goddam, boys, there's a body down there,' and when I looked again I could see it was a body of a man all right, stark naked, but the head was tilted sideways down on one shoulder so's you couldn't be sure at first what it was. Looked like some kind of squash, all mangled and sort of purplish."

There were diagrams in the papers to explain the operation of a catch-basin, showing a brick cylinder sunk into the ground, with a heavy wooden lid on top and a grating at the level of the ditch. Rainwater flowed into the grating and poured into a basin a few feet below, and the basin also caught the fermented stream from the city sewer. That's where Cronin's body was, face down, bobbing gently back and forth with the garbage.

"Funny thing is, none of us thought of Dr. Cronin," Rosch told the press. "He'd just about gone out of everybody's mind. We was just that shocked, y'know, didn't wonder who it was – didn't look human, even. I got back to Noyes's grocery store there to get a telephone message to Lakeview police, and left the boys here to figure out how to get the body up from where it was."

They did it by pushing a horse blanket underneath with a hoe and a shovel, and then hauling it up. They wanted to tie a rope around the blanket before they laid the body on the ground, but the corpse's arms, which had already burst open, fell off then, spilling putrid decay around their feet. Michaels, who'd had the worst problems about turning back for air, admitted that he had to back off a distance, and they left the remains as they were. Finegan stood over the waxy hump, but a little way off, until Captain Villiers got there. It was Villiers who turned the body over, taking care with the head, which was crushed into the collarbone.

"He knew who it was right away," Finegan said. "He said, 'My God, it's Dr. Cronin,' and I could see he knew, but I couldn't see how anyone could tell for sure because what was left of the face was all bloated, and the scalp had peeled away from his head and was hanging off. Lips were gone, too, turned over inside his mouth, mustache and all."

But it was the way the head had been hacked off at the neck that twisted it to dangle at such a queer angle on Cronin's shoulder, Rosch said. It had been bashed in on one side right from the forehead back, and hatcheted through at the base of the skull.

Villiers and his men took over then, and got the body in the police wagon, rolled in the blanket. The police wagon raced up Evanston Avenue, followed by the Office of Public Works wagon, with Rosch and the men on it. Rosch said that everyone on the road seemed to know something had happened just by looking at their faces; white as sheets, they were. By the time the body was lifted out in front of the police station, a crowd had begun to collect and five minutes later the first tipster got on to the downtown papers from the telephone in Noyes's grocery store.

That was when Tom heard the news. The reporter who'd answered the phone had cried out in a strange, exultant voice, "Hey! We got a murder! That Mickey doctor's been found axed up in a sewer!" Afterward it always seemed to Tom in some confused way that he had found out everything in one day, because by the time he got to bed at dawn the next morning he'd also heard about Camp 20 for the first time; and for the first time he'd sensed that in some way he would be not a little but very much affected by what had happened. But, of course, it wasn't really like that at all.

Huntley said there was only one possibility. Cronin was the victim of a feud and several people must have been involved in the killing; Mrs. Conklin had been right all along. But if Mrs.

Conklin knew more, she probably would have said more. That meant the only other avenue of information now was through the only other person who'd said Cronin had enemies. That was Tom's source.

They were in the saloon. Tom had a galley-proof of a vaudeville review wadded into his shirt pocket and he was a little bit worried about it. He'd simply stood up and walked away from his table when Huntley had beckoned him, without, as Mrs. Delaney was constantly remarking of the neighbors rude habits, so much as a by-your-leave. Huntley tapped him lightly on the shoulder. "You follow?" he asked.

"Yes, sure," Tom said. "What do you mean?"

"I mean your contact's the only person might get us a lead on this story."

"But he was certain that Cronin hadn't been killed. Absolutely certain. He told me Cronin was going to turn up in London anytime now."

"Well, somebody got to him first. That was on the cards, too, from what your pal said."

"And what about all those stories from Long? What about those?"

Huntley finished his beer and set the glass on the counter. "Well, now, that's where things do look naughty," he said. "Long was lyin', which don't surprise me none, but lyin' at such a nice, steady pace – such an inventive style, too, and consistent – there must 'a been more at stake than a few bucks. Somebody was directin' him, Tom. Somebody he wasn't goin' to cross." He considered a moment. "We should 'a sent our own man out to check it, I guess. Percy fell down there."

"And that Murphy girl. And the street-car conductor."

"They could 'a been mistaken," Huntley answered. "But then they could 'a been part of the plan, right along with Charley Long and even Frankie Woodruff. Only story looks like it stands up now was what them officers of Villiers saw the night Cronin disappears, a wagon with a trunk, and a wagon later with no trunk. But all the rest of it – a plan."

"A conspiracy."

"A conspiracy. So what I think is, you should go back to your source."

"My source." Tom shook his head. "Dick, my source is a man who writes poems about Ireland in his spare time and worries about feeding his family when he's out of work, which he is at the moment, as a matter of fact. He told me what someone else told him."

"He someone you know from Baltimore or Philly?"

"Philly? I've never been there."

"Thought you said you was born there."

"Pennsylvania. I was born in Pennsylvania. Pottsville. What's that got do with anything? I grew up in Baltimore, and I met my source, as I guess I now have to call him, when I got to Chicago. Jesus, he's just a friend of mine."

"All right, don't get het up now, boy; it's just my mind racin' off course." Huntley patted Tom's shoulder absently, staring at the counter. "This fellow's poems any good?" he asked.

Tom frowned and then laughed. "No. Well, they scan, you'd have to say that for them. But no, they're not. So what?"

"So maybe his information's like his poems, not so hot but it scans some. Think you should go see can you mine some more out a' him."

"You seem to forget I'm back at the desk job," Tom said, tapping the pocket with the vaudeville review. "I shouldn't even be here now."

"That I'm goin' to see Percy about in the next five minutes. Finish your beer. If that's all right with you, a' course?"

When they got out on the sidewalk the newsboys were already in full chant, lifting armloads of papers to show proof of fresh and urgent wares: "Cronin Murder!" and "Doctor Butchered in Lakeview!" The evening papers had put on an extra edition to meet the clerks and typists and businessmen now emptying the downtown offices. From what Tom could see, the two of them were the only people on the street not buying. "So you're going to ask Mr. Percy if I can get time to go back and talk to my source?" he asked.

"Think that might 'a occurred to Percy already. I'm sayin' I want you back to give me a hand generally, same as before. Percy's gotta put a few men on this story now, you done more legwork 'n anyone. I'll see can I slip around and catch him at his

99

supper — I know his usual place. Then, he agrees, first thing you do is hunt up your pal." Huntley was watching the news-boys. "Nothing sells papers like murder," he said. "War is good for business, but murder is best."

Tom didn't have to hunt up Andy, though, because Andy was waiting for him. He was standing next to the *Tribune* en-trance, searching faces in the hurrying crowd, and he was at Tom's side almost before Tom saw him.

"Tom," he said, grasping his arm. "They told me inside you were gone for a few minutes and I've been waiting. My God, this is terrible news."

Tom nodded. "It sounds like it was horrible, Andy."

"It's a curse on us, I'm telling you, a curse." Andy pulled off his cap and wiped his face with a handkerchief. "I just can't believe it," he said. He looked at Tom with distracted eyes and replaced the cap.

"Who told you I'd gone out?" Tom asked. "I'm meant to be on duty."

"Of course — Jesus, I can't take it in. If you've to go back, sure I can see you again," he said. "I just took a chance you might be free."

"It might be all right now, the way things are turning out," Tom said. "I guess the boss might let me go, but I'll have to go in and see. Will you wait?"

In half an hour's time they were on Michigan Avenue, walk-ing south to keep the wind to their backs and looking for a quiet coffee shop. Tom had been assigned to reporting duty once more with a few words from Percy, and more from Huntley, whom he was to meet at the Lakeview police station at ten o'clock. It had rained earlier and the evening smelled now of the lake and the start of summer, peaceful and full of promise. Andy was still agitated. "I can't believe what has happened," he said several times. "I can't believe it."

They stopped in a drugstore near Monroe. It was new and fitted with electric lights in the ceiling and had a black-and-white tiled floor that shimmered under them, and along the side wall there was an ice-cream soda fountain as elegant as a downtown restaurant saloon. They sat at a marble counter, side by side. Tom ordered a pot of tea, remembering that it was supposed to be better for the nerves than coffee; or so his mother used to say, a long time ago, suspicious of all things American. But Andy wouldn't drink any of it. He sat still with his head bowed and his hands clasped on the marble counter-top and Tom told him as much as he knew of the discovery of the body. He said very little, only "Oh my God" once or twice, when Tom described the way Cronin's head had been chopped partly off, and the way his body had swollen and begun to decompose in the rank sewer water.

When Tom could think of no more to say he finished his tea and watched Andy's reflection in the mirror behind the counter, wondering how he was to proceed. Would Huntley press a man whose clasped hands were trembling? Even Percy mightn't expect it. "Are you sure you wouldn't like something?" he asked Andy timidly, and when Andy shook his head, he added, "We could find a saloon for a jar, if you like. You needn't worry, the paper's given me a bit of cash for spending." He studied the pattern of tea-leaves in his cup, undecided whether that sounded more or less vulgar than "expenses".

But Andy lifted his head resolutely. "No," he said. "No. Thanks, though. Tom. No; what I'd like to do is walk up for a bit, if you can spare the time." He looked around him as if his surroundings slightly baffled him, and then frowned up at the ceiling. "I find these old electric lights very hard on the eyes, do you?" Then he looked directly at Tom. "There's a few things I'd like to tell you about. Have you the time?"

"I have. Of course I have."

They set out again all the way to Congress, where there was a park. It wasn't much of a park. A square of sparse grass, ragged at the edges where traffic had worn it away. But a dozen spindly young trees had been planted at intervals as a pledge to the future. There were benches where three or four citizens at a time could take their ease and examine the newest and best of Chicago's architecture, and Andy used the hand-kerchief to wipe the last spatters of rain from one directly opposite the arched mouth of the Art Institute before they sat down. Then he began to fumble for his cigar and matches; his props, Tom thought wearily, his lecturing props. But he felt guilty for thinking it, and as he watched Andy turned suddenly and pointed to the building on their left. "Have you been inside the Auditorium yet?" he asked.

"No," Tom answered automatically. He wrenched his thoughts around. "It's supposed to be fantastic inside, isn't it?" he added. "Mosaics made of millions of pieces of marble or something."

"It's a thing of genius, all right; but it's in the construction," Andy replied. "Jack Gallagher was on the crew. There's a platform of wood and iron and concrete underneath all that, five foot thick and built so that it floats, to get over the problem of being so close to the lake."

Tom nodded dumbly.

"An Irishman did that, Tom. Louis Sullivan. A genius of an architect." Andy jabbed his cigar toward him. "Do you think I'm foolish for saying that, that an Irishman did that?"

"No. Of course not."

"Others do. You can't help wonder sometimes. I like thinking we can show this city we can produce a genius or two. And more in time, too."

He chewed on the cigar, which had already gone out. "The truth is that I'm not that fond of the style. I prefer the Fine Arts Building there, and I like the old Art Institute best of all. What do you think yourself?" He was quite calm now. It was as if another person had replaced the distraught man of twenty minutes earlier.

"I don't know," Tom said desperately. "They're all nice in different ways." He stared at the buildings, trying to look as if there was nothing more immediate on his mind. The possibility that Andy had been temporarily driven witless by shock occurred to him. These things were said to happen. "They're all grand buildings," he said finally, to break the silence. "Imposing. That's the word."

"It's turning into a grand place, Chicago," Andy replied. "I'd like my children to grow up with this city and reach their dreams, a simple and universal aspiration of parents. Yours wanted that for you, me for mine, you'll want it for your children when you have them." He spoke in a deliberate, oratorical way, every sentence a distance from the next one.

"If I have them."

"Ah, you will. You will. And you'll feel just like I do when I look around me here, on a balmy night like this; feel that they should have wonderful lives and want for nothing and reach their dreams. But I don't want them to forget the past, either. Is that foolishness? I don't think it is. You must know where you came from to put any shape on where you're going. That must be true for everyone. You're thinking I've forgotten that I said I wanted to tell you about a few things, are you?"

The last was in the same hypnotic lilt as what had preceded it, and it took a moment to register. "No, I wasn't thinking about that," Tom answered. "Not at all. Honestly."

Andy removed the cigar from his mouth and leaned forward, his arms on his knees. "The truth is I'm trying to find my words. It's been a shocking day. It doesn't seem possible, sitting here in peace looking at beauty, that the world could be such an ugly place. What I want to tell you is what was meant to happen with Cronin. I'm in the Clan. I suppose you guessed that?"

"Yes. Well, I'd begun to think you might be."

"Well, it's not so astonishing. So are thousands of others. I've been part of it all for a long while, since before I met Liz; back home, in Mayo, and over here, in New York first and then here. In Chicago. But I've never been involved in anything much except being an ordinary member. An ordinary loyal member. I never knew anything about the dynamite campaign, now, except that it was happening; that kind of way. Do you know what I mean?"

Tom nodded in the darkness. But Andy didn't look around.

"But still, even being an ordinary member, you know things. Because it's a democratic organization, and its members represent the republic that will some day be in Ireland. We are responsible under a solemn oath to generations yet to come, and that's a privilege never to be taken lightly, even by the most insignificant member of the organization. Do you understand me?"

Tom cleared his throat. "Well," he said. "I'm not sure."

"What I'm trying to say is that the issue of what Cronin was about came up before the membership of the organization long ago."

"That he was a spy?"

"No, no. Before that. The issue of what he was doing to destroy the organization came up for discussion in a number of camps, including my own, Camp 20."

"What are camps?"

"Camps, branches. Cronin challenged the Clan executive on decisions they were taking with regard to the campaign in England. Now that's fair and usual. He wasn't the only one."

There was no one near them, but Andy had lowered his voice steadily; it was so soft now Tom had to lean toward him to hear. "What happened during that campaign was that a lot of camps disagreed with what was happening and their members left. Or they were expelled; it doesn't much matter. But the difference with Cronin was that he wouldn't stop. He was a proud man. Proud, haughty. He did things so against the rules that he was charged with treason, and tried before a special committee, back in '85, and he was found guilty. But that still didn't stop him; not him. He went on persisting, making more allegations, and there was another trial."

"About what?" Tom interrupted. "What allegations was he making?"

"Ah, he insisted we were all being deceived and misled," Andy said impatiently. "He wanted to know things that weren't his business to know, in my opinion. Thought he should be the one to make the decisions. The point I'm making to you, Tom, is that the Clan used all of its democratic machinery to give the man a fair hearing. But when he didn't get his way he refused to back down. He'd start in again. Over and over. There was something goading him, no one could work out what."

"And what happened?"

"There was a trial, a hearing – in Buffalo. Cronin was outvoted, and he started going around to different camps, reading out his own version of a report. Well, that's totally against reason. What would be the point of holding hearings if anyone who didn't like the results could say thumb-my-nose to you? Do you see what I mean? What the man was doing made no sense." He paused and when Tom didn't answer he started again. "Then last February Tom Beach – you know, Le Caron – told the commission in London there were several more of his own kind, spies, at work in America with the Irish revolutionary movements. That's when it began to come clear that what Cronin was up to was the downfall of the organization."

"But that's not proof," Tom said slowly, "that he was a spy."

"No," Andy said, looking at him this time. "No, that came later. I was told that later, the way I told you. By someone I trust completely – that Cronin's name was there, on a document, shown in London. But before that, there was a vote in my own camp to investigate why Cronin was defying the organization. And I know that, because it was my own speech that persuaded Camp 20 to vote for an investigation."

"And did you investigate?" Tom asked. Andy was still looking at him intently.

"That isn't the way it works," Andy said. "The way it works, the camp votes on a certain course of action, and it's up to the leader, senior guardian, to choose those who will be involved. That's what we elect him for. He chooses his men and tells no one else. Sometimes they don't even know each other. It has to be that way, to protect secrecy; only those who have to know are told. That way information doesn't get out. Do you see?"

"Yes, I see." Tom hesitated. He could hardly make out Andy's face in the darkness. He had begun to worry about the time. It must be past eight, and he would have to allow an hour to get back, find a hack, and get all the way north to Lakeview. "Andy, what I guess I don't see is what this has to do with Cronin being murdered."

Andy shook his head, impatient again. "But what I've been telling you, Tom, is that the only decision the Clan made – and they made it at an open and democratic meeting, the way the members make all their decisions – was to investigate Cronin. That was the decision. It was my speech that proposed that, and we acted on it."

Tom, trying without success to see Andy's expression, wondered what Huntley would do. "Well, somebody decided something different somewhere along the line," he said. "Any idea how that could have happened?"

Andy stared at him and then turned abruptly away. "The truth of that will never come out. It never does. Those are the secrets that men go to their graves with. That's not what I'm trying to say to you."

Tom nodded. He was no Huntley. "I'm sorry," he said. "I guess I don't understand." But I do, he thought. Andy and his speech, his speech that had inspired action. He could imagine the kind of speech, passionate and flowing and demanding a formal inquiry, all very important, a speech soaked with patriotic fervor. Wringing wet with it.

"What I'm trying to say is," Andy said emphatically, "that there's going to be a lot of terrible things said and you should know, it should be told, that the men in Clan na Gael never voted to kill Cronin. They had reason to suspect him and what they agreed to do was inquire into his activities. That's fair. There was reason."

"But, Andy," Tom began again. Then he stopped. The conversation was circular.

"The Clan is an honorable organization with serious aims, Tom. It mustn't suffer unfair damage from any single deed," Andy said firmly. "No matter how terrible."

"But, Andy! No one cares about that. All people want to know, all the police want to know, is who did this thing?" There was no answer. Tom heard the faint echo of his question in the still, dark little park, and dropped his voice to add, "I'm sorry. I didn't mean to speak so loud."

When Andy answered his voice had changed. "I'm only an ordinary two-by-four, Tom, I told you that before," he said dejectedly. "There's a lot of questions I can't answer. I don't want to see the organization suffer."

"I know that. But don't you think – Andy, you made a speech and everyone voted to investigate, and that's very straightforward. But it doesn't explain how this murder happened and that's what has to be explained now, don't you think? Don't you feel that everything must be done to find out who is responsible?"

There was no reply for a long moment, and then Tom heard Andy drawing in his breath, harsh and shuddering. "What I feel!" he said in an uneven burst. "What I feel? What I feel is that I can't trust my own people anymore! I can't trust them." He began to cry.

They sat for a while longer. Tom looked at the ground, listening in anguish, his arms folded tightly. At last the sobs stopped, and Andy straightened wordlessly and then stood up. Tom stood, too, and put a hand on his shoulder, and they walked together in silence back to Michigan Avenue. At the cab rank Andy said softly, "You're a good man, Tommy. God be good to you." Before Tom could say anything, he turned and hurried away.

XI

"**Y**A FROM ONE of the papers?"

"That's right."

"Thought so," the cab driver said with satisfaction. "Ya late, fellah. This is my third trip out there tonight, place is crawling with people."

Tom could see it as soon as they turned off Fullerton Avenue, the trickle of traffic growing thicker as they jolted toward the Lakeview station. Rigs, hacks, police wagons were ahead of them, prowling the streets like giant insects, carriage lamps glittering. There was no moon, and he could just make out the shapes of people watching, gathered on doorways and corners.

The driver said that if the cops had any sense, they'd have brought the body straight downtown to the County Morgue. "Little hick place like this, everybody be out like it was some kind of picnic. Know what I'd do to them bastards done this?" He heaved himself around to put the challenge manfully to Tom. "Know what I'd do?"

Tom sank back into the seat corner and shook his head, though he realized that the cabby wouldn't be able to see that.

"I'll tell ya what I'd do." He heaved back again and gave the horse a slanting lash of his whip. "I'd take them out and axe them to death just like they done to this Doc, good and slow, so they'd feel every crunch into their skulls. That's the only way to treat these bastards, only way to stop this kind of thing. Hang 'em, they don't feel a thing. The noose don't frighten nobody. You get murderers, they just laugh at it. Whole damn city gone to hell now. Which paper ya with?"

"The *Tribune*," Tom said. His voice sounded faintly hoarse. He coughed and repeated, "*Tribune.*"

"*Tribune.* Joe Medill set that up, right? Another liberal rag, you ask me."

"I'm not really sure."

"Oh, yeah, another goddam liberal rag."

"I wouldn't say it's too liberal."

"Well ya wrong there, fellah. They're all liberal rags, whining about the poor, we all gotta feel sorry for, they turn to lives of crime because they're so hard up. Well, let me tell ya somethin', I grew up in this town and I'm tellin' ya we knew what poor was and we never turned to lives of crime. My old man flay the skin off my backside I so much as stole an apple, and I respected him for it. This as far as I'm gonna be able to take ya. Look at that crowd. Think they'd stay in their beds at night. Ya okay now? Ya know where you're at?"

The police station was surrounded. There were hundreds of people jamming the entrance, their faces wild with excitement. In the pallid light from the oil-lamp at the door they looked unearthly, colorless and contorted.

Tom nudged his way through slowly to the cordon of police, whose billysticks were drawn and quivering. The crowd surged and subsided, as if it had a life of its own, back and forth in front of the billysticks. The first cop Tom showed his card to pulled him past their ranks and he scrambled up the steps, holding his privileged press pass aloft, without looking back into the envious eyes of the company behind him. Huntley was immediately inside the door, writing notes out on the window-sill, ignoring the stream of police, detectives, reporters and photographers that flowed around him.

"You were quite a time," Huntley said serenely. "Get anythin' much from your pal?"

"Nothing much, I'm afraid," Tom said. "What's happening here?"

"Well, now, don't rightly know just where to begin. Let you have a look at my stuff here in a minute, I'm just finishin' a holdin' story."

"Dick, there's hundreds outside. I can't believe my eyes."

"That surprise you?"

"Yes, it surprises me. What's the point of hanging around the police station? Do they want to come in here and gape at the poor man's body, or what?"

"They just want to bear witness to evil, that's all. Hopin' for a glimpse or a sniff a' the devil while they're assurin' each other how shocked they are at such unimaginable wickedness." Huntley stopped writing and looked at Tom. "Do you want to see the corpse? Press allowed. Right in there."

"No," Tom said. "I don't."

"You probably should." Huntley pondered a moment. "Well, I ain't gonna force you. Here, read this; I'm gonna duck back in, one or two things I gotta check before I get a cabby to take this into the paper."

Huntley's notes were concise, in longhand, ready for the rewrite man. Body identified by C's close friends: John Scanlan, Mortimer Scanlan, P. McGarry. Also Dr. John R. Brandt, pres., Cook County Hospital. Prelim medical exam by Brandt. Full autopsy to follow.

Five wounds: front parietal suture; vertex, right of sagittal suture; third one half-inch posterior to second; left temple, cheek-bone fracture; behind jaw-bone severed skull base, four to five inches deep. Considerable force all wounds, suspect variety instruments, one very sharp, also heavy weapon. No marks (arms, legs); evidence no struggle.

Tom folded the page neatly and put it in his jacket pocket. Once, for a brief time, he had wished to become a scientist instead of a priest, to deal with things that could be tested and identified, the visible and tangible. He had given up the notion when he couldn't overcome the persistent nausea induced by fumes in the seminary physics laboratory, but he remembered what he found satisfying now, filing the notes away. In the end, no matter how horribly, no matter in what circumstances, people died of things that could be located and named.

Huntley returned with Captain Villiers behind him. "Tom, you remember Cap'n Villiers here?" he said. "He's got a question I thought maybe you could answer. Ever hear of a' Ay-nus Day?"

"I'm sorry?" Tom looked from one to another. "Agnes? Aonghus?" he asked.

"This is a thing, not a person," Villiers said. He looked offended, as if at an unpleasant smell. "One of my men said it was called an Anus Day. Mr. Huntley thought you might be able to enlighten us about it. If you'll come inside and view the corpse, I can show you."

Tom glanced at Huntley quickly, but Huntley was quicker. "Whyn't you just describe it for him, Cap'n? You got half a' Chicago in that there morgue as it is."

"It's a charm of some kind," Villiers said crisply. "Religious, I presume. A heart-shaped object hung by a ribbon around the dead man's neck. Colored red, with an insignia of some kind on it, letters and so on."

"Oh. Agnus Dei," Tom said, pronouncing carefully. "It's what's known as a scapular."

"A scapular? Can you tell me just what that is?"

"Well, it's nothing very important," Tom said. "It's a kind of religious emblem, that's all. Lots of people wear them that way, around their necks under their clothes. It's just a special – a sort of token, a badge. A reminder to pray, that kind of thing."

"What does it mean?" Villiers asked with distaste. "It's Latin, isn't it? What does it mean?"

But Huntley interrupted. "It means God's lamb, doesn't it, Tom? Haven't forgotten as much as I think I have. A token to say, I am God's little lamb."

Tom smiled faintly at him and said to Villiers, "I don't think it's a very significant thing. Lots of people wear them as a devotion. Catholics, I mean; lots of Catholics."

"I see," Villiers said. "Perhaps you'd think it was significant if it was all that was left on a dead man's body. Whoever the brutal killers of this man are, they removed every item of his clothing and threw him naked into a sewer. But it appears they may have placed this item around his neck before they disposed of him."

"Oh, no," Tom said. "No sir, Captain, why, I'm sure Dr. Cronin must have been wearing it. No one would have any reason to put it on him after – there wouldn't be any reason to do a thing like that."

"That's another possibility, naturally. I assure you we'll be looking into everything." Villiers looked at him coolly. "But this is a strange murder, Mr. – I'm sorry?" He inclined his head toward Tom, elaborately polite, and Tom said quickly, "Martin, Tom Martin."

"I think you'd agree that there is something particularly strange about this murder, Mr. Martin? Strange as well as vicious. Macabre, I think is the word you writers might use. We can't rule anything out when we're trying to assess what is, as you put it, significant." Villiers turned and offered Huntley the same inclination of the head. "Thank you both for your help." He turned away, and disappeared through the door to the back room.

"That man is crazy," Tom said to Huntley. "What is he imagining?"

Huntley shrugged. "From his viewpoint, which is the peak a' affectation and ignorance, I expect he's imaginin' blood sacrifice in a medieval torture chamber with Old Nick runnin' the mysterious charms concession."

"But scapulars are just a bit of piety. The Church encourages people to wear them – there are probably fifty of them hanging around the necks out there in the street."

"I take your word for it. The question is," Huntley said, "what kind of men would chop a man to death, rob all his clothes, dump him in a filthy sewer, but leave him with a holy doodah around his neck?"

"Well, not necessarily agents of Satan," Tom said crossly. "I suppose I'd have to say superstitious Roman Catholics, yes. They're hardly the same thing and, anyway, most people of any religion or none would respect – oh, this is ridiculous. This is crazy."

"Yep," Huntley said. He sighed, an unexpectedly deep sigh. "It's a crazy thing, I agree, to be standin' here discussin' what murderers respect and what religion they might be. The problem with that there God's lamb trinket on poor Cronin's neck is that it just suits Villiers and others like him down to the toes. It fits in with everythin' they fear about peasants from Europe who love martyrs and worship statues. It scares hell out a' 'em, like them pictures a' mutilated hearts Catholics seem to be so fond a'." Tom looked up sharply and Huntley put up both hands. "No offense now, Tom, you know that." Tom began to laugh before he meant to and stopped again abruptly. He felt a little crazy himself. Maybe this is how Andy had felt, too.

Huntley added notes on the Agnus Dei scapular to his story and gave it to the cabby. He left Tom with instructions to go over the evidence of the three workmen and the details of the body's location with the sergeant on duty. Tom found the sergeant, a man accustomed to the mathematical precision required in courtrooms, who was able to specify that the sewer basin was exactly one hundred yards from the Chicago and Evanston railroad depot, and three-quarters of a mile from the point where the trunk was discovered.

Huntley was back in time to get quotes from Cronin's friends; a dozen or so had turned up to identify the body. Mr. Conklin, the landlady's husband, stirred some interest because up until then his existence hadn't really been noticed. Mr. Conklin indicated that his wife was not up to the harrowing task, and went resolutely inside to view the corpse. When he reappeared before the cluster of waiting reporters he cried, "Monsters! Oh my God, what beasts could have done this?" The sight of the Agnus Dei scapular had torn his heart out, he told them. "A holy sacramental the dear, devout man never removed, even when he bathed, even when swimming." Tom looked around for Villiers, but he was nowhere in sight.

When the last of the witnesses had been shepherded back to their rigs by the police, the crowd began to disperse, drifting away in twos and threes. There was still a question over when the autopsy could begin, and it was becoming urgent. Despite the new and ingenious automatic water sprinkling system set up to moisten the corpse, decomposition was proceeding at an alarming rate. "Cops'll likely wait till there's no one about and then whisk Cronin down to the County Morgue for the autopsy," Huntley said. "Not much sense us waitin'; we may as well head in."

It was after midnight by then. In the hack, Tom started to relate what Andy had said, keeping his voice down to evade the ears of the driver. But he was cut short with an angry snarl he hadn't imagined was in Huntley's vocal range: "Well, that's the most damnfool thing I heard yet from a grown man."

"Why?" Tom asked, startled.

"I got it right?" Huntley snapped. "This fellow solemnly informs you that a roomful a' men didn't vote to commit a murder? You tell me when they ever did? One good reason why people keep an otherwise tedious thing like democracy is committees and such seldom vote to kill people, even the ones they don't like. That's a damnfool thing to be boastin' about."

"I don't think he was boasting," Tom hissed, watching the driver. "He was making the point that the Clan had reason to feel that Cronin was behaving oddly and decided to investigate, that's all."

"So what?"

"So — his point is the Clan shouldn't be held responsible for the murder."

"Does he know who should?" Huntley hissed in return, and Tom shook his head.

They were silent for the rest of the journey. In front of the *Tribune* Huntley paid the driver and waited until he'd started the horse up and rattled away before he turned to Tom and spoke. "Don't want to argue with you or trespass on your friendships," he said. His voice was gentler than usual. "You know that."

"Yes."

"But I think I oughta say to you that you're gonna have to make your mind up about this here situation." Huntley paused, his face earnest, studying Tom for a response. "It ain't a vanished doctor we're dealin' with now; it's a murder, and an ugly one, and it was done by more 'n one person, and it's more 'n likely they got some connection with your pal's Clan na Gael. You'd best think about where you fit into things before this situation gets any worse."

"I've said a hundred times I don't hold any brief for the Clan. You know that," Tom muttered.

But Huntley shook his head. "You're gonna have to stand back a space and think about what you do hold a brief for, and who. That's all I'm sayin'. Hope it don't sound pompous."

"No. All right. I guess I get what you mean. The thing is, what nobody understands . . ." Tom waved at the *Tribune* building a little wildly and stopped.

"Go on," Huntley said.

"What nobody understands, I mean about me, is that it hasn't got anything to do with me. I heard all this history, over and over, all this – this righteousness about poor little Ireland, and what I always thought was, so what? They aren't the only people who ever suffered. So that's all I'm saying – I don't fit in, as you say, at all."

"Where'd you hear all this history?" Huntley asked.

"Oh, in school, in the seminary. There was this priest, Father Farrell, supposed to teach European history; all he ever talked about was Ireland. Look, it doesn't matter, I get what you're saying. I'm just, you know, tired of being misunderstood."

Huntley said easily, "I'll keep that in mind. You keep your pal in mind, where you fit in with him. That's all I'm sayin', and I don't mean no offense by it." He slapped Tom on the shoulder, a little tentatively. Tom shrugged.

They sat together in the newsroom for another few hours, working in the rhythm Tom felt he could now maintain in his sleep; he reading and methodically checking the other papers through each edition, Huntley tapping out copy, one page after another, and the copy boy hustling each sheet off to be processed as it fell limply from the typewriter. The newsroom was deserted and dim, only the light over Huntley's typewriter left flickering when they reached the deadline for the last edition.

They went together down the back steps. They could hear the presses below them warming up, humming with anticipation – any moment now, any moment now. On the ground floor there were men running in every direction, their shouts blotted out. The drone picked up steadily, a little faster, a little faster. Any moment now it would lift off, full tilt and away, no turning back. The men scurried, demented, up and down ladders, as they did every night. Now; now; Tom and Huntley waited in mutual accord until the thing screamed: now. Huge sails of paper, taut as bedsheets, pitched into the great iron mouth and a few minutes later the overseer handed them the first two copies of the final edition, still warm.

They slipped along the wall and out into the loading bay. The wagons were already drawn up, close together and waiting. On the sidewalk the delivery boys waited too, butting each other and wrestling in aimless exuberance. Tom and Huntley side-stepped them and found two cabs on the corner.

It was almost dawn. Tom asked the driver to go along the lakefront though it was a bit out of the way. It was just light enough to see the lake lapping up on the beach at Oak Street. He slouched into the cushions and thought, finally, about Andy. Of course, it was possible that Andy knew more than he had told him, Tom knew that. That's what Huntley was wondering – not so much where Tom fitted in with his source as where the source fitted in. But the touching part about Andy was that he was, in the end, just what he said, an ordinary two-by-four who trusted the word of men above him. Not the sort of man who'd ever know much. How silly he must seem to Huntley; Tom's garrulous, simple-minded contact. Tom felt sleep coming in waves. The lake smoothed out before him to a perfect arc on the horizon, outlined in an uneven blur of pink like something stroked on with a child's paintbrush, and promising nothing more complicated than another lovely May morning.

XII

LESS THAN TWENTY-FOUR hours after Cronin's body had been lifted from its watery tomb, Mrs. Carlson decided to tell her secret. It was a remarkable piece of luck for the police, since she had to be one of the few remaining Chicagoans who had never heard of Cronin, alive, dead, missing or discovered. Mrs. Carlson didn't trouble her life with newspapers. She couldn't speak in anything but Swedish, which made her statement largely an exercise in mime; she couldn't read in any language at all. What she had grasped without difficulty was that when the Lakeview police turned up in squadrons to visit Patrick O'Sullivan's ice-house on Thursday morning, it was time to direct someone to the cottage.

The cottage was on Ashland Avenue, just off Roscoe, about one hundred and fifty feet away from the rear entrance of O'Sullivan's shed. It was a single story over a basement, five rooms. Fifteen years ago when Jonas Carlson had built it, Mrs. Carlson must have had her dreams, even her floor plans, for the way it would look sometime, furnished with pine sideboards and tousled, rosy babies. But Jonas was a man work seemed to evade. Fifteen years later she and Jonas were still in the two-roomed shack at the rear, and still relying for survival on the rent the cottage brought in. The cottage was weatherbeaten now, the attic was still unfinished, and the rosy Carlson babies had grown up and moved on.

She was pleased, if perplexed, when Villiers plied her with fresh coffee and insisted on settling her in his own chair. Through a process of gesticulation and grimace, Mrs. Carlson made it clear that the last tenant had left a terrible mess behind, the sort of mess that would make a law-abiding citizen feel uncomfortable.

Captain Wing, who been drafted in to assist Villiers in Lakeview, drove to the cottage with two officers where he saw immediately that the two Carlson premises and O'Sullivan's ice-house were not desirably located for much apart from crime. They stood alone in a patch as large as a city square, and a prairie rolled in every direction around them, dotted only remotely with neighboring cottages. There were no streetlamps out this far. At night, Wing could see, it would be black as a cave. But in the mid-afternoon sun, he could see enough on the porch to set his pulse ticking pleasantly. There before him lay a trail of pea-sized spots, dried and dark but familiar to his eye in that state; a trail of blood.

One of the officers forced the lock, crashed back the door and then drew in his breath. It was an impressive sight, not easily interpreted. Someone had painted the floor recently, or at any rate slapped a brushful of muddy brown down in looping, random strokes. The smell of paint mingled sourly with something tangier in the stuffy little hallway. At the entrance to the parlor on the left, the painter had left his stamp in the paint, the distinct print of one naked foot. Inside the parlor, he had apparently abandoned the job after a few wild sweeps in the center of the room. The rest of the floor was swamped in a great deal of blood. The captain cursed softly and looked carefully and methodically around the room, starting on his left.

There was blood splattered from the doorway to the skirting-board and then up across the white wall, where it had clotted in clusters like patterns of spring blossoms. Blood had pooled in the center of the floor and from there streaked in one crooked, broad path to the right corner, as if something long and heavy and saturated had been rolled across the room. To Wing's immediate right was a cane rocking-chair, the seat and legs coated in blood. One arm had been wrenched off and was lying on the floor.

Wing sent an officer back to Lakeview to call in Forensic, and inside an hour every city newspaper had the news in precise and comprehensive detail. Tom thought of Mrs. Carlson, blowing discreetly on her coffee in the station house, while Wing and his officers sniffed the rancid air in the cottage.

"I'm not sure I want to see this," Tom said to Huntley.

"You won't," Huntley answered. "Whole place'll be cordoned off while Forensic dig around. We'll have to find us a bored cop to talk to."

By the time they arrived, with a score of other reporters, there were plenty to choose from. Some looked as if they may have been up most of the previous night at Lakeview station, Tom saw, as harried and gritty-eyed as he was himself. Hands behind their backs in the regulation stance, the police stationed themselves every few feet around the Carlson lot and up Ashland Avenue and ignored the public, who were also gathering in jubilant horror. Lakeview, Huntley observed, wouldn't recover from the thrill of this May for years. The press distanced themselves from all but each other, pushing as close to the cottage as they could. Huntley left Tom with a crowd pressed against the picket fence. "You watch here a piece," he suggested. "I'm just gonna saunter around a while, see what I can pick up."

Tom watched. There were men moving behind every window at the cottage, but he couldn't really see what any of them were doing. He thought he recognized Captain Villiers once, speaking tersely at the door to what seemed to be a plainclothes detective. Every few minutes a police wagon arrived or departed, collecting or delivering more men. An hour passed, and some members of the public melted away. They were replaced by others. The two policemen at the gate of the cottage shifted their positions a fraction, and began mumbling to each other. Tom shook his notebook from his jacket pocket, wondering whether he should begin asking questions now that the shield was lowered, however slightly.

"You press?" He turned hastily at the voice behind him, and saw a face with an antic grin at his shoulder. He nodded.

"Dunne," said the other. "*Times.*" He was even younger than Tom. "Bad pay and sore feet, that's what they're talking about, and they've got my sympathy. Amazing to think how many people think the press lead fascinating lives. Feel like having a gawk elsewhere?"

"I can't," Tom said, "I'm under orders."

Dunne winked and went off and as Tom watched him he saw, finally, someone he knew, someone he might possibly ask questions of. Coughlan, the detective from Chicago Avenue station, was leaning lazily against a police rig up the street, smoking a cigar. He had to mention Huntley's name twice before Coughlan extended his hand lazily. "So. You playing the boy, while Huntley noses around?"

Tom didn't reply, and Coughlan laughed. "Professor Huntley, hayseed philosopher for hacks. Treat you all right?"

"Yes. Fine."

"Put his paw on your knee, whisper little thoughts from the folks back home?" Coughlan laughed, studying Tom's face. "Want to watch out for that. Well, what can I do for you?"

"I thought maybe I could ask you a few questions about what's been found in the cottage."

"Lot of blood, I guess, is the answer. Lot of blood, some bashed up furniture."

"And it looks like it may have been the place where Dr. Cronin was murdered?"

"Couldn't say anything like that for certain – this place's been vacant a long time, as I understand it. Whatever went on could have been months ago."

Tom nodded, and wrote a few words in his notebook. "Is there a way of telling about that? I mean, can the, ah, forensic people, can they tell by examining the blood in the room and Dr. Cronin's body?"

Coughlan was still leaning against the rig. He looked at Tom with something almost tender in his eyes, sweet and sardonic. "Cronin's body's been in a sewer for three weeks," he said. "Do you know what human carcass is like after three weeks soaking in a sewer, Mr. Martin? Not much you can learn from it." He flipped the cigar into the road. "Afraid I got nothing much to tell you. I'm sure it'll all come out in the wash. Isn't that what they say?"

"I guess so."

"Whatever it means. Well! Nothing attributed to me, right?"

"No," Tom said. "Right."

Coughlan looked at him again, with the same expression. "Give my regards to the Professor," he said, and walked away.

It was another hour before Huntley came back. By that time

Tom had pocketed his notebook and given up hope of finding anything to report. He was leaning on the fence with the residents of Lakeview, viewing the unending movement inside the Carlson cottage with dull eyes. Huntley's face was happy. "Got a good little story," he said, clapping Tom on the shoulder. "Hope you wasn't too overwrought with excitement here."

"Rigid with it," Tom said, straightening up. "In fact, I'm so rigid I've got a cramp."

"Want to hear what I got?"

It was a good story. Huntley got it from the county pathologist's assistant, who'd been instructed to have a hack waiting at the Carlson cottage at two o'clock to collect samples for the laboratory. But there was a dispute between the county laboratory and police headquarters on Harrison Street as to what constituted forensic evidence and what constituted samples, so the pathologist's assistant was still waiting at quarter to five. Huntley told him he was in the pharmaceutics line himself, and the assistant enthusiastically repeated everything he'd gleaned from the laboratory analysts on the way out to Lakeview.

He gathered from their remarks that the corpuscles in human blood were larger and more compressed than those in animal blood, and were much easier to identify under a powerful microscope. The same microscope could compare two blood samples, and expert examiners should be able to decide – fairly accurately – whether they came from the same source, on the basis of the degree of resemblence. The theory hadn't yet been applied, he explained to Huntley. But Dr. Brandt from Cook County Hospital had been waiting for just this kind of opportunity. They were even at that moment setting up their microscopic equipment.

"And they been hoarding that little store a' blood from the Lakeview trunk for three weeks in the pathology ice-box, just hopin' their chance would come," Huntley said gleefully.

Tom repeated the phrase he felt had become his recurring line. "I never thought of that," he said, and then added suddenly: "But Detective Coughlan never thought of that either."

There was a press conference that night in Harrison Street. Dr. Brandt presided, with Chief Hubbard, Captain Villiers, and

Captain Wing. There was general disappointment that the scientist had discarded his white coat and was not bearing laboratory vials brimming with samples, and it didn't lift any when Dr. Brandt cleared his throat, asked for attention and opened the press conference with a comprehensive explanation of the technique of blood identification. Dr. Brandt nodded occasionally, like a giddy hollyhock, toward Chief Hubbard, who returned the gesture graciously. The reporters wrote diligently if somewhat sullenly.

Major breakthrough, exhaustive research, impact on medical circles. Tom listened, lulled, and waited for the falling note that would signal a new rising tone of summary. But authorities more expert than Villiers had arranged the staging this time. The door was flung back just as Dr. Brandt had reached "my thanks to my colleagues", and the State Attorney, J.M. Longenecker, was ushered into the room by a uniformed policeman.

Longenecker took a place modestly at the end of the line of men, hands folded. Dr. Brandt wavered slightly and a reporter toward the front took the advantage, asking quickly whether the tests had been conclusive.

"Oh, yes, without question," Dr. Brandt said mildly. "There is not the least doubt in my mind that the blood in the trunk and that taken from the floor of the house came from the same person."

A babble of questions followed. Chief Hubbard lifted a hand. "Gentlemen," he said. "Please. There will be time for questions afterward. Dr. Brandt has given you the results of his investigations. If we can ask your patience for just a few moments, the State Attorney, Mr. Longenecker, has taken time from his busy schedule to be with us tonight to discuss the consequences which must follow on today's developments. Mr. Longenecker?"

Longenecker's voice was resonant, practiced, pitched to be heard. "Chief Hubbard, Dr. Brandt, gentlemen: may I first pay tribute here tonight to Dr. Brandt for giving so generously of his time and his very considerable skills . . ." A weary little sigh barely rippled through the ranks of reporters as heads bent again over notebooks. It struck Tom that public representatives found murder just as useful a boost as newspapers.

XIII

IT WAS GOING to be the most majestic funeral Chicago had witnessed since the obsequies for Governor Stephen Douglas. Church had deferred to state: since Mahoney's Funeral Parlor couldn't start enbalming until the autopsy was finished on Friday, and Mahoney said there was no way the corpse would make it to Monday, the Archdiocese waived normal arrangements and agreed to a Sunday funeral. There was no question about the venue. The doctor's friends reserved the cathedral for a Solemn High Requiem at noon with the services of the full choir and accompanist.

By the time the body was delivered to the First Cavalry Armory late on Saturday afternoon, every newspaper office in the city had posted the details of time and place in the front window to avoid further enquiries. The public was frantic for information, yearning for details of his burial as only yesterday they had yearned for details of his death. Cronin missing had been either faintly sinister or faintly comic, a curiosity piece; Cronin murdered had become a martyr, a reverential figure. An act of reparation, Huntley said, by a terrified city. The *Herald* said that many a hero would pass from this life with less than the show of honor and respect that Chicago with its generous heart would accord in sympathy to the tragic victim of evil forces. The *Times* said thousands upon thousands would be present at the final tribute, stirred by a desire to testify, in their humble way, to the city's sorrow and indignation that such a crime had befouled its fair name. The *Daily News* said the funeral would be a public demonstration of revulsion toward secret assassinations which the world could not fail to heed.

Percy said that the story was bigger than anything in years and he didn't want any veiled smart-alec stuff about morbid curiosity-seekers in Huntley's copy. "That goes for you, too," he told Tom. "Everything solemn as hell, okay?"

"Yes, sir." Tom said. It was his first actual writing assignment, though he was only one of four reporters assigned to the job. Huntley said nothing. He'd just come back from the Armory, where the mourners were lined up for two blocks waiting to view the coffin.

"That doesn't mean you can't keep your ears open for any little development in the way of news," Percy said. "There's bound to be people at this funeral who know goddam well the whys and hows and whos of this murder. Something just might leak your way. Right?" he nodded at both of them and walked away.

"Long as you write it good and solemn," Huntley said. He inserted a page of copy paper into the typewriter and sat back. "I intend to give this both barrels now for the mornin', just to start us off right."

"Give what both barrels?"

"The solemn and heart-wringin' scene at the Armory the night before the funeral," Huntley intoned. He began to type vigorously.

"The most august lyin'-in-state this city has accorded a citizen since we shoveled under the man who almost beat Abe Lincoln. The prize catch a' Digger Mahoney's career, and a most deservin' fellah he is, too."

"Where Dr. Cronin comes from," Tom said, "it's called a wake."

Huntley snorted and went on typing. "Ain't no wake when the deceased is hoisted up on a platform under a canopy a' black silk, and there's four fellahs with feathers in their bonnets and gloves up to their elbows wavin' swords over the coffin. Tom, boy, this is called lyin'-in-state."

"My God."

"Presume He'll be impressed, too. That ain't all: listen." Huntley ended his first paragraph, removed the page and consulted his notes. "A six-foot cross a' white roses and carnations. A four-foot-high candelabra with seven lighted tapers. Two black flags and the Stars and Stripes, draped from the beams a' the roof to the catafalque . . ."

126

"The what?"

"Catafalque. Banked on all four corners with hydrangeas and over it all . . ."

"Who are the fellows with the feathers and swords? And why the American flag, anyway? I thought that was only for war veterans and politicians."

Huntley flipped back a page in the notebook. "Knights a' St. Patrick," he said briefly. "It's plumes, to be precise, not feathers. Later to be relieved by sentries a' the Hibernian Rifles. Listen a minute. Over it all – this here's the best part, don't want you to miss it – a crayon portrait a' the dead man, five foot high and half that wide."

"Oh, God."

"So the grievin' public can make sure they got the right corpse. On account a' Mahoney couldn't do anythin' with his best touch and choicest embalmin' elixir to make the poor Doc fit to be seen. It's interestin' about the flag, though, isn't it? Cronin's friends are sure anxious folks see him as an American gent and not some kind a' dirty foreigner. Climate a' opinion at the moment, they'd wanted the Liberty Bell to toll, they'd probably a' got it."

Huntley went back to the typewriter and Tom picked up the lead page and read it: "All that was mortal of Patrick Henry Cronin was last night brought to lie in state in the First Cavalry Armory on Michigan Avenue. Today the murdered physician's remains will be laid to rest in Calvary Cemetery, after the most solemn rites of the Roman Catholic Church in Holy Name Cathedral. But as the procession moves through the streets and the muffled drums send their solemn tremor through the discordant air, the tragic mystery of his death will tear at every heart and its every phase will be discussed in whispers throughout this city." Tom looked from the paper to Huntley's face, wrinkled his nose, and turned away.

"I know, it's ripe stuff," Huntley called after him, and looked back at his notes. "Haven't even got to decribin' the casket yet. French walnut. Mounted in gold – come back a minute, Tom – a continuous rail a' silver on each side instead a' handles, decked with silver tassels."

"Good night," Tom said from the newsroom door. "See you in the morning."

Huntley went right on. Tom could hear him all the way down the hall. "Ornamented with double motifs a' silver flowers. I'm gonna write the Doc up to heaven and swing the pearly gates off their hinges for him when I finish. And two large wreaths a' gold intertwined with silver roses on each side of a silver plate . . ."

On the sidewalk Tom ran for a street-car headed north. It was still early enough to drop in on Andy and Liz. He was troubled by the way Andy had left him the night they'd talked, by his tormented face; his tears. The ordinary two-by-four bard of Kilgubbin, jibed by his friends for his patriotic plays, rocked to tears because it appeared that he had set something off with his fervent speeches. Tom wondered what else had happened at the meeting, what Andy hadn't told him; and in the next moment, wondered if Andy hadn't exaggerated the facts in what he had said. But he meant it when he said the most important thing was that the Clan should not be held responsible. That's just what Andy would believe. Huntley could not be expected to understand that.

The cottage was dark when he got to Locust Street, but as he came closer Tom saw a light fluttering somewhere inside. He knocked lightly and in a minute or two a face gleamed at the window, white against the dark pane, and then vanished. Kate opened the door. "I'm not to let anyone in, but I saw it was you. I'm in charge." She held dingy playing cards in one hand, pressed to her thin little chest.

"Are your papa and mama both out?" Tom asked.

"Mama took the baby to the doctor," Kate said, with emphasis on the last word to stress the consequence of the occasion, and then, apparently satisfied that Tom had registered that, she added sociably, "But she says it's only to be on the safe side. We're playing cards. You can play if you like, it's all right for you to come in."

Tom nodded. "Well, I hope everything is okay. And do you know when your papa's coming home?" Over her shoulder he could see the light again, fitfully tossing shadows on the kitchen walls.

"No. Mama said she couldn't wait any longer for him and that's

128

why I'm in charge. You can play with us, we're playing devil's card."

There was a sudden shuffling in the kitchen and Robert appeared with his handful of cards carefully fanned before him. "Hurry up!" he shouted. "Kate!"

"It's awfully dark," Tom said. "Will I put on the lamp for you?"

"I'm coming now! The thing is," Kate said, frowning at Robert, "I put it out so's we could play better. It's meant to be spooky."

"How do you mean?" Tom said. He sighed. "I guess I'll come in a minute."

Kate followed him into the kitchen, where the three small boys were sitting at the table. Their faces were washed white in the light from the candle in its center, and they stared at Tom cagily, not quite sure whether they had been caught at something or not.

"Did your mama say it was all right to light a candle?" Tom asked Kate, who said, "She didn't say I couldn't," rapidly.

"I think I'll light the lamp for you, okay? And blow the candle out."

"It's scarier with a candle," Robert explained, and Tom nodded, busy with the lamp. "See, you have to keep choosing one card after another and you don't know which one is the devil's. Do you want to play?"

"Not tonight," Tom said. "Tell your mama and papa I came around, will you? And no more candles. Promise, Kate? They're dangerous."

Kate thumped into her chair, shrugging, and Robert said, "Who cares, I wasn't scared anyhow." Tom considered whether he should stay until Liz or Andy came. But no, better to be a responsible friend who steps in and sets things right quietly, and goes, not hanging about looking for thanks. He left them arguing about whose turn it was, feeling, he realized, discreet and somewhat absurdly pleased with himself.

He got to the Armory just after nine the next morning. He had to concede that if public interest was the gauge, Huntley hadn't overdone it. The doors had been open for two hours and the cop on duty told him there was a crowd waiting even then. There was a line now stretching to the next block, waiting for nothing more than a glance from lowered eyes at a casket and a crayon portrait. The mourners filed obediently into the building in two orderly lines and out at the far door at the same doleful pace. He couldn't see Huntley, who'd been told to get a spot as near as possible to the hearse; he was probably chatting up the driver somewhere with a line about his former days as an undertaker, Tom thought broodingly. There were two more reporters to be stationed at the cathedral by noon, and one of them was to leg it out to the cemetery to secure a graveside position as soon as mass started. Tom was the mop-up man, delegated to follow, mingle with the mourners, get a little color if he could; nothing inappropriate.

He took up his post a short distance from the cop, pulled out his notebook reluctantly, and began writing. "Laborers beside merchants, tradesmen beside bankers," he noted. "Old men and young, white-haired matrons and girls, children and aged men. Memorable scene." It was quite true, too. And it would go on for another hour, and it would take another hour to get the few short blocks to the cathedral. He turned up his jacket collar, for even the weather had changed to suit the city's mood, and was grayer and sharper than it had been for weeks. It might even rain. Perhaps God was impressed.

When he'd been watching and scribbling sporadically for almost an hour, Packy Ryan's Clare accent sidled forward from somewhere near his right elbow. "Tom Martin," he said. "It's yourself."

"Packy! God, I'm happy to see a friendly face."

"You were looking fairly miserable. Are you working, then?" Packy was a small man, with small, merry eyes and a voice that matched. Tom always had to lean forward to catch his words above the noise in Gleason's. It was no different, he found now, in a street even as unusually subdued as Michigan Avenue this early Sunday morning. "Working?" he repeated. "Yes, me and every other hack in Chicago."

"Aye, Andy said you might be." Packy looked up grinning, his eyes puckering into two slits. "He was to come with us today but he fell foul of a few balls of malt last night."

"Oh," Tom said, "that's where he was. I went round but he was out."

"He got a day's work with overtime and his joy was uncontained, you might say. He'd a terrible head this morning when we called down for him. Couldn't move from the bed, now."

Poor Liz, Tom thought. "Who's us?" he asked.

"Jack Gallagher and Pat Cooney and myself are over beyond. Will you join us, or does your work nail you next to the bulls?" Packy tipped his head toward the policeman a few feet away.

Tom pocketed the notebook promptly. "I'll join you, if you don't mind," he said. Company would not only be a relief, it would also probably prove helpful. He followed Packy through the crowd, which had multiplied dramatically. Looking right and then left along the boulevard, Tom realized that thousands were gathering there who weren't joining the line of those filing into the Armory. They were merely waiting, with the same strange watchfulness of the crowds outside the Lakeview station and outside the Carlson cottage, still and alert.

Gallagher and Cooney had positioned themselves on a low, broad window-ledge in the building angled away from the Armory entrance, and when Tom had scrambled up next to them he saw why. Though they couldn't see the entrance from there, with just a slight craning of the neck they had an unimpeded view of the steps and sidewalk, which had been cleared by the police. He and Cooney reached down to help Packy, and as they were hauling him up there was a hoarse murmur from the thronged street signaling that something new had happened at last. "Doors must have closed," Packy said, straightening. "Just about time."

"Won't be long now, lads," Gallagher said. "Should be spotting some familiar faces."

There was barely room for the four of them on the ledge. Tom looked over Packy's head at Gallagher's flushed face; he could have been at the racetrack, speculating on the horses about to trot into the starting gate. Beyond him Cooney, his narrow face pale, was impassive. Cooney was one of those ageless types, Tom thought; maybe thirty, but could be a few years either way. Gallagher was a good fifteen years older, and Packy was yet older, though he had a deceptively unlined face and a jaunty style, common enough in little wiry men.

131

Tom thought he must look like a boy next to them. Someone's son. Immediately he saw his father as if he stood before him, bleary-eyed and slumped with exhaustion, his mouth an angry line. The picture was so sharp that for a moment Tom was frightened, and saw himself in the corner bed, too cold to sleep. He squeezed against the window-frame and concentrated on the faces, trying to separate them into separate people, individuals in a group. In a few minutes there was another stir, and when he twisted his head he saw men descending the Armory steps slowly, bent under the weight of a casket the size of a sideboard.

"Begod, John Devoy! First pallbearer!" Gallagher said excitedly over the hush. "Do you see him, Pat?"

"I see him," Cooney said laconically. "Keep your voice down."

Tom struggled to get his notebook out. "Which one is he?" he asked in a whisper. "Do you know the others?"

"I do, indeed," Gallagher said agreeably. "Mr. Devoy of New York. Tommy Tuite, Eddie O'Meagher Condon ... is that Luke Dillon?"

"It would be, of course," Packy said, though it was doubtful whether he could see anything, even standing on the tips of his toes. "The Philadelphia swank."

"Is he important?" Tom asked meekly.

"Devoy's representative on earth," Packy snapped, and Gallagher laughed and answered easily, "One of Devoy's henchmen, got himself elected chairman of the Clan executive a few years back. Here to drive it home that himself and Devoy and the east coasters are dealing above board. Will I name them again for you?" Tom nodded, and Gallagher repeated the list. Packy interjected: "No friends of Chicago, that lot," his little voice hard; then he asked eagerly, "McGarry and the Scanlans toting the coffin as well, Jack?"

"That's it. And Marty Kelly."

Gallagher went on, to the honorary pallbearers and the organizations they represented: the Illinois Order of Catholic Foresters; the Independent Order of Foresters; the Ancient Order of Hibernians. Huntley would certainly have all of it

132

accurately, but Tom wrote anyway, as much as notice to anyone looking that he was on official duty as anything else. When
Gallagher finished his list Tom looked hastily around to catch
what was happening and then jotted down what he could.

The hearse, drawn by four black horses, pulled around the
corner and stopped. The pallbearers slid the casket inside, its
walnut and silver splendor on final public view through the
glass-panelled sides. From a side street a platoon of police rode
forward with military precision and behind them, four abreast,
marched columns of men in uniforms, olive and gray: drum-
mers, sentinels with rifles; then the plumed Knights with their
swords safely sheathed. More men followed, not in uniform
but in formation, with black armbands on their jackets and
arms flat to their sides like toy soldiers. Gallagher reeled off
identifications buoyantly: the Hibernian Rifles guard of honor,
the A.O.H., the Knights of Columbus. "And P.J. Cahill at the
top, grand marshalling to beat the band," he concluded, and
extracted his waistcoat watch, a rather grand object suspended
from a shabby leather strap. "Twenty past. Odds on it will be
half an hour before we shift. Any takers?"

No one answered because the drums had begun, recalling
them to the moment. Tom put away his notebook in the interests of propriety. The hearse rolled forward and then, in row
after row, the official mourners moved past in a steady tread.
There was no sound but the drums, slower than a sleeping
heartbeat. Then the police cordons motioned the mute thousands into the street and when the movement became general
Cooney crouched and jumped lightly down from the ledge.
Packy and Tom jumped after him. They reached up to help
Gallagher, who puffed a bit as he clambered to the ground and
then squinted at his watch. "Twenty-two minutes," he
grunted. The four of them fell into place.

Down Michigan to Chicago Avenue. Tom matched his pace
to the others, Packy and Gallagher to his right, Cooney on his
left. He wondered what Huntley and the reporters were seeing
from their vantage points. What he could see was massed hu-
manity on every side. There were people packed in along the
sidewalks, jammed together in every window, lined in an un-

tidy fringe along the roof-tops high above the street. Black crêpe streamers furled from lampposts and doorways, and banners and flags, in red, white and blue, hung from window-sills. Here and there, he saw a green banner waving.

He turned to comment on that to Packy, but Packy was listening to Gallagher, his head tilted up to him. He turned to Cooney, whose face was composed as always. An intimidating type, Tom thought, the quiet man who could be thinking anything. He spoke in a suitable undertone. "I was just noticing the green banners," he said.

"Yes. Lifts the heart, doesn't it," Cooney replied shortly. There was no change in his expression to indicate he'd savored that experience, and Tom, unable to think of an appropriate rejoinder, said nothing else.

Near the corner of Rush Street Packy nudged him. "There's Mike McDonald, do you mind him there ahead of us?" he whispered, pointing discreetly with the cap in his hand. Tom followed the direction and recognized the face from newspaper cuttings. The most powerful Democratic boss in the city, they said, a saloon-keeper who ran a gambling shop known simply and elegantly as "the Store". Packy gave him another companionable nudge. "Jack and I were just saying," he added, "that every politico in town is here. Dan Corkery and Mick McInerny from the south side; Johnny Powers out of the 19th Ward. Anybody you could name."

Tom nodded. Someone else would no doubt note all that down, he decided. The procession crossed Rush Street with no diminution in the numbers lining the streets. After a bit he mentioned the green banners to Packy, who answered with spirit: "I saw them myself; and I don't know whether to applaud the defiance or condemn the compliance."

Tom looked down at him, bewildered, but another question had intervened in his rambling thoughts. "What about Alexander Sullivan?" he asked. "Is he here? I've never seen him."

Packy darted a surprised look up at him and his eyes crinkled in a smile. He dropped his voice to a decorous whisper. "Lord love you, lad, don't you know that Alex Sullivan and Cronin were sworn enemies?"

134

"Well, yes," Tom said, "but I thought maybe under the circumstances . . . you know, everyone being here . . . "

Packy's smile vanished. "Sure, it may be an occasion not to be missed by the likes of us, but there's no way Alex Sullivan would pay his respects to that oul' fraud, dead or alive."

Tom retired again in confusion, and they trudged on in silence.

Rush Street to State Street was a tawdry stretch, though there were new brick three-story buildings now, and excavated lots with scaffolding, cheek to cheek with the rickety older neighbors whose wooden porches were collapsing. What an ungainly city it was, Tom thought, raw and ugly but full of its own promise, like the youngsters swinging from telegraph poles and perched in flocks on the scaffolding.

They followed the dulled drumbeat toward the cathedral and the steeple rose high above them. When the procession came to a sudden standstill the drums stopped with it, leaving an odd empty ring in the air. Gallagher's jovial voice rose in the new silence like a swimmer surfacing: ". . . so when Grogan's widow said she hadn't worked in thirty-five years, Johnny said he said nothing about work, he said there's a job for you if you want it in headquarters." Packy chuckled appreciatively.

A moment later Cooney, who had not spoken since he had replied to Tom on Michigan Avenue, turned and addressed all three of his companions. "Now lads," he said, "the question is whether we wish to get into the church or not? I've had a word with Dan Coughlan, who can arrange it if I give him the nod, and it beats standing outside. On the other hand, we could slip away. Tom, what about you – have you special marching orders?"

"Dan Coughlan the detective?" Tom asked blankly.

Cooney looked at him. He had very black, very large eyes. "The very same," he said evenly. "You know him?"

"Why, yes. I do," Tom said. It astonished him that he and Pat Cooney would know the same person, independent of Andy and Gleason's.

"So," Cooney said, not quite smiling. "Not such a big town

135

after all. Well," he said to the others casually, "what about it?"

"It's a bit too early to bail out," Packy offered, "but we'd be wisest to stay well back in the cathedral, in case we change our minds, you know."

"You won't be landed in the front row, don't you worry," Cooney said.

They edged their way off the street and through the crowd on the sidewalk. They inched forward, close to the buildings and in single file, Tom trailing last. At the corner, near the new Cathedral High School, Cooney and Gallagher went ahead to search out Dan Coughlan.

It was then, pressed up next to Packy slightly back from the crowd, that Tom had the only conversation of the day that he remembered long afterward. It had taken him a while to recover from their last exchange and think of what it was he wanted to know. "Packy?" he asked, he hoped in a conversational tone. "Do you remember when the pallbearers came out, and you said they were no friends of Chicago – John Devoy and the others?"

"I do," Packy said. "What about it?"

"I just wondered what you meant."

"I meant that these boyos from the east think they own the Irish nationalist movement and they find Chicago a great embarrassment to them," Packy said serenely. "We're the wild men here, didn't you know?"

"No," Tom said. "Are we?" There was probably a joke there somewhere. He forced a laugh which sounded frail.

Packy watched his face and then laughed back, a laugh so bitter and jeering that Tom's smile died. "Oh, that's us," Packy said, "that's us. Rednecks in rawhide. Can't be trusted to discuss fine points of strategy over decanters in Dublin. We're the ignorant yahoos who want to taste blood. And since '81 we've had the reins in our hands and the boys with the eastern twang don't like it. That's what I meant, Tom. That make it clear to you?"

Tom could feel his face growing hot. He looked away, into the crowd. It was impossible to see what was happening in front of the cathedral, but the people in front of him were shuffling, rustling about, pushing forward expectantly. In a moment Packy spoke again, his voice remorseful. "I'm sorry, Tom, I'm terrible sorry. I've a harsh tongue and, God knows, no reason to turn it on you."

"It's all right," Tom said in a swift mutter.

"No, I mean it. Forgive an old man."

"It's all right. Honestly. Nothing to forgive." Tom began to concentrate on separate people again. Apart from a few elderly women, no one seemed to be either praying or grieving. They were straining to see, men twisting their heads, hats in their hands, and women peering unabashed from the shelter of veiled hats.

"The truth is I am bitter," Packy said softly at his elbow. "I don't give a tinker's curse for their opinions, and I don't trust them."

Tom looked down at him and said "I can see that" in a way he hoped could be taken without sarcasm if Packy so wished it. The little man rewarded him with an acknowledging grin, and Tom smiled back a little stiffly.

"There's John Devoy there," Packy went on. "Look at him. Thirty years ago he was the most daring young fellow in Ireland. By God, he was mighty! Infiltrated the British garrison in Dublin. Organized Stephens's escape from Richmond Jail and was caught himself and sent down. You wouldn't think a man like that would have spent the best part of ten years now just chatting: chatting to Mr. Charles Stewart Parnell about forming alliances with English liberals, and to Mr. Michael Davitt about new laws to protect Irish tenants from their landlords. Trying to make polite agreements with the devils who watched the tenants starve to death and then flung them out of their rotten hovels on the roads!" Packy spat venomously on the sidewalk and Tom glanced around hastily. No one had noticed.

"I don't know much about it," he said to Packy.

"You should, then," Packy said, cocking his head up. His small eyes were glittering. "Isn't it your past as well? Isn't it why every damned one of us is here? Exiled over oceans in hundreds of thousands."

Tom said nothing. He had not quite shaken off the image of

137

his father, and he did not want to talk about the evils of history. As if he sensed that, Packy said: "We have to take the past with us; no one escapes that."

"We should try to change the future, I think," Tom said, carefully diffident. But Packy went on as if he hadn't heard him. "I know too much," he said. "I know too much to be impressed with what Mr. John Devoy's about."

"Perhaps he just changed his mind?" Tom ventured. In spite of himself, he found he was curious. "Cooling his heels in jail?"

"Not to hear him tell it. A dedicated revolutionary as always, he says. But the revolution now is about Mr. Parnell thundering words around in the House of Commons in London, and himself and Mr. Davitt lathering the tenants up to skirmish about with the National Land League, and Mr. Devoy telling all the rest of us to bide our time. "

"And what is Mr. Parnell's attitude?" Tom asked, thinking of Percy.

This time Packy laughed outright. A woman ahead of them turned and scowled. "The man who answers that question," Packy said, lowering his voice to a whisper again, "will have something to say, because Mr. Parnell keeps the cards close to the chest. But I can tell you what the attitude of the muck savages in Chicago is, if you'd like to know. We learnt our lessons well, and what we say is there's no hope for Ireland in constitutional politics. Never has been and never will be. The only message England understands is the one that's carried by the bomb and the bullet. And I've contempt for any man squandering time on anything else."

Tom was once more at a loss for an answer and they stood locked in uneasy silence while the crowd began to spread, creeping forward to fan out in front of the cathedral. He was working himself up to suggest that they should move with the others when Packy spoke again. "I've contempt for all of this, too, if you want the truth. Not that I stand over what happened to Cronin, because I don't. But in the broad span of things, it's nothing."

Tom turned to see his face but saw instead Cooney and Gallagher heading toward them, with Dan Coughlan just behind. When the three reached Tom and Packy, Coughlan stepped forward and shook hands with Tom first; it was obvious that Cooney had mentioned his presence. "Well, Mr. Martin," he said. "It seems we have mutual acquaintances."

"I guess," Tom said. "One anyway," he added and then realized foolishly that since Cooney had made no introductions, Coughlan apparently knew the others, too. But Coughlan merely gave him a languid nod and repeated "I guess," and then narrowed his eyes in the general direction of the cathedral.

"You boys want to follow me, there's a side door handy enough here. I can smuggle you in near the choir loft – view ain't great but I presume you know what an altar looks like by now. Prime spot for hearing uplifting music, anyway."

They set off, Tom again at the rear, and Coughlan cut through the swarming crowds deftly. The uniformed police stepped aside for them, and they went in a side door of the cathedral and paused briefly. Tom looked all around; a proper and pompous cathedral, he decided. For the poor parishioners to take pride in. Every pew was filled and the funeral had not yet begun.

Coughlan waved them on, into the dusky recesses of the choir loft stairwell, smelling of damp wood. The others settled near the back, and Tom edged forward to see what he could through the door which had been left slightly ajar. Coughlan handed him a folded sheet of paper before slipping away. "Your scorecard," he said. "So's you can follow the game." It was the choir schedule. Tom read it through listlessly. Schmidt's *Requiem Mass in D Major,* Mozart's *Redemptor Mundi Deus, Agnus Dei* by Reisinger. The Misses Coffey would sing. He remembered that he was meant to be working, refolded it for reference, and put it in his pocket with the notebook.

The funeral went on a long, long time. Occasionally Tom roused himself and stepped out the door to determine whether there was anything to watch, but the congregation only shifted from their knees to their feet to their seats in the eternal way of congregations, sighing and creaking. From the loft above, the music soared and sank, and the throb of the organ shivered along the bannisters. When the sermon began he forced himself to follow for a while in case reference was made to murder. Eventually he heard ". . . an atrocious death! In the fulfilment of his mission, in the very carrying out of his avocation, he met his own death. Therefore the lesson is brought home to us to be always prepared lest God should strike us, for His angel is always coming from him to touch the young and the old . . ."

He tried counting and locating the random coughs, as he had when he was a child, but his thoughts drifted and tumbled through a chaos of memories, dim as the place he stood in.

There had been no funeral for his grim, angry father; they never found his body. Perhaps there was some kind of service, but he was certainly not taken to it. His mother's funeral he wasn't told of until it was over, and she was buried in the asylum grounds. Better that way, the nuns said.

The priest worried and warned and scolded on. Behind him he heard Gallagher's rumbling murmur: "You didn't see Frankie Agnew? Ah, God, Packy, I was taken aback, he's not looking at all well . . ." and then Packy's tiny wheedling whisper, "But he got that contract despite all the carry-on, I believe?" From far away Tom heard the lamenting sing-song of the final rites and knew the priest was circling the casket. In a minute he would smell the sweet musk of incense. He wondered suddenly where Huntley was. In the sacristy, probably. Passing for an aged sacristan.

Coughlan reappeared and led them back to the sidewalk. The others weren't going on. They shook hands in turn with Tom, hoping to see him soon, and vanished into the crowd; amazingly, there was still a crowd, several thousand at least, on State Street. The casket was returned to the hearse for the journey to the depot of the Milwaukee and St. Paul. There were special trains organized, a complement of thirty-six cars. Tom dutifully joined the mourners headed for the station. It might take two hours to get to Calvary. With luck he might find Huntley there, and come back in a hack to write. What, though? The rain that had held off all day began to fall with a great fury.

XIV

ATRICK O'SULLIVAN WAS arrested in the ice-house in Lakeview on the morning after the funeral. Shortly before midnight, Dan Coughlan was locked into the cell beside him in Cook County Jail. Percy said it was a nice break for the morning papers; O'Sullivan's arrest was a good story, but Coughlan's was sensational.

It was Mrs. Carlson's evidence that tied down O'Sullivan. Mime had been sufficient to dispatch Captain Wing to her cottage, but Captain Villiers wanted the kind of nuance that leads to convictions. While he was serving Mrs. Carlson coffee, the investigative forces of Harrison Street were winnowing through their files of citizens under obligement. In a matter of hours they'd produced a Swedish baker whose Fullerton Avenue shop was testimony to the skills of illegal-alien assistants. To Mrs. Carlson, who had been trying to interest her husband in the vagaries of his tenants for weeks, it was a pleasure finally to meet someone who listened avidly to her every word. She gave full fluent Swedish detail for an hour, and the baker hurtled it all over in English to Villiers. It didn't take long for Huntley's contact to pass it on, almost sentence by sentence.

The cottage had been rented on March 20th to an Irishman named Frank Williams. Usually Mrs. Carlson's husband dealt with prospective tenants, since his English was passable. But as it happened her son was visiting that day and he discussed the terms with Mr. Williams, who was happy to pay twelve dollars for a month's advance immediately. Mr. Williams said he would be moving in with his sister, who would keep house for him, in a few days' time. Three days later he came back with a haulage wagon, and indicated to Mrs. Carlson with extravagant sign language that more would be delivered the following week. Mrs. Carlson watched from her window, and when she saw him make his way to the ice-house and speak to O'Sullivan, she assumed he was prudently ordering ice for the summer months.

But no ice-box arrived. No more furniture arrived, and no sister arrived. In mid-April Williams returned. This time, as far as Mrs. Carlson could make out, his gestures indicated that his sister was ill, very ill. He paid another month's rent and departed. Mrs. Carlson told her interpreter that she liked to see people moving in once they'd rented a place; it didn't look good to have the cottage vacant. This time she noticed during her vigil at the window that Williams talked to O'Sullivan a long time, long enough for Mrs. Carlson to conclude they were speaking of matters other than ice deliveries.

"Old lady says she thought they must be friends," Huntley told Tom, "a couple a' Mick cronies. When Williams doesn't turn up for another few weeks, she sends the husband to O'Sullivan to ask about him. 'Course, O'Sullivan says he never saw the fella before and he was makin' enquiries about the price a' ice, and so on, and Mrs. Carlson thinks this is funny but she waits it out. On May 3rd a stranger turns up on her doorstep. He lets her know Frank Williams won't be taking the place after all and offers her another's month rent by way a' compensation.

"Mrs. Carlson thinks, well, okay, the sister must 'a been worse 'n he realized. She's glad to have the next month's rent, but figures if she moves fast she might get a tenant for that month too, so she tries to get him to get the furniture out. Fella says he'll be back for it. But when he doesn't come back after a week or so, Mrs. Carlson has a peek through the windows a' the place. What she can see, it looks like the Micks had a bad brawl. Just as she's wonderin' what that might mean, she sees the cops knockin' at O'Sullivan's door again, and she starts to wonder maybe the brawl is somethin' to do with him, and Williams, and the strange fella and who knows who else. And that's when she makes her mind up she wants the cops to know it's nothin' to do with her, whatever it is."

Tom thought of O'Sullivan, pulling his mustache, in a station interrogation room surrounded by detectives. "But that's not enough, is it? It's not enough to charge O'Sullivan with murder," he said.

"No, it ain't. But they also talked to this Justice who introduced Patrick O'Sullivan to Doc Cronin a month before he was done, and the Justice says it annoyed him at the time because O'Sullivan pestered him so much about it. And in retrospect, the Justice says, it looks pretty fishy since he happens to know O'Sullivan is a chum of Alex Sullivan's. And he knows more; he knows O'Sullivan is in the Clan."

"And that's enough?"

"These days, that's enough." Huntley looked speculatively at Tom. "You thinkin' maybe you should tell your pal that?"

Tom shrugged. "I guess he knows. He told me he couldn't trust his own people anymore."

"Well, from what I hear he's not alone," Huntley said. "There's plenty a' other Mickeys feelin' the same. Percy says there's telegrams floodin' in condemnin' in the name a' Ireland whoever did this dreadful deed, that kind a' thing. And I'm told there's Clan men already standin' in line to go state's evidence so's to be seen they don't hold with murder. That should soften up the outraged natives some, anyhow."

"Who told you that?"

Huntley smiled. "My contact," he said.

Huntley's contact had also given him another angle – the story on the furniture. The police had traced what was in the Carlson cottage to A.H. Revell and Co. furniture store, and the salesman there found dockets showing that it was bought and paid for in cash on February 17th by someone named J.B. Simonds; a youngish man, the salesman said, twenty-five or thirty; reddish brown hair, dark eyes, mustache, wearing a brown overcoat and a derby. Mr. Simonds had everything delivered the next day to an upstairs apartment in Clark Street, the building directly opposite the Windsor Theater.

"The apartment he brought the cops to has a box-seat view a' Cronin's old office," Huntley said. "Theory is that the first plan was to trap Cronin right there, then they changed their

143

minds and decided it'd be safer to get him out to a nice lonely spot like Lakeview."

Tom examined Mr. Simonds's furniture requirements: one "Solid Comfort" spring, $1.50; one mattress, $2.75; one comforter, $1; one cane rocker, $1.95; one trunk, $3.50; one chamber suite, $14.50. Apart from the suite, the trunk was the most expensive item on the list. It was also the only item missing from the official police inventory on the cottage contents. The police brought the Revell salesman to the Forensic Exhibits room in Harrison Street station, and he identified the bloody trunk without difficulty as the one he'd sold in February.

Tom watched Huntley type for a while, and then went back to the Morgue. Percy had detailed him there to put together a good background piece on Alex Sullivan. It was only a question of time before he was nailed, Percy said. But he stood over Huntley's shoulder railing at him: "Why can't we firm up this story? Can't we get one miserable source in this city to pin Sullivan down?" Huntley paid no attention. He had already tried everyone, he said, several times over, and though the whisper that had linked Sullivan's name with Cronin at the start had now become a wind-storm of rumor, no one would talk, on or off the record.

Much of what was in the clippings only tended to bear out what Andy and Jack and Packy had said about Sullivan; it seemed long ago now to Tom. There were reports on Sullivan's speeches from public platforms going back years, on the dignity of the laboring classes and the iniquity of Chicago's bosses, on the rights of unions, on the just claim of the working man to a share in America's wealth. Whatever speech Alex was making, Tom noted, he never failed to mention his own impoverished origins, his immigrant parents, his years of studying law by nights. He was involved in as many Irish societies as Cronin, but the references were in a different tone. Sullivan's words on the pain of immigration echoed all that Packy said: "Not a social necessity, but a political oppression."

The rest of it was there, too. The arson charges and financial irregularities and the 1876 Hanford trial. But nothing had ever stuck against him. If he was a man with a whiff of sulfur about

144

him, there was an equal suffusion of incense in the cuttings – reports of Catholic Benevolent Society dinners with Alex and Bishop Feehan sharing the platform.

He finally found something worth taking the stairs, two at a time, up to the editorial floor. Huntley saw him coming and stopped typing. "Look," Tom said. "January, '83, annual dinner of the Irish National Land League of America. Guest speaker, Dr. Patrick Cronin. Who introduces him? Alexander Sullivan. Go on, read."

Huntley pushed his glasses up on his head and read aloud: "'Most distinguished guest, a man who serves the land a' his birth with the same unstintin' dedication as he serves the poor a' Chicago in his new position at Cook County Hospital.' Well, shows they were pals only six years ago."

"Exactly," Tom declared triumphantly.

"But that stands to reason."

"How?"

"Poor old Doc probably wouldn't 'a got his job at Cook County without Alex Sullivan givin' him the nod. Like I said, the man's got clout. He can get people out a' jobs or into 'em. That's next best thing to havin' a say on life and death. Can't find anythin' else in the line a' Irish scandal?" Huntley turned back to the typewriter.

Late in the afternoon, Huntley's contact reached him again. "Appears it'd be worth our while to be in Chicago Avenue station by ten or eleven tonight," he told Tom, "so if I was you, I'd get a bit a' rest, bite to eat, meet me back here by nine." Tom nodded. Mrs. Delaney had not become accustomed to his exits and entrances at strange hours. He wasn't sure if he would ever grow accustomed to them himself.

"My landlady thinks I'm a burglar," he said to Huntley.

He stopped to eat in a German beer-hall off Wabash, lingering over the choice of sausages and pickles, sliced and mixed, or whole, the size of turnips. Associating with Huntley was, in any event, broadening his palate. Huntley still had a taste for European food, and in the short time they'd been spending their days together Tom had eaten Greek, Italian, Polish food; and Jewish food, kosher corned beef and feathery pancakes from the stalls at Jefferson and Canal Streets. He liked the German beer-halls best, though. There was something placid and snug about them; even in the quiet late afternoon like this, there were always a few old men at the tables, playing cards or conferring over beer-steins — elders of the family, perhaps, or regular customers who felt as if they were. Irish saloons were crowded with men who stayed on their feet, drinking and talking rapidly, like passengers watching for a train. Germans, from what Tom could gather, liked to eat when they drank, and to do both in comfort. These were places where large families might come on festival nights, grannies and babies and plump wives. Tom, smiling to himself, spiralled the sauerkraut on his fork. My God, what a martyr he was to sentimentality.

He was in the police station just after nine. It was eerie, unusually quiet, only the gaslight flickering fitfully in the glass globe over the sergeant's desk. Huntley left him on the visitors' benches and went to have a discreet word with his contact. Tom thought about Coughlan. He'd meant to mention his encounter with him at the funeral to Huntley, but had forgotten in the morning's hustle. An insolent type. Tom couldn't see him joking and laughing with Packy and the others in Gleason's on a Saturday night. But it wasn't odd that they should know him, since half the police force must be Irish. It seemed a long time ago that he had been at his ease in the saloon with the others, nothing more on his mind than the novelty of his new life, out in the world, a man with better prospects than most. He wondered how the men would be taking news of Coughlan's arrest, and, with a twinge, he thought of Andy and Liz. He must make time to see them soon.

The quiet began to oppress him. There wasn't even a policeman about, and no one waiting to see a policeman, report a missing child or a stolen horse. The homeless who crowded in to the station all winter would be in the city's squares, parks and doorways tonight. Once the weather warmed, they didn't court police company. By July, all through August, they would be down at the lakefront. And so would plenty of respectable families, families whose frame shanty houses turned to dry ovens in the summer, who fled down to the beaches to find relief and sleep.

The door opened and Huntley appeared, beckoning. "Hold on to your boots," he said when Tom reached him. "This beats all."

The inside room was a box with high, barred windows and there was only one person in it, a thin man of about sixty with a face like a cross gnome and a hat balanced on one knee. "Mr. Dinan," Huntley said to him, "this is Tom Martin, works with me. Tom, this here's Mr. Patrick Dinan, runs a livery stable up on North Clark. Mr. Dinan, okay with you, I think both of us will just take down a full note a' what you got to say."

"Okay with me," Mr. Dinan said. Without rising he gave Tom's hand a single shake as if he were flicking water off his wrists. "You want me to start the night the doctor disappeared, or before?"

"Before," Huntley said.

Before, and for quite a long time before, Mr. Dinan had been providing a regular service to the detectives in the Chicago Avenue station, supplying them with horses and rigs as they required. It was not unusual to be asked to have a rig ready at a certain time and to keep quiet about it, which is what he was asked on the morning of May 4th by Detective Coughlan.

Coughlan told Mr. Dinan that a man would call at the stable at about seven o'clock and would need the horse for no more than a few hours. The man came early, Mr. Dinan said. "Thin, dark fellow. Black mustache, seedy-looking. That didn't strike me peculiar, I know in their line of work they got to dress all ways." What did strike him was the agitated way the man objected to what was waiting for him, and how adamantly he objected to the white horse, and the absence of side curtains on the rig. "Coughlan didn't give no special instructions. Blacksmith said the white horse was the only one available unless he wanted to wait, because the sorrel needed shoeing. This fellow just wouldn't be reasonable, insisted he couldn't wait and said he couldn't have no white horse neither."

He nosed around the stable, saw a black horse and demanded that one, Mr. Dinan said, but Napier Moreland, Mr.

Dinan's hostler, said the black horse had been worked pretty hard that day and needed a rest. "Fellow went on and on till I was tetchy myself and told him take it or leave it. I said it would take a while to get side curtains on if he was in a hurry, and he could always put the top up if he needed his privacy that bad. Then I told him, Detective Coughlan wants some special kind of horse and rig, time to say so was when he was making arrangements earlier."

The man didn't say anything after that. He put up the buggy top and drove off. Mr. Dinan watched him go north on Clark until he crossed Chestnut and then lost sight of him in the dusk. "I wasn't there when he come back, but Napier, he was real annoyed. Said he drove that rig into the carriage-walk, jumped down and then just took off. Never bothered to see was anyone there to look after it. Napier reckoned horse had been run hard and some distance, too." Mr. Dinan said he made up his mind then and there to speak up to Coughlan about the whole thing. But when he opened his paper on Monday morning and read about Dr. Cronin disappearing, the first thing that struck him was Mrs. Conklin's description of a white horse.

"Might never have taken notice of it," he said triumphantly, "but that fellow was so blame surly." He had his suspicions then, Mr. Dinan said, but he reasoned with himself that it could be no more than a coincidence. That's why he said nothing when the cops came around later that day asking whether anybody had hired a buggy and horse on Saturday of the description given by Mrs. Conklin. "I just kept to the arrangements I always have with the detectives and kept mum. They don't like the uniform boys knowing their business, I know that." What he decided to do, Mr. Dinan said, was to see Captain Schaack privately.

"Captain Schaack?" Huntley interrupted mildly. "That the captain right here in Chicago Avenue? Mike Schaak?"

"That's right," Mr. Dinan said. He'd gone around to see the captain that very night in the station, and when he discovered the captain had gone home for his dinner, he went around to his house and told him the whole story right then and there. "I figured once the top man knew where things was at, well then,

I could forget about it, and speak my mind to Coughlan about his bad-tempered cronies another time."

Mr. Dinan said he hadn't seen Coughlan since and the whole thing had slipped his mind until just last week when they found Dr. Cronin's body, and before the night was out the police were back resuming their investigations of every livery stable in the neighborhood. "Whoah, look't here, I says to myself. They're right back here asking did I rent out a rig and white horse on the night of May 4th, and Captain Schaack should have told them not to waste their time with me if Captain Schaack was doing his job. There's something wrong here, I says to myself."

Mr. Dinan nodded emphatically and looked from Tom to Huntley. Huntley said, "Yep, I see what you mean. What did you do then?"

What he did then, Mr. Dinan said, was go straight to the Chief of Police.

"Hubbard?" Huntley asked.

"Chief Hubbard," Mr. Dinan confirmed. That was yesterday. Tonight, from what he'd been given to understand, Detective Coughlan was going to be arraigned right here in Chicago Avenue station. "Pretty shocking thing, if you a' t me," Mr. Dinan said. "You know, I never did take to hi ," he added. "Always thought there was something about him, couldn't put my finger on it."

Huntley stood up and thanked him and Mr. Dinan said not to mention it. He rose, put his hat on firmly and snapped the brim slightly, gave them another hand-flick each and walked out of the box-room. Huntley shut the door after him. "So," he said to Tom. "Coughlan. And Schaack, too – he'd hardly be in the Clan na Gael?"

"Not likely," Tom said.

"Wonder does he owe them for his job. Coughlan, he could sure be a Clan man. Probably is in this up to his neck."

"Yes," Tom said. A number of vagrant thoughts were converging. "He could be, of course."

"The good citizens a' Chicago'll be very distressed to hear it. Crooked cop's one thing, a conspirin' cop is another. Did I say somethin' to you the other day about needin' a thick skin to ignore what you're gonna hear about your own people?"

"You say an awful lot of things to me," Tom sighed.

Huntley laughed and looked at him approvingly. "Well, I'm sayin' now a suit a' armor'd be more the thing."

Tom smiled faintly. "I'm still working on a brass neck."

Coughlan's warrant had been sworn out earlier in the day. His colleagues arrested him while he was on duty in the station day-room. They waited with him somewhere in the station, hidden from prying eyes until the judge arrived for the arraignment. Tom and Huntley waited, too, in the waiting room. They were gradually joined by reporters from every other paper as the contacts system cranked into action. It was after eleven when the sergeant broke into the excited uproar to call them inside. They were herded into the main office where Coughlan was standing before the judge, flanked by police and detectives.

The prosecution got a week's adjournment, and then Coughlan formally applied for his own bail. "Rejected," the judge said tartly. "Remanded in custody, Cook County Jail." He banged the gavel once, then rose and left the room.

It took five minutes for the patrol wagon to pull around for Coughlan, and the whole time he was pelted with questions from the press. He ignored everything, looking straight ahead. When he heard the horses stamping at the door, he turned to the cops on his right and left. "Well, boys," he said, "guess my bedtime's come," and he sauntered into the night between them.

XV

June, 1889

THE BAILIFFS HAD no choice but to close the door half an hour before the coroner's court proceedings were due to start on the first Monday in June, because every seat in the county building courtroom was taken. There were twenty reporters quartered on the press benches designed for a dozen, but the previous week had locked them into a beleaguered intimacy and they settled together like roosting hens. The *Tribune*'s regular court reporter, a dyspeptic man named George Preston who sucked peppermints, grumbled to Tom that Hertz was crazy for publicity, and a coroner should have more sense than to risk mass suffocation letting every layabout in the city into what was an official hearing to determine the cause of death. Tom said he guessed he knew what he meant.

They both knew, though, that there would have been hysteria if Hertz had tried to keep the citizens out. The inquest had officially begun one week before, with visits to the relevant sites – the roadside where the trunk was discovered, the catch-basin, the Carlson cottage. The public had been resolutely present every step along the way. They trooped after the press, who trooped after the coroner's jurors, and Tom imagined them trawling over all the repeated details with relish as they appeared again in the papers each day, padded with analysis of what the jurors' expressions signified. Tom had run out of synonyms for "shocked".

But the evidence of murder was still all circumstantial, and no one knew it better than the State Attorney. Longenecker was banking heavily on the personal testimony scheduled to start today at the coroner's inquest. It would have to be conclusive enough to put suspects before a Grand Jury; the Grand

Jury in turn would have to be convinced the evidence justified indictments. The names of the witnesses were technically a state secret, but all of the press bench and most of the public gallery could have listed them in correct order, beginning with Captain Schaack. Almost as soon as the gavel had silenced the room, he took the stand, holding his cap upright like a trophy.

"Poor old Schaak," Preston muttered. "He won't get much sympathy here for trucking with Mickey ward healers." He turned and exhaled some peppermint toward Tom. "God, I'm sorry, Martin. Nothing personal."

Schaack was famous for his work in the Anarchist case. Huntley had turned up all the Morgue cuttings for Tom on the trial, and the commendations in the annual report of the Chicago Police Department. Just two years ago Schaack had been Chicago's hero; when sixty cops were injured and one of them killed in the Haymarket riots, he was the man who'd led the hunt. None of his efforts or anyone else's had identified the person unknown who'd lobbed the bomb into the police ranks, but it was Schaack's work that got the trial evidence that sentenced eight men to death.

"You'd 'a been here at the time," Huntley said, "you'd wonder what it is about people. Two got sentences commuted and another one, Lingg, hid a dynamite cap in his cell and chewed on it till he blew up. No one admitted to bein' a little bothered about there bein' no real evidence any a' 'em ever threw a bomb, or got anyone else to throw one, and no one rested easy till the other five had swung. You'd 'a thought Chicago would 'a exhausted a passion for murder and conspiracy, but here we are again."

And here was Schaack, every sentence drawing a derisory and quite audible hiss from the courtroom. Hertz made no effort to bring the court to order. Schaack was for sacrificing. His testimony was so lame that Tom couldn't see the jurors had much choice. Schaack admitted that Mr. Dinan had approached him promptly with the information on Coughlan, and he admitted that he'd ignored it. His defense was that he thought Cronin was probably alive and the hunt for a body and a killer was a waste of time.

"You held this view even as early as Monday, May 6th, two days after Dr. Cronin's disappearance, despite the fears of Mrs. Conklin which she had expressed publicly and forcefully?" Hertz asked. He did, Schaack said. He couldn't say why. He'd also neglected to question a number of people whose names he had been given as likely sources of information. Among them, Alexander Sullivan.

"Won't be the last time that name crops up," Preston said when Schaack left the witness stand.

"What will happen to Schaack?" Tom asked.

"Ah, Hubbard'll suspend him indefinitely, I'd say. Neglect of duty. He couldn't do anything less than that. Wouldn't be surprised if there's others. Lot of the force owe their jobs. Even some of the Krauts and Eye-ties. More'll come out than we've seen yet."

But not, it turned out, on that day or any other that week. A raft of routine evidence was to be taken first. Everyone from Mrs. Conklin to Dan Coughlan's doctor, who thought his patient was of good character as well as excellent constitution, had to have a session on the stand before the important performers, the Clan members, would be called. Preston said that might thin the crowd down some, but Tom found himself struggling through the same throng every morning. The reporters had agreed to operate a "take" system for the courtroom evidence, relieving each other on the notetaking and then doing individual rewrites for their respective papers. But Percy had made it clear, yet again, that more was required of Tom. "I want you to listen real sharp when these Clan na Gael witnesses start talking," he'd ordered him that morning. "You never know, something might just click, some little piece of evidence set you off thinking of something else. Right?"

Tom had nodded obediently. There didn't seem to be any point in restating his growing conviction that he knew less than anyone else in Chicago about anything Percy would be interested in. When the inquest adjourned for lunch each day, Tom followed Preston and the other reporters out and down to the street, but he wasn't asked to join them when they headed for a saloon. He decided there was nothing deliberate in it. He seemed to himself to be invisible. Some days he spent most of the break right in the building, strolling up and down the main corridor of City Hall. It seemed to him like an indoor street market, except that the wares were unseen. Everywhere he looked, down the center of the wide hall or along the walls, there were men congregated in feverish conversation. Under the low ceiling, their voices echoed like dull clinking metal.

Sometimes he circled the building, scrutinizing the columns and statues high above, from La Salle Street to Randolph, Randolph to Clark, Clark to Washington and back to La Salle; a warren of law offices where the city's attorneys burrowed into books with pages as frail as onion skin.

Or he chose a direction at whim and walked. He liked looking at the city, it was still new to him. Where the midday crowds around him saw only chugging street-cars and mounds of horse dung to be distastefully skirted at every corner, he saw infinite variety and novelty. But perhaps he would be like them in twenty years' time. Or he might be somewhere else entirely. A noted columnist, maybe, highly regarded in some more distinguished place. There was always the ultimate sophistication of New York, taunting every American who wasn't born there; if you have only one life to lead, the place to lead it was in New York. Or, far more untried and romantic really, San Francisco. No one ever spoke of Chicago and sophistication, Chicago and romance. Even the farm boys who hiked there from Wisconsin and Indiana and downstate Illinois knew better than that.

According to Huntley it was the energy that drew them, the high charge of things moving; railways by the hundreds, cattle cars, Great Lake ships and riverboats, the fiery southside steel factories with furnaces that blazed and bellowed all night long. That and high hopes of hedonism. Courtesans and gambling dens, downtown saloons with silver spittoons.

Hedonism was a costly proposition, but you could look for nothing. Tom had done a lot of looking, downtown at night with Huntley, but in the day the city looked quite different. No carnival of sin now, it was all hustling crowds and commerce and action. And the city shone, beginning from Michigan Avenue where the marble-front houses were washed in sun behind trees. Great carriages clattered along the tarred streets, no dust, no mud, and the downtown sidewalks were paved in huge stone blocks, a pearly stone that shimmered with some secret diamond light in the sun. The new banks, new theaters, new hotels were all brick and stone, with high colonnades and glittering windows, and there were street lamps like sentries along the way, set sputtering to life in the evenings by an army of lamplighters. What you noticed most in the daylight, though, was no wood to warp and rot, and no wooden buildings to burn, not since the '71 fire. There wasn't any way they could make that apply to the rest of the city. The cheap pine tenements and cottages went up all over again after the fire, and the people just took their chances. It was amazing to Tom that behind all this spendor, only streets away, there were filthy rotten tenements swarming with skinny children. Hundreds of pine shacks, a half-dozen to a city lot; dirt streets that ran like open sewers in the rain and were alive with rats on open garbage piles.

He walked dazed through his lunch hour, and when it was up made his way back into the stuffy courtroom. Every day Preston growled that it was like being under siege, "No way yoú can get out for a leak or a smoke." Every day Tom nodded sympathetically.

But on the Monday of the second week, Preston forgot his lines, and Tom realized that the atmosphere in the room had perceptibly changed. Every reporter was sitting upright, pencils vigilantly poised. The clerk of the court droned "Joseph O'Byrne," and the room responded with a hungry little buzz. O'Byrne, O'Byrne, the first Clan witness. The real hearing was about to start.

O'Byrne gave his name, age, address, place of birth and present occupation, as quickly as he was asked, and then Hertz paused for some effect, and asked how he was acquainted with the deceased.

"He was in Clan na Gael, and I am myself."

"Do you hold a position in that organization?"

"I do."

"Can you tell the court what that position is?"

"Senior guardian, Camp 234."

The hungry buzz intensified to something more voracious and Tom, puzzled, looked up at Preston, who was studying O'Byrne intently. "What's the excitement?" he whispered.

"Camp," Preston answered. "That's some kind of secret codeword. Usually Clan men say they're in some kind of club or other." Tom was about to say something, but he stopped himself.

Ten minutes later the excitement had faded considerably. O'Byrne was a willing and voluble witness, but his exposition of Clan na Gael indicated only that it was largely a social and charitable organization for men of Irish birth or ancestry. He was quite sure, though, that Dr. Cronin had stated on several occasions that Alexander Sullivan was his mortal enemy. O'Byrne was followed by Michael McNulty, who said that he'd been told by other Clan members that Alex Sullivan was out to get Cronin. Then there was Tom Conway, who said it was generally known throughout the organization that Alex Sullivan would stop at nothing to get Cronin.

But no one was able to say why.

When the court rose for the day Preston stetched his arms above his head and yawned. "Well, see you bright and early. Tomorrow's the fireworks." When he saw Tom's vacant reaction, he laughed, exuding a dizzying drift of peppermint. "Hertz is a stage manager from way back. Keep 'em on the edge of their seats to the last act. Got to hand it to him, he can hang on to page one longer than anybody when he wants to."

And Preston was right, though the fireworks were slow to ignite. Tuesday began with a tantalizing promise in the distinguished person of Captain Thomas F. O'Connor. He was a man who put effort into meriting the description. Over sixty, silver hair, flowing mustache, pointed beard. "Military bearing," Tom wrote. Imitation Confederate colonel, he thought. O'Connor must have been disconsolate in the uniform of the Yankees, which had won him his title twenty-five years earlier.

After the usual preliminaries, Captain O'Connor was asked whether he was a member of Clan na Gael. He answered that he was a member of Camp 20 of that organization. Tom looked up, then across at the other reporters; then down again. The number would mean nothing, of course, to anyone else.

"Have you ever been asked to do secret work for that organization?"

"I have." An excited little stir in the courtroom. Hertz paused, busy with his notes.

"Can you tell us who asked you to do this work?"

"I cannot, sir."

"Why is that?"

The Captain looked sternly at Hertz and said firmly: "I cannot recall the name." There was a little ripple in the courtroom, but Hertz let the answer pass and went on. "Can you tell us if you consulted anyone about this request?"

"I did. I consulted Dr. Cronin. His advice to me, after discussing the matter, was that there were enough good, honest men behind prison bars already, and that I should keep out of it."

"Did this indicate to you that Dr. Cronin was not in agreement with certain policies advocated by Clan na Gael?"

"It did, sir. And other matters subsequently bore this impression out. Dr. Cronin did not agree with a dynamite campaign in England, nor did he believe the leadership of Clan na Gael was honorable in its dealings with its membership. For these reasons, I knew his life to be in danger."

The courtroom stirred again, stealthily. Hertz waited.

"Will you tell us why you believe this was the case?"

"I will. I was present at a meeting of Camp 20 on February 8th when Dr. Cronin was alleged to have spoken in the strongest terms against the Clan na Gael leadership. A charge was made that Dr. Cronin had read a circular before another camp which was antagonistic to the organization and the view was put – and put with great heat, I may say – that the time had come to get to the bottom of what was going on."

"And can you name the leadership of Clan na Gael to whom Dr. Cronin was so strongly opposed?"

Captain O'Connor straightened up so firmly he was leaning back, as if against a strong wind. He was prepared, he said, to speak. "The leadership of Clan na Gael in Chicago is effectively in the hands of three men known to all as 'the Triangle', and they are Sullivan, Feeley and Boland." There was an outburst of puzzled whispers across the room and reporters gripped their pencils, ready to set them flying across the empty pages. But in the space of the next few minutes, Captain O'Connor's resolve crumbled.

He wasn't certain what Dr. Cronin had said against the leadership, or what decision had been taken in Camp 20 following the charges. He believed Alexander Sullivan was responsible for Dr. Cronin's death, but he couldn't say how.

Twenty minutes later, when Hertz released him from the witness stand, the courtroom had settled back again and Tom put down his pencil and rubbed his wrist. He nudged Preston, whose eyes were closed. "Your take," he whispered. Preston opened his eyes. "Old boy seemed to cave in there, didn't he?" he said indifferently. "I guess he reckoned the posse'd be out for him."

The next witness was a plump railroad clerk named Hegarty, who promptly brought the room back to life. Calmly, almost cheerfully, he confirmed that he, too, was a member of Camp 20 of Clan na Gael, and that he believed Dr. Cronin was a traitor to Ireland. Alexander Sullivan had told him so, he said, and Alexander Sullivan had said the Clan should get rid of Cronin.

Hertz moved forward, closing in on the witness stand, and asked whether Mr. Hegarty would tell the court the circumstances surrounding this disclosure.

"Yes, sir," the clerk said. He directed his gaze uncertainly but politely toward the public seats. "You see, we knew that Scotland Yard had sent out undercover agents to the United States to find out about the movement. So every member was on the *qui vive*, of course, for infiltrators in the organization. One night I was walking to the car after a meeting with Mr. Sullivan and he told me he thought Cronin was a scoundrel and it would be a benefit to the cause if we could get rid of him." Hegarty nodded emphatically. "I must say, of course, that would be my view entirely. I can't hold with people who want to elevate themselves by getting the secrets of other people under false pretenses."

"Can you recall the exact words that Alexander Sullivan used?" Hertz asked. The courtroom waited. Hegarty considered and frowned. "Well, I couldn't swear to them, now. But certainly he wanted to be shut of the man."

"And you say you agreed with this view?"

"The word traitor makes an Irishmen feel very vengeful, sir," Hegarty said simply. "Mr. Sullivan wouldn't be the only Irishman who'd believe that an informer should be removed from our ranks. But, of course, I never would have expected him to be murdered the terrible way he was. I thought Mr. Sullivan would take steps to see he was expelled from our organization, and quite right that would have been, too."

The courtroom sank back in a single dejected movement.

And then, just before the lunch recess, Luke Dillon was called. Tom lifted his head from his notes. Devoy's representative on earth, a pope to the diety. He saw himself at Cronin's funeral, with Gallagher and Packy and Cooney. The court was jaded with expectation by now, and there was no urgent hush when he walked across the room, a big, broad-shouldered man with thick fair hair, his jaw squared. Tom deliberated and then wrote "dignified".

Dillon identified himself by name, age, address and birthplace in short, detached replies. When Hertz asked whether he was a member of Clan na Gael, he replied in the same impersonal tone, "I am one of the nine members of the executive of that organization, and I want it understood that I am here today to clear our name of the ugly shadow this diabolical murder has cast on it. I therefore propose to tell the court of the events within the organization that precipitated Dr. Cronin's death."

The room was immediately and completely still. Tom could suddenly hear the rumble of carriages and the clang of a streetcar far below on the street. After a long moment Hertz spoke, every word dropping separately into the well of silence.

"Members of the jury," Hertz said, "I beg you to listen closely to the details Mr. Dillon has agreed to reveal concerning Alexander Sullivan and the leadership of the Clan na Gael known as the 'Triangle'. They will, I believe, go some distance

159

toward enlightening the jurors as to the cause and reason for Dr. Cronin's untimely and terrible death."

Dillon leaned forward slightly, his hands on the edge of the stand, and looked directly at the jury bench. "In order to lay the facts before this jury clearly, I must present some information concerning my organization to this court," he began. "Some of you present here today may be under the impression that Clan na Gael is a secret society. That is true, but only in a specific sense. Clan na Gael is an organization dedicated to the removal of British power in Ireland, and its members are therefore required to take an oath which binds them to take action when and if the day comes when their native land, the land of their forebears, requires them to come to its aid. The nature of our commitment is such that we must guard against infiltration by agents of Britain, and for that reason our business is confidential and our public demeanor cautious."

He paused and looked around the courtroom, and then resumed, slowly and emphatically. "But there is nothing in the obligation of membership to Clan na Gael which is contrary to the constitution or laws of the United States of America."

Dillon stopped again, almost as if to accommodate a challenge, even a comment. "There is nothing," he continued, "nothing whatsoever in our commitment, which would require a member of Clan na Gael to engage in the most minor infraction of those laws, let alone to contemplate the heinous crime of murder." His voice fell dramatically on the last word and he stood back. When he began to speak again, the courtroom all but swayed forward to catch his words.

"Now, as to the immediate background of the dispute between the late Dr. Cronin and Alexander Sullivan . . ." he went on, in the manner of a historian, a disinterested historian, relating established facts. Due to the confidential nature of the organization, many present may not have been aware that tens of thousands of Irishmen had sent their representatives here to Chicago in 1881 to a national convention, but such was the case. That convention agreed to a five man executive board, of which any three could form a quorum.

"The object was efficiency. The result was dictatorship,"

Dillon said tersely. "Three members of the board became the operating quorum at all times. They became known as 'the Triangle' – Dennis Feeley, Michael Boland, and Alexander Sullivan of Chicago."

His pace was perfect, Tom realized, not too fast for the less skilled speedhand writers, but fluid enough to keep his audience absorbed, sentence after sentence. He was used to speaking, and speaking for the record, and the Clan, it was becoming clear, was rather more devoted to records than might be expected of a secret organization.

"Within months these three men had taken complete control," Dillon said. He was gathering feeling into his voice now, disdain and outrage. "They ruled with the proverbial iron rod, and one of their first decisions abolished the system of exacting only a ten per cent levy of branch funds from every Camp. The Triangle decreed that all monies raised by members across the country should be centralized in one account, whereas previously every local area paid only a ten per cent levy to the national organization. If I tell the jury here today that this was no small matter, my point may perhaps be clear only if I also say that the decision brought into the treasury of Clan na Gael an aggregate sum of about a quarter of a million dollars." The court gasped in unison.

"You may well wonder why no objection was raised to this dramatic move," Dillon went on, irony tinging his voice now. "I ask you to cast your minds back to the years between 1881 and 1885. You will recall that a series of dynamite explosions took place in England. You may also recall, if I refresh your memories, that a total of thirty-two men, Irish Americans, were convicted on charges related to these explosions, and of these, I may add, twenty-two are still languishing in Britain's prisons today.

"The Triangle at the head of the Clan in America asked their members to empty their coffers into one central fund to finance this campaign, and the hard-pressed and loyal sons of Erin here in America gave without complaint because they felt it their duty to support the cause closest to their hearts." Without warning, Dillon stopped. Tom, his wrist and fingers aching,

161

stopped writing and looked up. The big man was gazing slowly around the courtroom in silence; and then he cried: "I have three statements to make about these matters!" The whole courtroom and the press benches jumped slightly.

"The first is that this senseless campaign did not have the support of the great majority of Irish patriots, here or in Ireland! That must now be stated for the record." His voice dropped again. "The second adds insult to the injury of wrongdoing, insult to those who gave so generously. The money in the organization's treasury disappeared so rapidly, so completely, that it became increasingly evident to some that little of it had gone toward any campaign against Britain. The third is simply this: the man who demanded an investigation, who first said that the members had a right to know what had happened to their money, the man who had the courage to ask whether it had gone instead into the pockets of the avaricious opportunists at the helm of the organization, was Dr. Patrick Henry Cronin."

There was a long and satisfied sigh from the courtroom. When it had subsided, Dillon finished in two swift sentences. "The most powerful of this vicious triumvirate beyond all doubt was a prominent lawyer in this city. The man who had everything to lose had Patrick Cronin lived, was Alexander Sullivan."

Hertz had planned to intervene with a short adjournment at just this juncture, but the press benches had emptied almost before the gavel fell on the desk. "Well, no shortage of copy there," Preston said. He clapped Tom on the shoulder in sudden and intimate camaraderie on the way to the press room. "You want to type up your story and I'll check it against my notes? Or vice versa, of course, if you like."

It was all good stuff, Percy grudgingly remarked several hours later in the newsroom, and Dillon was worth running in full. "Looks like you were right about these 'camp' things," he added brusquely. Tom, who was pounding out the last pages of the day's evidence, smiled with what he hoped was the right mixture of self-deprecation and gratitude. He accepted that Percy would have been really pleased only if he had managed somehow to come across Luke Dillon himself and smuggle him into Percy's cubbyhole office without any other paper knowing about it.

But Percy's attention was shortly afterward diverted by far more rousing developments, because at five o'clock the jury had agreed that no more evidence was required. They retired to the coroner's office, and all across the city chief copy-editors were praying for a verdict on deadline. Shortly after ten o'clock Preston phoned. Not only had the jury reached a conclusion of murder by conspiracy, but they'd named four people as either principals, accessories or persons with guilty knowledge who should be held to answer to the Grand Jury.

Percy listened to the crackling voice, nodding, and then hung up. He waved Tom to his side. "What's-its-name, Woodruff; O'Sullivan, the ice-house geezer, and Dan Coughlan. They already got them, and they're arresting Alex Sullivan tonight. Find Huntley, will you? You might as well go with him, if you're through with your own stuff." Tom turned and hurried for his hat. Most of the staff, he saw, were watching him with embarrassed but appraising eyes.

Tom told Huntley afterward that though he didn't know what to expect, never having seen an arrest before, what he had in mind was a cross-section of important senior police and associated officials coolly discharging their duty, collaring a villain who would be either cringing or snarling, an animal trapped. Something like that, he said. At the very least, he imagined he'd get a good look at the infamous Alexander in his hour of shame and defeat.

What he did see was a cross-section of important senior police and associated officials milling irresolutely about Oak Street, until one detective plodded slowly up to the door of number 376 and rang the bell. The door was opened by an elderly wisp of a man who said: "Yes?"

"Is Mr. Sullivan at home?" the detective asked politely.

"Why yes, but he's sleeping. Is it anything urgent, or may I help? I am his clerk."

The detective said that it was urgent, actually, and concerned Mr. Sullivan, and the clerk said agreeably that in that case he'd waken Mr. Sullivan. The detective went inside and the door closed. The police and officials talked to each other in insistent whispers on the sidewalk and the assembled reporters shifted back and forth, watching the door. It opened in twenty minutes, and the detective emerged with a rather short and slim figure beside him, well-dressed down to lemon yellow gloves, a fedora hat smartly pulled down over his brow, shading his face from view. They walked together at ease to the police carriage and climbed inside. It pulled away, with the rapid fire of reporters' questions still ringing in the air.

The rest of the police, the officials and the press piled into an assortment of hired hacks and rigs and followed at high speed to Cook County Jail. They were just in time to see Sullivan bow courteously to the bailiff on gate duty in the jail yard and stride inside. The gate closed, and after a few minutes of sullen muttering the entourage returned to their vehicles and departed. Huntley saw Tom into the hack and said he'd meet him back at the paper after he tied up a few loose ends.

"All I found out in the end, though, was that Sullivan was the soul a' charm to all concerned," he told Tom later. "Palmer read the mittimus and asked had he anythin' to say, and Sullivan says not tonight, what he has to say he'll say in court."

"Who was it you were talking to?"

"Jailer. He said ten minutes after he locked him in he had a squint through the gratin' a' the cell, and there was Alex, curled up on his cot, sleepin' like a brand new baby."

164

XVI

IT TOOK ALEXANDER SULLIVAN three days to get out of jail. His law partners, and Al Trude, one of the city's most powerful attorneys, were in court when it opened the morning after the arrest, looking for a writ of *habeas corpus*. At three o'clock that afternoon the prisoner entered the court looking very much like he'd spent the night down the street in the Grand Pacific Hotel: Prince Albert suit of black diagonal stripe, black cravat, turndown collar and linen of snowy white – Huntley had it all in his front page story.

"A goddam affront to justice," Percy growled.

"And to Longenecker," Huntley said. "He looked like he wanted to string Alex up by his fancy cravat right there."

Preston did the report of the court proceedings. Sullivan's petition for release on bail charged that his arrest was based on evidence before the coroner's jury which was wholly insufficient and largely hearsay, incompetent and irrelevant testimony calculated to create prejudice. Counsellor Trude argued that unless there was positive proof, or a strong presumption of guilt, the accused could not be detained pending trial. Mr. Sullivan, he pointed out, had made no effort to flee. He was at home in his bed when arrested; he certainly wasn't on the same footing as a felon.

Longenecker represented the people. He argued that guilt or innocence was a matter to be decided in another court, but that there was no doubt that the coroner's jury believed the accused was connected with a conspiracy to murder Dr. Cronin. It took him most of an hour to make the two points. After what Huntley described as penetrating questioning, the judge remanded Sullivan in custody while he read the evidence of the inquest, and let him go forty-eight hours later.

The decision was the lead item in every Saturday paper. Almost every customer in Gleason's seemed to have a copy when Tom arrived with Andy that night, bearing out Huntley's views on the benefits of murder to the news business.

But the focus of attention in Gleason's was not where it had been the night before in the *Tribune*. The angle Percy, Huntley and Preston had agreed the paper should lead on was the size of the bail bond, followed by the judge's comments. Bail wasn't often fixed at $20,000. It wasn't often that four bondsmen turned up anxious to stake the accused, all of them highly respectable merchants and real estate dealers.

As for the judgment itself, there wasn't much choice in the end. Even Percy admitted that. There was no rule of law which could allow Dr. Cronin's well-publicized fear of Sullivan as evidence in a murder trial.

"No impartial man can think it would be possible for a jury to convict the petitioner on the legal evidence that remains after all other is struck out," the judgement concluded. "A man cannot be deprived of his liberty on the grounds that more evidence will be produced to show him guilty."

What had absorbed an hour's considered discussion last night in the newsroom got only passing comment from the Gleason clientèle. Sullivan's release, the size of the bail, the style of the bondsmen, all seemed to be taken as matters no less predictable than sunset. What everyone wanted to talk about was the story Tom had handled himself, an inside-page piece under the headline, "Irish Leaders Say Sullivan's Arrest Is a Serious Mistake." When Jack Gallagher came in an hour later, he had a paper under his arm which he laid almost reverently on the counter. "Have you read it?" he asked Andy.

"Sure, of course I've read it," Andy said. "Isn't it only what was to be expected?"

Andy was in good spirits. He was working again, on a southside building job that might last through July. And, as he'd been expounding to the group at the counter, he was pleased with the legal system. The sound principles of jurisprudence had triumphed over a slack operation that accepted slander and bias in the coroner's court.

"But Davitt and Parnell!" Gallagher cried. "And the length of their statements!"

"And plenty of others, too," Andy said.

"Yes, but Parnell. And Davitt," Gallagher repeated. "I didn't think they'd be paying that much attention to us here. What with all they have on their plate."

"Are you mad, man?" Andy lifted his whiskey glass high in a grand gesture. "Where's the place more important to Ireland now than Chicago? And who's more important than Alexander Sullivan?"

"You're right, of course," Gallagher said. "You're right. What are the pair of you having? I feel like buying a drink. It must have been a moment in there in the paper, Tom, when this statement came in to you. Was it over the telegraph wires, or what?"

"Yes," Tom said. "The wire service." He ran a finger around the rim of his glass. Percy had flung the story down on the chief copy-editor's desk snarling, "I want every line of that in. Damndest nerve I've seen in a long time. A couple of puffed-up patriots in some miserable swamp hanging off the edge of Europe decide to tell the American people how to conduct their business. Who do these boys think they are?" And then Percy saw Tom, back where he'd sent him himself, on the copy desk. For a breathless moment, it looked as if Percy might even say he meant no offense, as everyone else did these days.

The others stared at him until the chief copy-editor handed him the wire copy and said, matter-of-factly, "Take care of that, will you, Tom?" and they all went back to work.

Parnell and Davitt said much the same thing in their statements – Sullivan was an honest man, unassailable character, devoted to the cause of Irish freedom, appeared to be victim of serious miscarriage of justice. A score of other statements from lesser Irish nationalist luminaries to the same effect had also flashed over the wires, from Dublin and Detroit, Sydney and Syracuse. All of it served to confuse Tom further, especially since the great majority of Chicagoans did not share the opinion of Gleason's clientèle on Sullivan's release, and the letters to the papers seethed with frustration that no evidence had yet been found that would put him back behind bars. It didn't look as if anything would, either, no matter how assiduously Longenecker courted the press.

The Grand Jury sessions had started, and every evening Huntley appeared faithfully at the copy desk to fill Tom in on the details of the day's hearings. Grand Jury proceedings were supposed to be strictly confidential, but Longenecker was generous about briefings from non-attributable sources. He had, as Huntley said, a lot at stake. But the witnesses before the Grand Jury were mostly the witnesses who'd been before the coroner, and even Huntley couldn't find a fresh angle.

"Seems like an almighty waste of time, doesn't it?" Tom said.

"Democracy's a very repetitious business," Huntley answered. "Seems to be some fundamental human need to scratch up the same ground a few times over before we can move on."

Tom had begun to wish Huntley would stop his nightly visits, which reminded the others of his Irish links and stirred their unease. But he couldn't bring himself to say anything, and the weekend after Sullivan's release something happened that forced him to accept that the unease was far more general than he had wished to believe.

Nanda turned her back when he arrived in the dim little grocery shop at Clark and Kinzie, busying herself with a parcel. Tom was at first deeply flattered. It's because I haven't been in for a while, he thought, and checking that Mr. Chakonas was nowhere in sight he called out "Hello there, how've you been?" in his breeziest voice. She turned and looked past him, drying her hands on an apron, and went into the inner room. A moment later Mrs. Chakonas came out and rushed past the counter with the olive jars to the door. "We close now," she said. "You must go." Her face was composed and she too avoided looking in his eyes.

Tom stared at her without comprehension and then mumbled something and left. When he looked back the door had closed and the striped awning was jerking downward over the window.

He strode furiously up Kinzie, remonstrating with himself. Anything – it could be anything. Perhaps her parents had betrothed her to someone else; they did that in these Mediterranean countries. Perhaps there's some family battle going on. But he thought of how Mrs. Chakonas had joked with him over the olives, how Nanda had promised Greek sweets, and he heard himself prattling about green Irish fields and his face flamed again. How dare they.

He went to Foy's early that night, hoping for a cup of coffee and a chat with Liz about nothing in particular; just a sample of ordinary life to flavor his week. But Andy took Tom's arrival as a cue for departure and had his jacket over his shoulder, two cigars in the pocket, before Liz had offered a chair.

She stood at the door with them looking up at the evening sky. "You won't be long?" she said to Andy.

"I won't be long," he promised and she smiled at him doubtfully, the dimple in her cheek a tiny furrow. "I want you to talk to the boys, Andy. They're running wild now that school's out. Look at the time, and they're nowhere to be seen."

"I'll talk to them in the morning. First thing." Andy leaned over and kissed her. "You worry too much."

"Don't be too late, then," Liz said. "Tom, you'll bring him back early, won't you?" She gave a little laugh and nod, to show it was a joke, when she saw Tom's disconcerted look.

Andy threw his head back for a moment, scanning the heavens. It was a clearer night than usual, bright with stars and an almost full moon. A beautiful evening, he said, and set off, whistling abstractedly. Tom had to walk briskly to keep up with him.

"Listen, before we get to Gleason's, I've been meaning to ask you," Tom said.

"What about?"

"About this Cronin thing; something Packy said to me the day of the funeral." Tom went on, summing it up quickly, Packy's remarks on Devoy and Parnell and Davitt. "But if there's this – well, this division of opinion, wasn't it strange that they sent messages about Alex Sullivan when he was arrested?"

169

"Not a bit of it," Andy said. "There's divisions, all right. But they're what you could call internal. At least when the rest of the world is looking at us. It's only right that the leaders of the Irish nationalist movement should denounce wrongful arrest of a prominent Irish American."

"But John Devoy, Luke Dillon – they're convinced Sullivan had something to do with it. "

"They've their own axe to grind," Andy replied shortly. Tom tried to see his face, but Andy looked straight ahead.

"Wait," Tom begged. He put a hand on his shoulder to bring him to a halt. "Just a minute, before we get there and start talking to the others. I just don't understand."

Andy looked at him, but his face was in shadows. "And you want to understand, do you?" he asked abruptly. "Yes, all right, you do. That's fair enough. All right."

He drew in a breath and then started walking again, but slowly. "Alex Sullivan is a very strong man, very powerful. Very clever. For which reasons, John Devoy and Luke Dillon and all of their ilk hate him – it's the same old story, old as the world. But Parnell and Davitt in Ireland, others who take a broader view, they know Sullivan is the man we need. And they know it would be a terrible day for Ireland if he were to be condemned for a crime he didn't commit because of the jealousy and spite of his rivals here. That's why the message was important. It was a message to the movement in America, as well as a statement to the world." He glanced over at Tom. "Am I making sense to you?"

"Yes," Tom said. "But, Andy, somebody did commit the crime. Somebody murdered Dr. Cronin. Somebody in the movement. Everyone knows that."

Andy nodded, looking down at the sidewalk. "I'm not denying that," he said. His voice was sad, as it had been the night they sat in the little park on Congress. "What can I say about that? I've told you what I think. I think the Clan should not suffer, no matter who did it."

"And you don't think," Tom said, still hesitant, "that Alexander Sullivan could have had something to do with it?"

"No," Andy said, "I don't. Not at all. That's just badmouthing."

They walked on a bit before Tom said, "You think an awful lot of him."

"He understands his own people," Andy said simply. "Us. Here. Devoy doesn't, nor the others. I don't know why that is, but it's the case. Alex Sullivan is the man to lead us because he knows that we have to live here and get on, but that we'll never forget what's behind our backs. He knows what drives us on and why we won't give up, not ever. Never."

He stopped and faced Tom. They were just out of range of a streetlamp and in the reflected light his pale eyes were almost white. "What about your own people? Your father was a Mayo man. What did you learn from him?"

"Nothing. Nothing at all. I was too young when he died."

"What about your mother?"

Tom drew in a breath and let it out slowly. "She had a hard life," he said finally. "I don't think it made much difference to her where she was."

Andy shook his head dismissively. "Then talk to Packy sometime about why he's involved," he said. "Packy's from the parish of Clare Abbey, ever heard of it?"

"I don't think so," Tom answered.

"He left Clare Abbey in 1847 when he was twelve years old, because the whole townland was devastated by the Famine. His family took a boat from Liverpool to Canada. Packy was the only one who survived Grosse Isle. Do you know about Grosse Isle?"

Tom shook his head.

"Ask Packy sometime," Andy said. He turned his long light eyes away, staring into the street ahead. "I'll tell you what I know. My father was a young man with a family in 1847. Before I was born. He walked from one end of the county of Mayo to the other, pleading for work on a public relief scheme. He saw men falling dead with hunger still trying to work, dropping with the shovels gripped in their hands. He saw women and children going into the fields and pulling up roots to eat raw, and when there were no more roots they ate grass. He saw his own neighbors die of hunger, one after another, shrieking with hunger, skeletons with nothing left to them but eyes and bellies. Women with dead babies at their breasts.

"And all the way along the road he walked, he saw these starved shells of men and women and children, some of them still writhing and vomiting and some of them dead in the ditches. Sometimes the animals ate them where they lay because there was no one with the strength to bury them. And all the time the people mobbed the workhouse, screaming for God's mercy, for food, until the constabulary was called out to beat them away, or shoot them away."

He stopped, and spat on the ground as Packy had at Cronin's funeral. "And all the time the big wagons full of grain rolled down those roads to be loaded on to English ships and sailed off to English tables. Did you know that, Tom?"

"No," Tom said.

"My father didn't know that then. He found that out later. He told me. He said those who were let live out of all who died were let live for a reason. That's what he told me, and I will tell my sons the same if the day doesn't come in my lifetime to satisfy that reason."

He began to walk again, and Tom caught up with him after a moment. Chicago Avenue was just ahead. Tom stole several sidelong looks at him, but neither of them spoke again until they were just outside Gleason's. Andy straightened then and smiled as cordially as if nothing had passed between them.

"I'll bet the boys are scouting around for fireworks for the Fourth. Ever do them when you were a kid?" he asked Tom.

"I used to try – never got away with it."

"I love them. Only takes a bit of know-how, and they're great fun. Come on, we'll lift a few. No more gloom tonight, let's drink to it."

They entered the crowded pool of noise and laughter and Andy pushed ahead to the bar, waving to catch the barmen's attention. But his arm was seized in mid-air. It was Jack Gallagher, who tugged him aside.

"Come and sit down, I've a table and a pitcher there. There's terrible news," he said.

"Lord have mercy, man, what is it? You're the color of ashes," Andy said.

"It's in the late extra, the boy was just in selling it – you won't have seen it?"

"No," Andy answered. "What is it, quick?"

Gallagher propelled them to the table. Packy was sitting there with another man, a pug-nosed local precinct captain named Cunningham, with the paper spread out before them.

Gallagher picked it up but held it to his chest a moment, speaking to Andy. "This Grand Jury investigation. Someone identified the man who rented that Carlson cottage from a photograph of the Clan at the unveiling of the monument in Mount Olivet, and they got him today in Winnipeg. Andy, you're going to be upset about this, sit down."

"In the name of God, tell me," Andy said, standing still.

"It's the young fellow just over that you got the building laborer's job for. Martin Burke."

Andy sat down and took the paper from Gallagher, and Cunningham, who had a voice that rasped like sandpaper, said, "Arrested boarding the *Atlantic Express* with a ticket for Liverpool in his pocket. Looks like he was flitting, all right."

Andy put his head down on his hands, all the buoyancy of a moment before gone. "My God Almighty," he groaned, "this can't be happening."

XVII

FROM THE END of June, the city began to simmer. There was a new menacing whir over the newsroom clatter every afternoon now, when the new electric fan was switched on. The reporters took off their collars, mopped their foreheads and went on typing. Damp circles of sweat spread under their arms. And the temperature was still only at the ninety degree mark; worse would come.

The police were looking for someone. The man who'd bought furniture from Revell's salesman under the name J.B. Simonds had also been identified from the photograph in Mount Olivet Cemetery on the day the Clan na Gael plot was consecrated. Huntley's contact said his name wasn't Simonds, but Huntley couldn't get any more than that.

The Grand Jury was flinging a wider net, calling in new witnesses by the dozen every session. On Tuesday, Longenecker's mouthpiece had something to brief the press with. Mr. Byron L. Smith, receiver for the failed Traders' Bank of Chicago, produced receipts showing that Alex Sullivan had deposited $100,000 in the bank in May, 1882, and drawn checks to exhaust the entire amount over the next five months.

The checks were all payable to a Chicago Board of Trade broker named John T. Lester, who was duly ordered in with his books, which disclosed that Sullivan had tried his luck in railroad and telegraph stocks almost daily for months at a time over the next few years. He scored some substantial successes until 1887. The wheat corner break in Cincinnati that year lost him $95,000, and seemed to have had a chastening effect.

Tom told Andy. He saw the light on in Foy's on his way home and knocked lightly; Andy opened the door almost im-

175

mediately, a little disheveled but still dressed. He was having trouble sleeping, he said. When Tom told him it looked like Sullivan may have played with Clan funds, Andy replied with an irritable sneer: "Byron L. Smith? Byron *L.* Smith?"

He folded his hands primly and addressed the empty street: "Gentlemen, I assure you that the accounts which you have before you record transactions which were undertaken in good faith with a person whom we believed to be of honorable character."

Tom laughed aloud. It was a perfect reproduction of the midwestern upper-class drawl, just slightly flat and just slightly nasal. "You could pass for a banker," he said. "But, Andy, it seems bad, doesn't it?"

"I don't know. Maybe he did, maybe he didn't. Maybe he was trying to raise more money. Anyway, that's not proof he used funds wrongly, is it?" That was just what Huntley had said to Tom; there wasn't enough evidence to charge Sullivan with embezzlement. "Who'd listen to financiers?" Andy went on. "They'd all love to gut Alex Sullivan now like a dead fish, and the rest of us along with him. Why wouldn't they cook the books?"

Afterward Tom lay on the narrow bed in his airless little room and resolved that he would not ask Andy again to weigh up information. He was not an impartial observer. And would you be, Tom addressed himself in the darkness, if everything you believed in was at stake, everyone you trusted suddenly suspect? There was no answer. But unlike Andy, he didn't believe in much or trust many. Maybe that was worse.

It wasn't just Andy, though; something was happening to everyone. Even the little world around Locust Street was furtively touched now. On Wednesday Mrs. Delaney went to an early mass. "For the repose of poor Mr. Delaney's soul, God be good to him," she told Tom, pouring out his mug of coffee. Her hand was shaking. "And what did I see on the way out of mass but ugly great signs chalked all along the wall of the church. Of the church!" The signs said that the murderering Mickeys should go back into the hole they crawled out from, she said.

Tom told her only fools wrote words on walls, and drank his

coffee. He returned his morning copy of the *Daily News* to his pocket, depriving Mrs. Delaney of the opportunity to read the statement from the recently formed American Protective Association, which said that the Cronin murder case was only further proof, if proof were needed, that tougher legislation on immigration restriction was essential if the United States was to remain a civilized country.

He saw Liz in the distance as he left the boarding house for work. She was balancing on the window-ledge of the cottage, scrubbing the pane of glass with a handful of wet newspaper, and as he came nearer he saw the buggy with the baby in it outside the door. The other little one was seated on the doorstep with an enamel bowl of water before her, crooning as she ladled it all about her with a cup.

Tom called out when he was close enough, but softly, not to startle her. "Where do you get the energy for it, in this weather?"

"I have to keep myself entertained, don't I?" Liz answered over her shoulder. "The worst of the sun is it shows up what you needn't notice all winter."

"The worst of the sun is this much of it. Is everyone well?" Tom asked. He peeped into the buggy at the baby, who looked up wanly.

"We're all managing," she said, watching him with a slight smile. "Have you a minute? I need some advice about something, now you're passing."

She gave the glass a last sweeping wipe, dropped the newspaper neatly to the ledge and swung around. Tom stepped forward to give her his hand, but she sprang nimbly to the ground beside him before he reached her. She smelled of vinegar, from the washing water. Her hands were ruddy and puffed, but her arms were white and sprinkled with freckles all the way to the shoulders, where she'd rolled her sleeves.

He followed her inside. The curtains had been stripped off the windows and lay in a sullen heap on the floor, and in the glaring sunlight the room looked pitifully exposed. Tom saw bald patches on the narrow sofa he hadn't seen before, and the splayed legs of the rocker. The wallpaper pattern had faded to

177

an indistinct blur. The pictures, though, stood out more than usual owing to a very recent shining with the vinegar and water: a color portrait of Liz done before her wedding, her eyes tinted to match her blue hat; a sepia photograph of both her and Andy on their wedding day. On one wall there was a large painting of Robert Emmet in the dock, and facing it was one of the Sacred Heart, Jesus pointing with an aggrieved gaze to his afflicted organ. Several limp palm leaves, remnants from the last Palm Sunday, were stuffed behind the frame.

Liz went to the kitchen and opened the potbelly stove, idle for the summer. "I've hidden this here till I think what I'm going to do," she said, unrolling a brown paper parcel. "Look at it. I found it under the boys' bed." It was a slingshot, a truly magnificent one, made from black leather. It was a good eight inches long and just flexible enough to allow near-perfect aim control.

Tom ran his fingers along the twin prongs, listening to the squeak. "It's awfully big for their small hands, isn't it?" he said.

"Big! It's a weapon. Where did they get it, what do they want it for? And these, look at these – they're like bullets!" She unwrapped a smaller piece of paper in the parcel and Tom saw six or eight metal balls, misshapen and oddly colored, but distinctly intended to fit the broad rubber strap of the slingshot.

"They look wicked, all right," Tom said. He picked one up and rolled it on the palm of his hand. It wasn't as heavy as it looked.

"What do you think – what in God's name am I supposed to do?" Liz demanded, and gave the paper an exasperated shake. "It's for these battles the boys are having, nearly every night now. You must have heard."

"I've heard," Tom admitted. The ugly tension had seeped down to the children, and there were constant reports of boys from the Irish neighborhoods responding to taunts with bricks and bottles along the river at night, up and down Erie Street. "But Liz, your fellows are too small for that. They wouldn't be let fight by the older ones."

"That's what I thought. And they're not let out on the street anymore than I can help, though I'm at my wits' end keeping track of them. But Tom, God Almighty, look at this thing."

178

"It's not as bad as it looks, Liz. Honestly. It's pretty light-weight, really. And these things – you'd hardly call them bullets, now. They're only melted down bottle caps – look closer. Feel them; there's no weight in them." Tom put the pellets in her hand and closed her fingers over them. He hesitated, not quite wanting to say they were absolutely harmless, which they weren't.

Liz looked down at her closed hand. "I don't want them at this kind of thing, Tom. This is a rough city and there's a lot of evil out there, and if they start this now, God knows where they'll end up. In jail, without a doubt. Or maimed for life, or dead. But sometimes I feel like I can't cope with them anymore, they're growing too wild."

Tom put his hand on her shoulder in a kind of awkward pat. "You haven't shown it to Andy, have you," he said, a declaration rather than a question.

"Not yet. I suppose I must." She took the slingshot back and re-rolled the parcel slowly. "I can't bear to keep after him about anything just now. He's too distracted. Things have been said to him on this building job he's on, insulting remarks – that kind of thing. Then the other day a gang of little hooligans from the public school jumped on a girl Kate knows, going to the bake-shop for her mother. Tore her dress and chased her home, called her shocking things."

Tom shivered in spite of the heat. They walked back outside, and he told Liz what Mrs. Delaney had seen that morning, and Liz leaned against the doorway, watching the child, who was still preoccupied with the water basin. But her eyes widened fearfully. "On the church!" she said, as Mrs. Delaney had.

"It's only ignorance, Liz. It has to be ignored. You know that," Tom said. "Andy must have seen this sort of thing before."

"It's not just that, though." She shaded her eyes against the sun, frowning. "Friends of Andy's are being called to this Grand Jury now, every day someone else. Johnny Beggs has been there twice, and he's said he'd been summoned to go back a third time. Do you know Johnny?"

"No. I don't think so."

Liz bit her lip. "Well, he's the top man in the group – in the Columbia Club." She looked at Tom and when he didn't show any sign of recognition she added: "Camp 20. The Columbia Club is the other name for Camp 20. Andy said he told you."

"Oh," Tom said, startled.

"So," she said. "Things are worse now than they've ever been – oh, dear!" She broke off to snatch the cup from the little girl, who was about to dispense its contents affectionately on her sister. Tom shifted the buggy into a safer position at Liz's direction and then took his leave. He walked to the Clark Street car, still brooding, fanning his face with the folded copy of the *Daily News*.

The only person Tom felt he could talk to about any of this was Huntley. But Huntley only glanced through the *Daily News* story when Tom thrust it before him and then pushed the paper aside. "Why, that ain't too bad, Tom; as prejudice goes, it's pretty civil," he said calmly. He was eating a peach, carving it in quarter-moon slices, one by one, off the stone. There were more in the paper bag on the desk. The heat had forced a plentiful early crop, and they were cheap. Tom was suddenly and unexpectedly irritated with him, his calm sarcasm, his preoccupation with food.

"No, I suppose you're right," Tom said. "We dirty immigrant peasants should be thankful there's no cartoons showing Paddy the Irishman in his stovepipe hat with a monkey's face and spiked teeth, cutting somebody's throat."

"It's the long upper lip," Huntley answered evenly, examining Tom's face. "You've somethin' a' one yourself. That's where the suggestion a' monkey comes in. Niggers get fat lips and saucer eyes – apart from the obvious, a' course – and dagos get black hair slicked down with grease. Cartoonists like a nice easy national characteristic. Seems to me, for someone who was sayin' not too long ago all this had nothin' to do with him, you're pretty sensitive. Here, have a peach."

"It has something to do with me now because I know the people who are the butt of this. They're all around me. Neighbors. My friends." Huntley looked at him but didn't reply. "And maybe I understand a little better what it's like,

180

that's all," Tom said. Huntley remained silent, and Tom took the bag, rooting through it until he found the smallest and firmest peach. "All I really want to ask your opinion about is how much worse it will get," Tom said. "Maybe the cartoons are still to come? Maybe there'll be whole neighborhoods burned out?" He told Huntley about Mrs. Delaney and the church, and the girl Kate knew, talking between loud bites into the peach.

Huntley listened soberly. When Tom had finished he said: "Listen, Tom. When I was a student, on the east coast, in the '50s, not thinkin' much about anythin' but enjoyin' myself, a lot of things went on all over. Ever hear of the Know Nothin's? Otherwise known as the American Party. Hated immigrants, hated Catholics 'specially. In Chicago they disguised themselves as the temperance movement and got the women on their side, but it was never about no prohibition on drink, it was always about clampin' down on the Irish in saloons and the Germans in the beer-halls. Lots a' ways, Chicago wasn't the worst place on account a' the Irish had a good grip, even then, on politics. Tell you what else, they was smart boys to get that grip early and hang on. I were in their place, I'd 'a done the same."

He dipped into the bag and retrieved another peach. "Cronin's murder is gonna stir it all up some, but not too bad. If Cronin had 'a been a native, and not one a' your own – well, that'd be different. Things ain't gonna be pleasant, but they ain't gonna be too bad either. You can live with that."

Tom watched him slice the peach. His irritation had passed and he was ashamed of it. "I'm always afraid to eat more than one of those at a time," he said. "I'd worry about getting sick."

"Live risky, have another." Huntley pushed the bag at him. "You ain't got no religion anymore, so maybe it's hard for you to remember how worked-up people get about it."

"I never said I didn't have any religion," Tom said. "I said I didn't know that I believed anything anymore."

"Hah!" Huntley jabbed the air with a peach slice. His eyes blinked happily behind his glasses. "Now there you are, my point exactly! Religion means somethin' different altogether.

181

Thing is, Tom, religion is more often about war against whoever has a different one than anythin' else. Take your family
name, for example. You and half a' Europe are named for a
saint that went to war, did you know that?"

Tom sighed. "Go ahead and tell me."

"Martin a' Tours. Turned back the Turks and the Pope or
somesuch immediately says all the peasants across Europe –
who up till then didn't have no last names and didn't need 'em
– are to be called Martin."

"Where did you hear that one? I don't believe it."

"Story's somethin' like that anyway. Think about it, there's
a Martin in any language you care to name – Spanish, German,
whatever." He resumed carving his peach as judiciously as if
he were sculpting something permanent. "Now, as it happens,
there's a few things goin' on you'd be interested in knowin'
about. This Friday night there's gonna be a big meetin', platform full a' nobs, to honor Doc Cronin and rally public opinion
to capture his killers."

"Rally public opinion? Isn't it rallied enough?" Tom cried.
"My God, what do they want?"

"An eye for an eye, if they can get it," Huntley replied. "Anyhow, that ain't the main thing that's interestin'. What's worth
goin' along to see is all the Clansmen who'll be standin' right
next to Judge Richard Prendergast and Mr. Robert Lindbolm a'
the Board a' Trade and Mr. Louis Nettelhurst a' the Board a'
Education. Not to mention Mr. William Penn Nixon a' the *Inter
Ocean*. He says right here in his esteemed paper that Dr.
Cronin's murder and the Haymarket riot were caused by one
and the same vile force."

"What?"

"Don't be so indignant. Didn't see that, did you?" Huntley
put the paring knife down and leaned to read the newspaper
lying next to his typewriter. "He says: 'In each case the motive
power was contempt a' American law and the purpose was to
make the will and decrees a' a secret cabal supreme over the
lives and fortunes a' American citizens.' He ain't the only one
thinks that. Hand me a nice hygienic piece a' copy paper there,
will you?"

182

Huntley took the paper from Tom's hand and began to arrange the peach slices on it neatly. "So I took the liberty a' suggestin' to Percy that you come with me on Saturday night for a look-see. That all right?"

"I don't want to go," Tom said mutinously.

"Well, me and Percy, we ain't really givin' you a choice. Here, catch." Huntley threw him a peach from the bag. Tom bit into it viciously.

The meeting was in the Central Music Hall. Three months before, when Dr. Cronin had sung at the Robert Emmet commemoration, Tom had filed in with Liz and Andy and been impressed in spite of himself at the numbers of Irish faithfully turning out in high March winds to pay their respects to the nationalist cause. On Saturday night, even an hour before the scheduled starting time, it was obvious that the numbers turning out in sultry June would be twice as high.

This time Tom walked behind Huntley to the row reserved for members of the press and tried not to gawk at the stage. Two American flags the size of blankets were draped on each side of the rear wall, tucked in all around with banks of flowers. There was a banner swaying between them, suspended from the organ loft: the Statue of Liberty, the figure of Columbia and the American eagle shared the space on it more or less equally.

But what had arrested Tom upon entry was the main prop of the evening, set stage center in front of the speaker's podium. It was the five-foot crayon portrait of Dr. Cronin, salvaged from the Royal Armory and newly trimmed in black crêpe streamers.

Tom squirmed down in his seat and took a quick look at Huntley, whose face was suffused with pleasure. He looked like a Botticelli cherub, gazing demurely at the stage ahead of him. "If the organizers a' the Personal Rights League a' America catch you scowlin' with distaste at their choice a' decorations," he said softly to Tom, "they're more'n likely to take the view you're guilty a' un-American sentiments."

It took twenty minutes for the audience to settle into their seats and another twenty minutes for Colonel W.P. Rend, presiding officer for the occasion, to present letters of regret from dignitaries unable to attend – two Senators, several prominent clergymen, and a dozen others whose names Tom couldn't place. There was a musical tribute from the combined choirs of the Swiss and German community before the speakers took their places.

"Should I take notes?" Tom whispered.

"Won't be necessary. Copies a' them speeches been sittin' on Percy's desk since noon. Just get a feel for what's goin' on," Huntley answered. "You could always listen, too, a' course." But that was, in fact, not easy. Before the speeches began, the entire hall was exhorted to rise for a rendition of "The Star Spangled Banner" which brought the meeting to a peculiarly climactic pitch from which it was difficult to retreat.

The local but minor Irish speakers were called first. Tom concentrated on styles, hearing sentences in snatches. Congressman Frank Lawler used the imperative: let us not condemn the race that gave us the heroes of Bull Run, Gettysburg and the Shenandoah Valley – a Corcoran, a Meagher, a Smith, a Mulligan, a Shields and a Sheridan – just because that race is now bowed down with a Coughlan, a Burke and a Sullivan. Judge Richard Prendergast preferred the declarative: no man who was asked to express himself on the topic of this foul murder could remain silent. Colonel Rend himself kept to a straightforward eulogy: Dr. Cronin was a model citizen and became a martyr to Ireland's sacred cause for the highest motive.

It was a courteous audience. The Irish speakers were applauded thoroughly but a little distantly. Then Mr. Lindbolm took the podium. He didn't get past his opening sentence before the audience cut in and clapped with thunderous approval for his views, which were that they had gathered there to emphasize their rights as men and as American citizens, and to protest against these rights being dominated by foreign influences and conspiracies. It was the same for Mr. Nettelhurst.

And then finally John Devoy took the podium. He looked remote and disdainful, an Old Testament prophet with his untamed beard. He stared deep into the audience as if his eyes would burn into the souls of the conspirators and bring them forward there, before the podium and the mute crayoned face of their victim. His voice was dry and crisp and Tom lost track of his meaning, feeling he was being tossed forward on words toward some cataclysmic moment.

Something must be done, something would be done. Treachery. Redress. Vindication. Vengeance. The whole Central Music Hall rose together and affirmed with wild applause the resolution of the night. They would get the murdering conspirators and bring them to justice.

The next morning the Sunday papers gave the names the audience thirsted for. After examining more than two hundred witnesses – a number unprecedented in a criminal case – the Grand Jury had indicted seven men for Dr. Cronin's murder. Four of them – Dan Coughlan, Patrick O'Sullivan, Frank Woodruff and Martin Burke – were expected. But there was news in the fifth and sixth names. John F. Beggs, senior guardian of Camp 20, had been arrested the previous night and charged with organizing the murder plot; and an international bulletin had that morning been issued seeking the man identified as the purchaser of furniture in Revells. It was Pat Cooney.

The seventh man was the real surprise. The cops had pulled in an unemployed drifter named John Kunze on a vagrancy charge, and someone recognized him as one of Coughlan's street contacts. They put him on a routine check before the Grand Jury witnesses, and two of them linked him positively enough to the murder to warrant a manslaughter charge. Kunze was a German immigrant with no Irish connections, and only a rudimentary command of English.

There was no mention of Alexander Sullivan.

XVIII

August, 1889

THERE HAD ALWAYS been boundaries, but Tom only really understood that now. Now he knew them defined as if by customs posts. Kilgubbin was marked off by Erie Street all the way from Wells Street on the east to the north branch of the river. It stretched past Locust Street as far as Oak Street. It was named, he discovered for the first time from Mrs. Delaney, from the village in west Cork where the first immigrants had come from. Goose Island began on the other side of the river and went all the way to Halsted and Division. Most of the shanties built in the '50s and '60s were still there. No pigs anymore, but geese and hens and goats still shared human quarters in the shacks crouched along the river and the canal.

Within a few days of the Grand Jury indictment at the end of June, everything changed in Kilgubbin and Goose Island. Scalded with shock and still uncomprehending, the people there saw that they had been chosen to pay. The ugly threat that had hung over them since Cronin's body was discovered now became a reality, and suddenly it no longer mattered who had killed Dr. Cronin. Without planning, without effort, they came together in a tight and often wordless unity.

When they did speak it was a short muttering. Even Mrs. Delaney had taken to muttering about "things": things that weren't going to be let go on like this and things that had better been let lie and things that could come to a bad pass. What Tom heard, in the shops and on the streets, in Gleason's waiting for a pail of beer to bring back to Foy's, he could not have imagined before. There was no justice, there was only vengeance. There was no proof, there were only victims. Johnny Beggs was Gleason's own first cousin. Pat Cooney's

187

aunt had delivered half the babies in the district. Martin Burke was no more than a boy.

The battles between the Kilgubbin boys and their adversaries were open and vicious now, and patrol gangs stalked Goose Island in the hope of ambushing slogan writers from enemy neighborhoods. Every day there was fresh fuel to their smoldering resentment in one newspaper or another: an editorial denouncing secret foreign societies as a threat to the fabric of American life, a statement or a letter warning of the sinister primitivism of Roman Catholicism from the United Order of Deputies or the American Protestant Association.

Huntley still held the view that it wasn't all that bad. He pointed out that when you analysed all the statements and letters and editorials, most of them stuck to attacking Clan na Gael, and not the Irish in general. What Tom couldn't really explain to Huntley was that the distinction didn't seem to mean anything to the people in Kilgubbin and Goose Island. Later Huntley said that it wasn't even the Clan that was drawing the fire anymore, it was just that section of it that supported Sullivan. Everyone could see now that the other wing of the Clan was as anxious to hang Cronin's murderers as Longenecker. And Tom couldn't explain to him why that was worse.

The sun bleached the grass to hay and scorched the dirt-paths until they burned underfoot, yet softened the tar streets downtown to putty. At night the heat settled down close to the ground, a blanket sealing the city. Andy's work had dwindled to two days a week, which is why more often than not now on Saturday evenings Tom went into Gleason's only long enough to get a pail filled to take away. "I'll just go to roll the growler," he'd say, exaggerating the "r"s, lampooning the local expression, which at least provoked a slight smile from Andy. Sometimes he brought something for the children, too, lemonade or the fizzy bottles of what they called "brown pop," but he was careful to be frugal. Liz would worry about spoiling them. But there were no more good-natured protests at his generosity and there was no pretense that someone else should pay.

If Liz was there she sometimes had a glass of beer with them, though Tom suspected it was more to deplete the store left to Andy than anything else. Usually she left the house, pushing the buggy in an effort to lull the fretful baby to sleep. Tom sometimes wondered if that, too, was a device, holding Andy at home to watch the smaller children. They were the only ones untouched by heat or anger, and while the two men sat on the back stoop they squealed and raced in and out of the cottage and around the little square yard. Occasionally Andy was called on to adjudicate in a dispute, and some nights he had to convert glass jars into jails for their captured fireflies. Now and again one of them would come and collapse against his knees, and he would stroke the child's hair and sing a little. Those were the only times Tom saw him at ease, diverted and himself again.

Most of the time Andy was like someone trapped, turning the same points over and over as if searching for some hidden combination of words that would spring a lock. Sometimes he turned without warning to fanciful conversations. One night he began the game of wondering what he might have done with his life if he had been born rich, or a member of the English royalty. "I suppose I'd have justified all manner of what I'd now consider conceits and injustices, eh?" he remarked playfully. "Isn't it all a great charade, imagining we come to eternal truths independent of our circumstances?"

"But you might," Tom answered idly. "I mean, you might come to conclusions that aren't, you know, that aren't in your own interests. People have."

"Only if they're well enough off to start with, Tommy. That's the trick to achieving altruism: start from the high ground."

Tom straightened up, his interest flickering a bit. But the back door slammed and the smallest boy came out, snuffling pathetically. "I don't wanna play," he whimpered, clutching his father's knees.

"Cry-baby cry," Robert chanted in the dark kitchen.

"Kate!" Andy shouted inside. "Come out here! Robert, you don't be taunting this poor child." He glared at Kate, who emerged with a clatter of the door. "What's going on in there?"

"Nothing!" She said crossly. "He always wants to play and then he cries if he gets the devil's card. It's not fair! If you get the card you *have* to do what the dealer says, and he just cries and says he won't! I told him he's too small, it's not my fault."

The little boy cried louder into his father's knees and Andy growled, "Put away those damned cards and come out and play tag or something. I swear to Jesus I'll burn them yet. Shush, George, stop crying boy." Tom thought he could heroically offer to play with them. But the fact was that he was there for Andy's benefit, to keep this vigil with him, really, until something happened that would propel him forward toward some new stage.

At the very least, to keep him company, perhaps distract or amuse him if he could. And Tom tried, but his mind often wandered listlessly. He was too spent with this dreadful summer to concentrate, and usually Andy was coiled up in concentration. Pat Cooney had vanished; that stunned him more deeply even than Martin Burke's arrest, and he sat for long periods in silence, hunched, his fingers laced. When he did speak, his words burned with feelings Tom could only identify imprecisely: grief and anguish and fear, and bitterness. Poor Martin Burke, poor Johnny Beggs; God help Pat Cooney, on the run like a felon, in hiding somewhere, God knows where. God help the Clan, God help us all; and God damn John Devoy and all he stands for.

It was the Cronin Committee the people hated now, and Devoy, who was behind it: Devoy, who couldn't contain his disappointment that the Grand Jury had found no plausible way to indict Sullivan; Devoy, who was so poisoned against Sullivan that he would heedlessly destroy them all. Devoy and his henchmen couldn't stop. Giving evidence was not enough. They had joined the friends of Rend and Scanlon and McGarry, and shared platforms with the businessmen and the bankers, the native citizens who railed against foreign conspirators and demanded revenge.

The Committee put down money to finance its own investigations, flaunting the news to tempt informers. Slowly the papers began to reveal its successes. The Committee exposed

190

Charley Long's connections with the Sullivan supporters in the Clan, and traced his dispatches to persons close to the Triangle in Canada. The Committee identified Annie Murphy as the daughter of one of Sullivan's allies. The street-car conductor who'd backed up her story was another Sullivan supporter. The Committee moved through Chicago, pointing to policemen and politicians whose jobs were gifts from Sullivan. The press followed them, snatching greedily at every new name.

From Kilgubbin and Goose Island the people watched the Committee, waiting for it to move close enough to be bitten, deeply and, with luck, lethally. And then, at the start of August, the Committee moved in range by announcing a rally in Cheltenham Beach to be held on the same day as the annual picnic in Ogden's Grove. The picnic in Ogden's Grove was held near the Feast of the Assumption and called the Lady Day picnic; but it was also a commemoration of the 1798 rebellion. The collection always went to the Irish National League. The Committee proposed to take up a collection for the Cronin murder trial prosecution legal fund at Cheltenham Beach. The Ogden Grove organizing group said their annual picnic would go ahead anyway, on the same terms as usual.

The people on the front steps fanned themselves with their newspapers, and they smiled grimly when they muttered.

"They don't see it the way you do," Tom said to Huntley. "As far as they're concerned, it's a test of loyalties."

"It ain't gonna be seen that way," Huntley said. "Way it's gonna be seen, they don't give a hoot about murder when the murderers happen to be their own crowd."

"They think the men are innocent," Tom said. "Some of them, anyway," he amended. "Anyway, they say there's no real proof."

"Maybe they think whoever knocked off the Doc done the right thing?" Huntley removed his glasses and wiped them carefully dry of sweat. They bothered him in this weather, slipping constantly down his nose.

"I haven't heard anyone say anything like that. Not once. In fact, they say the opposite." He quoted Packy. "They all say they don't hold with what happened." It was the way most people prefaced their remarks, that was true. He didn't add that, now, more and more of them said that they didn't hold with what happened but it might be so that Cronin had, after all, been a spy. "These are just ordinary people, Dick, people with families and worries about paying the grocer. They don't approve of murder any more than anyone else does, but they feel like they're being persecuted, like they're under siege."

"And they think turnin' their nose up at the Committee's gonna prove somethin'?"

"It will show that the Committee doesn't represent them. It'll discredit Devoy." Huntley remained silent, and Tom added, lamely, "You don't know what it's like to live there."

"Haven't lost my imagination, either." Huntley replied, and adjusted the glasses on his nose. "Hope you ain't gonna start tellin' me I can't have a viewpoint on somethin' I ain't experienced. That particular fallacy's a dangerous sort a' ignorance."

Tom felt that way, though. He felt himself inhabiting two worlds, and in one of them no one spoke under his breath. In work they spoke in full, deliberate sentences about the impending trial, about Longenecker's frustration at the continued absence of evidence against Sullivan. Apart from Huntley, though, no one spoke directly to him about any of it. Sometimes – though he wasn't sure of this either – he felt that they stopped talking when he came near. He was careful not to be curious. But he knew they approved of the Committee, and Devoy, and Tom thought privately that they might be right. He also agreed, very privately, with Huntley: if it weren't for Devoy and the Committee denouncing murder and murderers, things might well have been much worse in his other world.

But when it came to the conflicting events scheduled for Lady Day, he knew where he would have to be.

Four horse-drawn street-cars had been hired for Locust Street alone. They came early, in a cavalcade that summoned shouting children from every house. Tom went out on Mrs. Delaney's doorstep and watched them racing in circles, dodging past the harassed drivers to peek inside. He saw Kate and waved, and she ran toward him.

"Tom Martin," she cried, "are you coming with us?" She

had taken to calling him by both names, an ingenious solution, he thought, to the dilemma of familiarity but unequal status.

"I certainly am," he said.

"What are you bringing?" she demanded, jiggling up and down.

"Beer," he said. "And a bit of cold pork."

"Ooohh. Pork." Her eyes widened respectfully.

"It's not very big," he said hastily. "But I got lemonade as well, and some chocolate." She grinned at him and ran back screeching to her brothers.

Liz was no less impressed when he arrived in her kitchen twenty minutes later and showed her his parcels. "You shouldn't have," she said, "It's too much altogether." She put one arm around him and hugged him gratefully. Tom was too startled to reply, and Andy, who'd come in from the back wiping his face on a towel, laughed and flipped the towel at Liz. "Oh! Impetuous gestures behind my back, is it?" he said. "This is what comes of giving a woman a day off."

"A day off what?" Liz gave his wet mustache a tug with one hand and resumed stacking food into her basket with the other. "I've been up since dawn putting jam on bread for this army. If I hadn't a rake of children to mind, now, I might have time for impetuous gestures you'd have to sit up and take notice of."

"Sure isn't that what got you in this predicament in the first place?" Andy answered. They both laughed, and Tom fixed his gaze somewhere between them and smiled very slightly.

"Ah, Tom, I'm warning you," Andy said mockingly. He turned to comb his hair, frowning into the piece of mirror over the sink. "It'll all happen so fast you won't know what's knocked you down." He shook water off the comb and began singing:

"When a pair of sweet lips are upturned to your own
With no one to gossip about it,
You could pray for endurance to leave them alone,
And maybe you will but I doubt it . . ."

He broke off and studied his reflection. "What do you think, Tom? Wouldn't it have made me a fortune on Broadway?"

"What?" Tom looked at the face in the mirror.

"The song, man. It's one of my own, from the days when I fancied I'd get rich with nothing more than a good supply of paper and ink." He put the comb down and grabbed Liz by the waist, singing while he danced her around the kitchen: ". . . when a sly little hand you're permitted to seize, with a velvety softness about it . . ." Liz laughed and protested and laughed some more, still holding a breadknife aloft in her hand. Andy's eyes were bright as jewels

The mood had touched everyone. Locust Street was in a state of giddiness. They piled into the cars, one family after another, shoving their baskets under the benches. The children fought over the end seats where they could hang out the windows, and those who lost got lap space from an adult or a grumbling older child. Tom sat between Kate and Andy, each with a wriggling small boy on their knees. Liz held the two babies. He heard her say how well the little one looked, nudging Andy to get his attention. Wasn't there better colour in her face, all the same, she asked? Andy said there was. He blew the baby's scant fair curls gently, until the baby shut her eyes tight and giggled. All the way out to the city limits they sang. The verses drifted merrily from one car to another, "Oh! Susanna" and "Camptown Races" and "Oh, Them Golden Slippers."

When they turned on to the dirt road to Ogden's Grove, Tom began to see the dimensions of the demonstration they were making. Cars identical to the one he sat in were lined up ahead and pulling in behind, stalled at crossroads; one hundred, two hundred. Ogden's Grove was vast, a series of forests and pastures, and every road leading to it was similarly choked with rigs and wagons and cars bearing singing, laughing families. They disembarked at the first clearing that was vacant, and immediately the women began to spread blankets and food out under the trees while the men turned to the task of marking off a rough softball diamond on the open grass.

Tom began to relax. He hadn't played in a long time but he'd been good at it in the seminary. The ball they played with here was different, a huge sixteen incher and pudgy to the touch, but as soon as he picked one and threw it experimentally in the air he knew he would be good today. He was standing there, running his fingers along the seamed U-curve, when he heard Andy say, "Are you sure?" behind him, and someone answered, "It's Sullivan all right – and the missus."

There was a crowd near the clearing, growing larger. Tom hurried to fall in step with Andy. They had to push quite close to the front to see anything. The man at the centre was slim and short, shorter even than Huntley, and his head was slightly too large for the rest of him. Tom would not have recognized him from the night of his arrest. He was wearing a suit, in spite of the weather. It was cream-colored and of some crisp light material. Tom realized after a moment it must be linen. Everyone else looked hot and rumpled beside him, the men in their collarless shirts with the sleeves rolled past their elbows who pressed forward to shake his hand, their wives clumped together at the edge of the circle. The woman clasping his arm with both hands, leaning against him devotedly, he thought he might have recognized even from the single glimpse he'd had that day when Huntley had pointed her out on Michigan Avenue, walking with the editor of the *Herald*. Her hair was a particularly ripe shade of gold, and rolled in a distinct way at the nape of her neck. She was in white, and wasn't quite as young as he'd thought, but she was so attractive it was difficult to look away from her face.

He never quite smiled, and neither did she, but they looked pleased, pleased and knowing. He spoke to every man in turn, some a little longer than others. Tom went forward without thinking about it, next to Andy, and when Andy's turn came he heard him say, "Wishing you well, sir." Then Andy turned and said, "This is a young friend of ours, Tom Martin. Tom, this is Alexander Sullivan, and Mrs. Sullivan."

Tom put out his hand and the short man took it in his and held it for a moment. "Hello, Tom," he said mildly. His face was broad and rather flat, and this close Tom could see the network of fine bloodshot lines. He had a thin mouth and his eyes were heavily hooded. But it was the gaze that was disconcerting, bold and intimate at the same time, as if he had shared a secret with you that he knew you would keep. Tom said

195

something in reply, and Andy said, "Tom is a reporter on the *Tribune*, Alex."

The hooded lids lifted just perceptibly but the eyes never wavered. "Not my favorite paper, I'm afraid," he said in the same mild tone. He released Tom's hand and turned to his wife.

"I'm actually a copy-editor," Tom said indistinctly. He bowed in the woman's direction and she bowed in return without looking at him. Someone pushed Andy and Tom aside then, and they waited with the others who had been greeted while the Sullivans moved on to the rest, slowly, at their leisure. Everyone waited until they had completed the circuit, and with a brief final wave they went back to the rig waiting on the path to bring them to the next clearing in the Grove and the next reception. Like royalty, Tom thought. For all the world, royalty at the Irish republicans' picnic. He was, he knew, a little awed himself.

Andy whistled as they walked back. His eyes were brighter than ever. All around him Tom could sense a new charge in the air, and from the open ground ahead he heard someone roaring the cry of the ball-park, "Let's play ball!" as if it were a call to arms. He stopped at the blanket where Liz had set out their picnic to get some water from his flask, and it occured to him that she had never left her place.

"You weren't over to greet the famous man and his wife," he said.

"I was not. Were you shaken by the hand with the rest of Chicago?"

He laughed. "This part of Chicago, anyway," he said. "In this part of Chicago, he's like a king."

"Not to me," Liz said. "I never could take to him, no matter what Andy says. I always feel if he decided to, he could have the power to make me obey him whether I wanted to or not." She leaned against the tree, her arms folded thoughtfully, and then smiled at him. "And I don't mean what you're thinking, either." Tom stared at her, aghast, and mumbled that he was thinking nothing. Liz just laughed, and told him to go and play ball.

He headed for the diamond determined to put everything

else but the game out of his mind. It proved easier than he'd thought, too, because from the first inning it was obvious that the game was part of the demonstration, and while it lasted it was the whole part. You could feel it from every man on the field, tension and exuberance running along invisible lines from one to another. Tom could hear the heavy thud of the bat almost before the ball left the pitcher's hand, see it scooped from the ground by the shortstop and winged toward him at first base in one motion. He played splendidly. They all did. They played as if they had to win or die.

Afterward he couldn't see Andy, and he merged effortlessly into the young men's group, which soon meshed with a group of young women. He should have found himself there before now, he thought. He looked around at their laughing faces, some quite openly flirting with the ballplayers, bringing them water and offering towels to wipe faces with. The incident with Nanda still rankled, but there would be no rebuff for him here. Tom smiled tentatively at one or two of them but backed off to sit under a tree next to the shortstop, whose name was Tim Casey. They had established a sort of kinetic bond during the game and they were almost reluctant to part.

Shoulder to shoulder, they drank beer and talked through the game, improving everyone's performance in retrospect to a sufficient standard. Casey gave him a cheese sandwich and Tom ate it with an indifferent and passing thought for the cold pork, watching the girls near him covertly. Eventually someone said the speeches were due to begin and the group moved together, thinning out to a long line as they strolled to the far end of the Grove. Tom walked with Casey and a girl named Hannah who had frizzed curls like a rag doll and talked breathlessly the whole way.

He had never seen more people in one place. There were thousands ahead of them, thousands more on each side, to the left and right as far as he could see. The speaker was no more than a tiny figure somewhere far in front. He must have been standing on the back of a wagon. He seemed a mile away and his voice was a shrill pip into the sky. Then the thousands surrounding Tom began to roar "Sullivan, Sullivan!" Casey

197

shouted with them and Hannah jumped up and down, screaming and applauding. Tom stood a little away from them, shading his eyes with both hands as if it were imperative that he see
what was being said. But he felt the day begin to ebb slowly
away from him, leaving him beached and alone again with the
same tired fears and puzzles. He wondered whether Liz would
be annoyed that he had disappeared without a word. He hoped
she would, a little.

The speeches went on and on, one tiny figure replacing another. All around him people shifted restlessly and slapped at
mosquitoes, but no one left. Casey considerately took account
of Tom's local ignorance and filled him in on names – congress-
men and senators, John Finerty himself, editor of the *Chicago
Citizen*, a champion of Irish freedom of international stature.
Tom forgot them as fast as he heard them, but he knew when
the significant name was spoken, because every time it was
taken up it was charged with intensity for several moments:
"Sullivan! Sullivan!" There was a long resolution of some kind
passed at the end, with stamping feet and cheers, but then
Casey said he'd better get back to his family. He asked Tom for
his address and they shook hands shyly, hoping to meet again.

It took Tom a long time to find the Foys in the crowds
streaming now toward the cars, and when he finally did he ran
the last few steps in guilty haste. It was a scene of collapse and
distress, the jolliness of the morning turned inside out. Liz was
bundling things back into her basket, with two children pulling at her skirt beseeching her not to go yet. Kate paced up and
down, jostling the baby who was screaming in a rage so sus-
tained that Tom gaped fearfully at the small red face.

"Ah, Tom, you're a godsend. Could you take care of Andy
for me?" Liz rolled her eyes over Kate's head and mouthed
"drunk". He saw Andy then, slumped against the tree, asleep.
"If you could get him up, Kate and I will manage the rest." She
saw his stricken face and smiled wearily. "Don't worry, it'll all
calm down in a bit."

He woke Andy, who was effusively glad to see him. They
staggered to the clearing together and, leaning against him,
Andy told Tom in slurred whispers that he had been on impor-

tant business the whole afternoon. He and a very few others had been selected to slip away and rendezvous at an appointed place to compare notes with their infiltrators at Cheltenham Beach. Ogden's Grove had more than double, maybe three times as many as the Committee had drawn, he hissed – 13,000 to 15,000, as against 5,000 or at most 7,000 for them. Tom had trouble understanding him. So much, Andy said, for John Devoy; and Frankie Lawler who'd never get another vote from him, and the damned priests who were with Devoy, abusing the cloth and collar. He stopped suddenly, nearly pitching Tom over. "An' don' leddem ever say we favor murrer," he said excitedly, "'cause we passed public rezolushon, right here, sayen 'twas atroshus. Tha's our statemen' to the worl'."

Before he fell asleep again in the car, Andy announced the numbers aloud to everyone, apparently forgetting whatever restraint had prompted him to whisper to Tom. They were quoted all around with relish. Eventually Tom pieced together, from the conversation, what the reference to the resolution meant. The resolution that had been passed at the end of the meeting had denounced Dr. Cronin's atrocious murder, and declared that they, the Irish Americans of Chicago, were no more to be held responsible for the atrocity than any other element of the body politic. The resolution was for some reason almost as richly satisfying as the numbers.

It was as if they, all 13,000 to 15,000 of them, had crushed the opposition and then risen above it to do the generous, the magnanimous thing. Tom sat in the jogging car and thought about it. All the children were dozing, even Kate. Someone had begun to play a fiddle in the car ahead of them, a song so mournful and commanding that the scattered conversations fell off. Tom heard a voice behind him exclaim, "Crotty's Lament," and join in humming dolefully. Liz sat next to him, rocking the baby, who was deeply and peacefully still. She looked straight ahead.

"Do you think there's such a thing as an entirely rational decision?" he asked her. They used to have conversations like that quite often.

"I do not," she answered promptly. "The ones that sound

rational are only justifying something, and you can justify anything, can't you? If you believe whatever it is you start off
from, anyway. At least you know where you are with the ones
that sound irrational." She never turned her head.

XIX

Autumn, 1889

O N FRIDAY, SEPTEMBER 6th, Longenecker opened the case for the state of Illinois before Judge McConnell. They were present, Longenecker said, to try the seven men indicted on the charge of murder. However, Patrick Cooney had not been apprehended despite every effort of police forces throughout North America and Europe; and Frank J. Woodruff, he said, was not to be tried.

Judge McConnell evinced no surprise. Neither did the court, restricted under his order to jurors, members of the bar, and representatives of the press. Cooney had simply disappeared, erasing every trace of his existence; Woodruff had confessed to seven variations of involvement in Cronin's murder as well as several unsolved crimes on the police books, eliminating any hope of passing as a fit witness. The prisoners on trial were O'Sullivan, Coughlan, Burke, Beggs and Kunze – four Irish American members of the Clan, and a German immigrant whom no one knew anything about.

According to what Huntley said were unofficial sources close to the prosecution, Kunze had been either duped or bullied into service by Coughlan. There was no other explanation for him. The four Clan men faced Judge McConnell and the court impassively. Kunze, whose thick red hair was combed down on to his forehead in an odd kind of fringe, looked distinctly clownish, even in the befuddled way he scanned the faces of the jurors who were waiting to be sworn to duty.

That wasn't to happen, as it turned out, for weeks. Judge McConnell drew up a list of questions the veniremen were to be asked, beginning with, "Have you formed an opinion . . . ?" One after another, they admitted that they had, and by and large the opinion they had formed was that the men before them were guilty. One after another they were dismissed, twenty and thirty every day.

The occasional man who swore he had no view on the guilt or innocence of the accused was challenged peremptorily, by one side or the other. The state suspected secret Clan supporters and, more to the point, men who'd possibly been bribed or threatened by the Clan; though that allegation was neither stated nor demonstrated, merely let loose by unofficial sources to run wild in the corridors of the criminal court building. The defense suspected undisclosed bias against the Irish and the Clan. As even Huntley conceded, they had probability on their side.

Tom read the accounts every evening in the slack hour between the first two editions. Percy had transferred him again, this time to the City Desk, where he had to log the fire and police calls, taking notes over the telephone and converting them into stories appropriately solemn or clever. To his own surprise he enjoyed it more than anything else he'd done so far. For one thing, it was a day shift. He no longer breakfasted at noon alone with Mrs. Delaney, and he now left work with the sky still light, stepping into the stream of workers rushing home, part of the world of ordinary mortals.

But he also liked learning the news and telling it. "It's about things that really happen, no guessing or drawing conclusions or wriggling things out of people," he told Huntley.

"Daily ritual up in Court Three's really happenin', too, though it's hard to believe," Huntley answered. "Looks like there ain't a man in Chicago can establish he's an open-minded citizen a' independent means without doubtful associations."

Tom tried to give Court Three no more than perfunctory attention. He had taken a tentative step toward broadening his social scope by searching out Tim Casey after the picnic. Twice now he had spent Saturday playing ball with Casey and his friends in Lincoln Park and drinking with them afterward. They didn't discuss politics of any kind, but their responses, he saw, were mirrors of the responses in Gleason's. He found he had little to say and much to think, just as he did with Andy and the men in Gleason's. Still, on the long walk back to

Locust Street he gave a lot of consideration to moving from Mrs. Delaney's. Perhaps in the spring. Somewhere nearer Lincoln Park, near the lakefront. But there was no hurry. It was a snug and agreeable state to be in, having a new selection of friends and choices about his spare time.

Besides, he felt more strongly than ever that he was needed in Foy's. He cheered Andy up, Liz said. What she meant was that he still kept him company, even when Andy had no money for drinking. Andy had been on two new jobs, and neither of them had lasted more than ten days. It was Kate who brought home the only reliable wage packet now, a couple of dollars a week from the clothing factory where she stood nine hours at a time at the cutting table.

But when Tom met him in the evening, Andy talked at random and length about books and the theater, about his own plans to write more as soon as he could get a steady job again; anything but the trial. It suited Tom. Sometimes when he came out of work Andy would be waiting for him, and they would stroll a while before turning home. To take advantage of the only decent weather Chicago offered, Andy said, the cool and delicious autumn. Tom didn't tell Liz that he often stood Andy a drink somewhere along the way. Just one, and only over his protests. If it sometimes seemed that he might have had another one or two earlier, Tom didn't mention that to Liz either.

By the last day of September more than seven hundred veniremen had been examined and a total of four had been accepted by both sides. John Kunze caused the only major diversion. He jumped to his feet one morning and pleaded to be allowed to address the court. Fascinated and embarrassed, the press and the members of the bar and the roster of potential jurors for the day watched Kunze wave his arms and wail. It was like a vaudeville act. "Vat I am in chail for?" he cried. "Ein doctor no man can heal und he don't know he woondt!" Judge McConnell said he had Mr. Kunze's matter under consideration, and the prisoner subsided tearfully. The court looked away.

It couldn't go on much longer, Huntley told Tom. The defense had used up all but twenty of their allowance in peremptory challenges. It looked now like Longenecker's supply of respectable and unprejudiced men of industry and commerce would outstrip them in the end.

"Maybe you'd like to do some reportin' on the trial," Huntley said. "I could have a word with Percy. Why, hell, boy, you ain't no newcomer no more, you could mention it yourself."

"Maybe," Tom said. "I might. I'll think about it."

But he wouldn't. He was in fact wishing he could think of a plausible way to leave town when the trial began in earnest. He had no excuse to request any time off work, no unfinished business in Baltimore, no relatives to visit. He considered inventing an ailing aunt. These mornings, reciting his prayers before the shaving mirror, Tom acknowledged in himself an absence of honesty that was, he believed, new. It was a matter of deciding not to speak, to hold back. At some point he had begun holding back on Huntley. He had never mentioned that he knew Pat Cooney. It wasn't much to hold back, since he knew nothing at all about Cooney. There was no reason to admit an acquaintance with him to anyone. But sometimes Tom caught himself staring into the mirror with his shaving brush drying in his hand, formulating syllogisms – all deceit is dishonest, some silence is not deceit, therefore some silence is not dishonest; some silence is collusion, all collusion is deceitful, therefore . . . A fictitious sick aunt, though, was a different class of theorem. She was also impractical. Once invented he'd have to keep her and, whatever about Percy, he didn't think he could maintain the fiction to Huntley, or Andy and Liz.

Liz left a note in Mrs. Delaney's for him, asking him to call in some morning; she had a favor to ask.

"Poor unfortunate woman. Isn't it a great pity that man can't seem to keep a job at all?" Mrs. Delaney said. "Well, she holds her head up, I'll give her that. All those children to feed."

"They seem fine," Tom said.

"Aye. Well, I'll say no more, I'm sure," Mrs. Delaney answered. She closed her mouth like a purse and her chins folded solemnly in place.

The favor concerned the children. Liz wanted Tom to bring them to the *Tribune* and show them around; if such a thing would be permitted, she said.

"I don't know," Tom said. "But if it is, I'll do it, and with pleasure."

"I'd appreciate it so, Tom; you've no idea how much." She sat at the table in the kitchen with her hands clasped on the edge like a schoolgirl. "I've been wanting to ask you for ages."

"And why haven't you then, before?" he asked, astonished.

"I didn't know whether it was a thing that was ever done." She clasped her fingers tighter; she was flushed and diffident. "They want to leave school next year. To get jobs somewhere, like Kate. I'm determined they won't. I don't mind what I have to do, but they have to go on, go to high school, however we manage it. Even a year or two. I thought if they could see for themselves, that if they stayed on, there'd be a life for them ... do you see what I mean?"

"I think Kate should come, too."

"It would be too hard on her; oh, no Tom. There's no sense giving her notions. She'll be all right, in the end. But they won't unless they get a start in life."

"If it's to be an outing and nothing more devious, she must come, too."

"Well," Liz sighed. "All right, then. So you'll do it, if you're allowed to, and you'll say it's your idea? You won't mind?"

Tom said he thought it would be the most honorable deception he'd been involved in for a long time. It would be, he repeated, a pleasure.

And it was. They went on a Saturday, a rich October afternoon smelling of burning leaves. First they went downtown on the Clark Street car to see the skyscrapers. Tom had done his homework in advance, remembering Andy sitting awed before the Auditorium, and he marshaled them to the corner of Adams and La Salle to inspect the Home Insurance building on the corner. Ten stories high, he said casually, a steel skeleton with only the thinnest skin of masonry over it. Architects did that, he said, and engineers and draughtsmen and designers.

Robert turned his pointed little face up mistrustfully. "My Pa says him and Mr. Gallagher are the ones make the buildings," he said.

"Ah, don't be stupid," Kate growled, poking him.

"Yes," Tom said. "Your da and Mr. Gallagher, too."

"The architect thought of them, stupid," Kate said.

The Rookery was on the other corner. There were supposed to be six hundred offices in the Rookery. Tom and the children stood in a row with their heads thrown back, swiveling from one building to another, until Kate saw a messenger boy smirk at them as he ran past and said she'd looked up enough. Tom faced them around toward Michigan Avenue and told them to look ahead instead, to the Pullman Palace Car Company Building. There was a restaurant at the top, nine stories over the street. The city would be laid out flat as a map to study while you ate your lunch; someone could be there right now, looking at them. He started to say it would cost a week of your papa's wages to eat your lunch there, but he thought better of it. He took them to a drugstore, with tiled floors and a soda fountain, and bought them ice-cream.

Then they went to the newspaper. Percy's only bemused comment, when Tom had asked, was that he had better make it short and keep them out of the way. He was relieved to find that Percy wasn't there. No one else seemed to mind, and in any case Kate and the boys were rigorously well-behaved, obviously under stern orders. They got to examine the telephones and watch the wire machines typing away to themselves, and in the caseroom they watched the columns of type slammed together into pages and locked into their cases. The overseer printed their names out on scraps of copy paper. They were led up and across the catwalks to see the presses and promised they could come back, for sure, some night late to watch them roll.

But all else faded when they reached the new linotype room. It was early yet, only one was in operation. They stood in silent homage behind them, single units linking man perfectly to machine. Tom tried, as he always did, to follow just one single letter as it was swung up up, around, over, rolled into its channel and dropped into place. As always he lost it. After a long time George asked who had thought of them, an architect or who. A genius, Tom said.

He brought them to the Morgue as an afterthought, doubting it would be of much interest. But the librarian, who was having a boring day, brought them behind the counter and through the narrow stacks, and showed them how the photographs were stored against mildew, and volunteered to let them see the front page for the day that each one was born on. It was while they were engaged in their personal histories that Tom discovered Packy Ryan's history. He saw "Grosse Isle" marked on a file as he rambled by, and he pulled it down and read as he stood there, by the dusty light from the basement window.

There was a special feature on 1847, the worst year in the history of the little island in the St. Lawrence River that was the Canadian quarantine station. The medical officer in charge knew the previous winter that there were going to be problems. He asked for £3,000 to make preparations because reports from Ireland indicated that this year's take of immigrants would be very large, very destitute and in very poor health. He got £300, enough to equip a hospital for 150 patients. The St. Lawrence was frozen and impassable until late in the spring, and the first ship from Liverpool arrived on May 17th. There were 241 passengers on board, all Irish, about one-third of them suffering from typhus and fever. Four days later eight ships arrived, and three days after that seventeen more ships came, all of them with starvation and fever victims, living ghosts and skeletons. Inside two weeks there were forty ships anchored in the St. Lawrence, waiting to be inspected, and 1,100 patients on the island, in sheds and tents and laid in rows inside the little church.

The ships from Britain were joined by the ships from Sligo, paid for by landlords because passage was cheaper than the subsidy demanded for tenants in the workhouse. There were no medical staff on board any of the ships. The passengers were given a pound of provisions a day, mostly meal, and shut up in the hold, without air or light. By July there were 2,500 patients, lying on the open ground, rained on and then burned by the summer sun.

The quarantine was abandoned. Those who were well enough to leave were let off after fifteen days at anchor. The dead were ferried away by the boat-load, and the ill and dying were put off to crawl on shore. From where they lay they could hear singing and laughter from the German ships gliding up the St. Lawrence, crowded with immigrants from Hamburg and Bremen who were examined on board and waved on to the New World.

In October the medical officer in charge of Grosse Isle and the eighteen medical assistants who had survived put up a monument on the island.

> In this secluded spot lie the mortal remains
> of 5,294 persons who, flying from pestilence
> and famine in Ireland in the year 1847,
> found in America but a grave.

There was a statistical estimation compiled by the Canadian immigration authorities in a footnote to the story. Of the 100,000 who emigrated to British North America in 1847, almost 40,000 died at sea or on arrival.

Kate was watching him when he looked up. "I've been trying to guess what you're thinking about what you're reading," she said. "I can with some people."

Tom closed the file and slid it back in place. "I was thinking it's probably time to go home."

"You weren't either," she said. She slipped her hand in his when they came out of the stacks and Tom, touched and surprised, squeezed it.

There was a vast stew waiting for them, and a pie from the innards of a pumpkin; the skull sat on the window-sill, drying, waiting to be carved for Halloween. There was a jug of apple cider.

"You've outdone yourself," Tom said.

"I am a woman of great depth and resource when required," Liz replied.

Afterward when Kate brought out the cards Liz took them from her and said, "No old games now, they always end in tears. Sure it's nearly Halloween, I'll tell fortunes for the lot of you."

Andy lit his cigar and sat in the rocking chair with the baby and Liz settled the rest of them around her at the table by the window. She made each of them in turn place their hands on the deck before she shuffled, and then handed the deck back to be cut, and then laid the cards out with delicate precision murmuring, "Yourself, your house, your hopes, your end," over and over. Even the boys paid attention. Kate could expect good fortune, she said, and Tom, a fair-haired woman, but that was some time off; they all laughed. Andy looked sidelong at them, smiling. "Anything else," Tom asked, "a bit more immediate?"

"A surprise," Liz said slowly, turning the card around. "I can't say good or bad. But it won't matter, for the end is a good card."

Henry wished to know if there was a sign of genius anywhere. Liz pondered at length, frowning. "That's not a bad card, now," she said. "There's great promise, but there's hard work before you reach it."

"Ah, that's not in them old cards, you always say that," Henry grumbled and wriggled off his chair and away.

They laughed and laughed as the night lengthened, and everytime the laughter eased off Andy would start them again with another snigger, until Kate was giddy and Liz said her side hurt. It was the last good time Tom had with them, the Saturday night of the trip to the *Tribune*.

Two things happened in the last two weeks of October.

Alexander Sullivan was declared legally innocent of all complicity in the murder of Dr. Cronin, by reason of the failure of the state to find sufficient evidence upon which he could be brought to trial.

And the day before the trial proper was due to open, the prosecution announced that twenty members of Camp 20 of Clan na Gael had agreed to give state's evidence. Andy was one of them. "Sure, there was really no choice," he told Tom. "It was go when asked, or be taken and hanged for obstructing justice."

XX

November, 1889

"AN EPISCOPALIAN INSURANCE clerk, parents American," Tom said. "A Presbyterian sewing machine manufacturer, parents American."

"How about the law book salesman?" Huntley asked.

"Congregationalist. American parents."

"Think you could overlook his race and religion if you thought he read his own products?"

Tom ignored him and went on reading from the news clipping he'd pulled from his wallet. "A Methodist druggist, parents English! A Methodist-Episcopalian real estate agent? Must be a mixed marriage somewhere. Father, American, mother Scottish; didn't I tell you?"

"Ain't none a' 'em got but one vote, same as everyone else, Tom. That makes it a jury a' peers."

"Twelve good men and true, no Irish need apply, no Catholics either. No members of the laboring classes."

"I ain't sayin' it's perfect, but ain't no sign yet it's the Ku Klux Klan either."

Which was true. The jurors were behaving impeccably, appearing equally attentive to both sides. So was Judge McConnell, who'd enraged the State Attorney several times by sustaining objections from the defense to everything not strictly related to the murder. That included about everything Longenecker had to say on the insidious operation of the "Triangle," and since the case establishing a motive for conspiracy was based on the machinations of Sullivan, Feeley and Boland, the counsel for the prosecution was severely frustrated and showing it.

He wasn't having as easy a run as he'd hoped. In two days of opening speeches, Longenecker had made only two points. One was that the state was not, of course, trying Clan na Gael, it was merely exposing the nature of the organization in connection with the trial for murder. Judge McConnell had interrupted, reminding him to keep to admissible evidence. The other was that the evidence the state was going to present was mainly circumstantial. But then, most evidence was, he told the jury.

"Even if you are looking at a man holding a pistol and see him fire it at another, and see the man drop – that is all circumstantial," Longenecker said. "You see the man holding the pistol; you hear the report; you see the other man drop, and you are satisfied that he is shot, and yet you don't see what killed him. The bullet is found in his brain and you saw the man firing the pistol. But these are only the circumstances of the case; only circumstantial evidence."

Tom cut out that report and kept it in his wallet, too.

He was astounded by the newspapers, beginning with their observations on the calibre of the jurors who were finally chosen, after more than a thousand men were rejected. They were not only identified by the press according to occupation, religion and parental nationality, they were also assessed. The law book salesman was "a model juror," the real estate agent "a gentleman of impressive fairness and intelligence."

The commentaries disguised the fact that there was nothing new to report yet. Public interest had in fact lost some momentum after the first few days of testimony, when hundreds and hundreds were turned away from the court. Now it was down to picking over the details once more: Cronin's departure, the discovery of the trunk, the body, the cottage. But every word was transmitted to the public in six or seven columns across the front pages, every day. The papers faithfully refreshed memories, and the people bided their time, waiting for excitement, evidence that would put nooses around necks.

Some of the papers did a little firm guiding. The *Inter Ocean* gave their top writer, Pat Grant, a free run in the first column to analyze the performance of the previous day's witnesses and their effect on the court. He was bluntly partial in his opinions,

Tom complained, but Huntley answered that it was only a question of whether he was less fraudulent than the reporters who sidled opinions into their copy, as he did himself.

They were two weeks into the trial, and, to Tom's relief, so far no one had suggested that he should join the roster of newsroom reporters sent up daily to help out Preston and Huntley. He attended zealously to his new duties, clocking up fire alarms and police calls during the day.

But they didn't altogether distract him. Sometimes, in spite of himself, he wandered down to the criminal court building when his shift ended, to have a drink with Huntley, to listen. The reporters assigned to the trial had become an exclusive set, impervious to other news, other people. They ate together at lunch and drank together in sleek La Salle Street bars at the end of the day, raking the ashes of the case for hidden sparks of insight. There was something seductive about it, Tom had to admit. Huntley was good at sifting through the wrangles that went on all day over technicalities, and at sketching the characters – Luther Mills and George Ingham of Longenecker's team, confident and cold, versus the crafty and slightly desperate defense, Messrs. Forrest, Donahoe and David. He described John Devoy, sitting right behind the defense counsellors, sinking wrathfully into his beard. The prophet now delivering a wayward flock for judgment.

Officially admissible in the court or not, what there was of the Grand Jury evidence that hadn't been leaked to the press before percolated down to them now. Everything pointed to the knavery of the man who wasn't on trial. Dr. Cronin's friends said his documents showed that Alexander Sullivan had sent men to Britain without funds or directions. Many of them fell straight into Scotland Yard's net, and those who escaped roamed London's streets hungry and homeless. The saddest story, though, was the evidence from Willie Lomasney's widow, Susan, the account she had given Dr. Cronin of what befell her after Willie was blown to eternity on the futile effort to destroy London Bridge in 1884.

Mrs. Lomasney went to Sullivan for money to feed her children. He gave her $100 and a ticket back to her family in

Detroit. She had to go like a begging ass, she said, to camp after camp of the Clan. Usually they contributed when they realized her plight. But it wasn't enough, and the sheriff eventually put her and her children out on the street.

The twenty witnesses from Camp 20 weren't due on the stand for some time yet, but the change in Andy was visible. He was keyed up, but at the same time calmer than Tom had seen him for a long time. Some resolution had taken place and it showed, apparently even to employers; he got work bricklaying on the city tunnel, and it looked like it might last until Christmas. Tom was both relieved and afraid. Since Burke and Cooney had been identified, Andy no longer spoke to him about the case. Tom understood that Andy must have known about the two men; they were close enough, all in the Clan together. He might have guessed, or perhaps more, perhaps he was told. But that didn't mean he had decided to speak in court, and Tom ached for him, watching him when they met. He renewed his determination to prove his loyalty – almost his fealty, he felt sometimes – during and after the ordeal ahead. Ordeal, yes, that was the word. In line with what he saw as his new responsibilities to provide moral support, Tom broached it with Liz one evening on the doorstep as she saw him out.

"I know you must feel it will be an ordeal for him, Liz," he said. When she didn't answer immediately, he added tentatively, "He's talked to me about it, you know."

"Talked about what?"

"About how this Camp 20 got involved in deciding to investigate Cronin, and that things got out of hand afterward. But it's only a matter of revealing what he knows in court. That won't be easy, of course, but he has only to tell the truth about what he knows; they can't ask more than that."

Liz nodded and after a moment she said, "Truth is beauty. Isn't that what the poet said?" She shivered, wrapping her shawl tighter. "And it'll be in the eye of the beholder in that courtroom, too."

Tom decided her mood was further proof of the dark rule of polarity that governed marriage. If one was calm, the other must be nervous. While Andy behaved now with a new sense of purpose, Liz seemed to have grown edgier and quieter. He said no more. In any case, she didn't want to talk about the trial any more than Andy. It seemed to Tom they were concentrated on the deliverance that lay ahead. He approved. Whatever the outcome, it would be over.

He was making plans himself, or letting his plans fall into place. He'd accepted with surprised pleasure an invitation to spend Thanksgiving with the Caseys in Edgewater, and he'd come to a decision to leave Mrs. Delaney behind him in the New Year. But he wanted to make this Christmas a gift to Liz and Andy, as they had made last Christmas a gift to him.

"Come on, I'm insisting on it," he said to Liz. "Please let me get a turkey, and presents for the children. You'll have to tell me what they'd like, though."

"I think it's lovely of you," she said. "But we've a long way to go till Christmas. We'll talk before then, surely?"

Midway through November Longenecker had a piece of luck of the kind that attorneys pray for, worthless as admissible evidence but invaluable in the hearts of citizens, including jurors. Failmerzger's men did it again, investigating an obstruction under a Lakeview manhole cover. This time the sewer maintenance crew on duty dug out a foot-long wooden box, and they didn't have to send for anyone to link it with a name once they saw the disintegrating contents – splints, cotton wool, antiseptic fluid. It was Cronin's kit, and underneath was a leather satchel in an advanced state of rot, and a slimy bundle which turned out to be the doctor's clothes.

Next morning the public were wedged elbow to elbow in the halls of the criminal court building. Longenecker had a small bonus, too. The discovery of the box and satchel prompted the jail warders who'd divested Coughlan of his civilian clothes to recall an impressive pearl-handled pocket-knife in Coughlan's pocket, a surgical type of knife. A distressed Mr. Conklin identified it as the doctor's favorite for small jobs. Longenecker got a lot of news space for his comments on the sort of man who could plan a butchery, execute it, and then coolly rob the victim.

But Longenecker didn't really need the knife to pin

Coughlan to the murder plot; Napier Moreland and Mr. Dinan from the livery stable had already done that job. Now Longenecker began to draw in the rope on the others. Mrs. Carlson levelled her gloved index finger from the witness box at the man who'd rented her cottage, looking right at Martin Burke. The justice who had introduced Patrick O'Sullivan to Dr. Cronin told the court how the ice-house owner had pestered him for an introduction. Longenecker took his time, splicing the star witnesses' performances in between the exhibits of the bloodied trunk and scientific verification of blood samples and descriptions of the wounds.

The press expected that he'd take Beggs up next, tying down all four of the Clan men before he turned to the problematic task of explaining why a German laborer would get tangled up in an internecine Irish nationalist dispute. But the Grand Jury had done their job well, and the evidence against Kunze was surprisingly good. Willie James, a sixteen-year-old stenographer, testified that he had seen Kunze in March, from the window of the office where he worked, in a building next to the Windsor Theater where Dr. Cronin had his office. Kunze was in the window of the flat across the street, Willie said. He was going through some contortions to wash his feet at a little hand-sink, and the spectacle particularly diverted Willie because the work Willie was meant to be doing was exceptionally tedious. The court loved Willie. Judge McConnell had to wield the gavel repeatedly to reprove their mirth. Kunze only stared, his uplifted face dazed, the whole time Willie was on the stand.

And Kunze had been seen by two other witnesses. Just two days before the murder, a policeman attached to Chicago Avenue had seen him outside the station house talking earnestly with Dan Coughlan. The policeman had noticed because it looked to him like Coughlan had something on the man, and he liked to know who the contacts in the street were.

Bill Niemann, who kept a saloon in Lakeview, said he had seen Kunze on the night of the murder, and not only Kunze but Coughlan and O'Sullivan as well. They came in between ten and eleven that night, Niemann said, and drank wine, which was an unusual order in his establishment. He thought they

216

looked pretty rumpled, like they might have been drinking all day and weren't up to any more beer or hard liqor. They talked for a long time at a table in the corner, too low for Niemann to hear what they were saying. O'Sullivan paid the bill.

Now it was time for Beggs. Captain Thomas F. O'Connor and Pat McGarry supplied the court with instances demonstrating how heartily Beggs had loathed Cronin, but Longenecker said that the only way he could illustrate the central role John Beggs had played in the brutal murder of Dr. Cronin was to call on those witnesses who could testify to what had taken place in Camp 20. He proposed to begin examination the following day with eight Camp members: Dennis O'Connell, Patrick Nolan, Henry Corcoran, Michael Kelly, Anthony Ford, Stephen Colleran, John Collins, and Andrew Foy. Tom left a note under the Foy's door that night, wishing Andy well.

Twenty-four hours later, in a saloon near the court reputed for the high quality of its cheese and pickles as well as its beer, he found Huntley. Huntley said the best way he could explain what happened with the Camp 20 witnesses was by analogy.

"You know the Chinese proverb about twelve blind men describin' an elephant? Longenecker spent the whole morning replayin' the Grand Jury evidence. What Luke Dillon, this Cap'n O'Connor and the rest had to say about an assassination committee. He was tryin' to establish that this plot to murder Doc Cronin all came out of one meetin', took place on February 8th last. Then he calls up his twenty witnesses and they give twenty different versions a' the meetin' – those that can remember anythin' about it at all."

"I'm not following you very well," Tom said.

Huntley finished off his cheddar, brushed away the crumbs, and got out his notebook.

O'Connell remembered only that there were allegations about a report which Dr. Cronin had made, reflecting badly on the executive of the Clan. Nolan recalled a motion calling for a committee to be established to report only to John Beggs. Corcoran said there had been uproar at the meeting because Captain O'Connor had said that the real traitors in the Clan were in the Triangle. Kelly said that Foy had made a speech which inflamed Captain O'Connor and after a lot of shouting a motion was passed which resolved the dispute, he couldn't remember how.

Ford said that Foy had made a speech and Captain O'Connor had replied, but he couldn't remember whether there had been a motion finally put to end the disturbance. Colleran said he remembered that remarks had been made by Foy and Captain O'Connor and that there was talk of a secret committee being appointed, but he did not recall a motion being put. Collins said that Foy had said there were spies in the order who should be routed, and the meeting had agreed to find out if O'Connor was telling the truth.

Foy behaved peculiar, Huntley said, flipping another page. "Walks straight up full a' bravado to where the prisoners was sittin' when his name is called 'n cries out, 'How are you, Martin?' to this Burke fellow. Shocked the court to the skin. Probably why he did it."

Probably, Tom thought. A slow wave of dismay washed over him.

"Foy says he recalls sayin' a few words to the effect that any spies in the organization should be routed. Cap'n O'Connor implied somethin' offensive about the Triangle that he took exception to, so's he left the meeting to get a drink and cool off, and that's why he wasn't present when any motion was actually put, which didn't mean that a motion hadn't been put." Huntley closed the notebook and pushed his glasses up on his nose.

Tom was silent, and then, realizing a response was expected, asked briefly, "Well? What do you think?"

"Tell you what Pat Grant thinks. Talkin' to him there in the gents, he says the Triangle instructed the whole bunch to get in there and flummox the jury with contradictions, and that's just what they did."

"Maybe they were really confused. Maybe they were scared. People react different ways."

"Maybe." Huntley chewed his pickle reflectively for a long time. "You won't take no offense if I say it's just as well this here Clan ain't takin' control a' the land of your forefathers for a while yet?"

In the days that followed Longenecker got little more satisfaction. He had a surprise witness who thrilled the court with the poignant finish she put on the murder scene. Mrs. Hoertel of Lakeview had been out hunting for her wayward husband and passed the cottage in time to see a tall, well-built man leap from a carriage and run up the steps carrying a case. She was even in time to hear him cry "Jesus!" as the door closed and she went on her way. "Too intent on findin' Hoertel to do him some bodily harm to stick around," Huntley said.

And when the full roster of witnesses was exhausted, there was nothing more substantial to grasp in the way of a plot than there had been on the morning that Mrs. Conklin reported her tenant missing.

XXI

December, 1889

O N SUNDAY, DECEMBER 1st, Tom bought every paper from his newsboy and hurried purposefully back to Locust Street. He spread them out before Liz on her kitchen table, opened to the advertisements for Christmas.

"Look," he demanded. "Holiday books at cut prices. Edna Lyall's books for children, all ages. Guizot's *History of Civilization*, 75 cents. Laboulaye's fairy tales, 95 cents. Or what about Charles Kingsley? Would they like that, do you think, Kate and the boys?"

"For $5.75?" Liz cried, reading over his shoulder. "That's scandalous."

"But it's eight volumes, cloth bound. I'd like to give them something like that, sort of permanent."

She handed him a cup of coffee and bent to stir the fire in the stove with a poker. The cottage was warm and peaceful, in a Sunday morning mood. The two little ones were asleep. Andy had gone with the older children, to mass first, and then to inspect the pine trees already beginning to scent the city, shipped down from the Wisconsin forests to the corner lots where they'd be sold in the next few weeks. There was a promising smell of dinner in the kitchen. Tom had been invited when he arrived, but he was going to meet Casey in Edgewater for the afternoon. Liz tucked more coal into the stove until it blazed and then sat opposite him with her own coffee.

"It's too soon to think about Christmas yet," she said.

"No it's not. There's even snow forecast. Anyway, it cheers me up to think about it," Tom argued. "Doesn't it you, too?"

She only smiled a little in reply. She was warming her hands on her cup, staring into it, and she had never looked quite so drained to Tom before. It hadn't been a good year in any way for her, he thought. "How is the baby?" he asked.

"She took a few steps yesterday," Liz answered, her smile broadening. "She's almost through the first year, and that's the most dangerous. Please God, she'll be stronger from this out."

"Good," Tom said. He had no idea what gifts would be suitable for babies.

"Tom." She looked up at him suddenly. "Do you ever think about patriotism?"

"Patriotism? No, never."

"With all that's happened? This passion for the piece of earth you came from. What do you think about it? I've never heard an explanation that satisfies me."

Tom held back a sigh. "Well, people want to take pride in their own background, I guess," he said uncomfortably. "It's about identity. That's only natural?"

"How much pride is natural, though? Or identity? Why should it be the most important thing there is?"

"I don't think it's the most important thing."

"But a lot of people do. As if this were the most important thing people could share, that they come from the same piece of earth. It's a daft idea, when you think of it. It's something I can't talk to Andy about for two minutes."

"No. I could see that."

She looked back into her cup. "He goes mad if I bring it up. He says I have no political perception or I'd be able to see that national freedom is a fundamental right, and all others will flow from it. Do you believe that?"

Tom considered. "I don't think I have much political perception either," he said. "I can see some truth in it, I guess. I can see that it's wrong for one country to take over another, for instance."

"But it's not that simple. Suppose the Confederate Army had won the Civil War, then there'd be two United States and everyone would think that was right, and that Abraham Lincoln was wrong to try and take over the South."

"Everyone wouldn't, though. Some would go on saying they hadn't a right to be independent and there'd be a lot of arguing

222

and eventually there'd be another war about it." Tom grinned at her. He wanted to see her laugh. "And what about the Indians?" he added. "Suppose they'd beaten the Yankees?"

"Yes, that's just it. If you go back far enough, none of this national pride . . ." She put the cup on the table, and shook her head. "Never mind. Sure, I confuse myself. I just wonder, sometimes, how much of war is about achieving some right or other, and how much is because we're all savages at heart. Fear of other tribes, that's why savages kill. Revenge against the other tribes. No one can back away because if they do the tribe will abandon them. Or kill them," she added drily.

"Oh, come on. There is such a thing as loyalty."

"Yes. Loyalty and betrayal – that's all part of it. Victims and vengeance, loyalty and betrayal. The more death and suffering, the more we have to believe it was all for a good reason. So people go on killing because they're bitter, or ground down, or poor. But the truth is, for most people nothing changes. They aren't more free than they were."

"No." They sat in silence and Tom listened to the wind jiggling stealthily at the windows until he roused himself. "Can't we talk about Christmas?"

This time Liz did laugh. "You talk," she said standing up from the table, "and I'll peel potatoes and listen."

He pushed the page of book listings aside and took up another, advertising Walter Proby's dry-goods store on State Street. Furs and furnishings, imported silks and hand-stitched leather boots; he skipped hastily down the page to the small ads.

A cornucopia of genuine bargains that week only, he read out. Ribbon sale, ribbons of every description at less than the cost of raw silk, sixteen cents a yard, embroidery materials at unheard of low prices, best Angora wool at ten cents per spool. Liz peeled steadily, the potato skins spiralling on to the far edge of the newspaper.

"I think I'd like to go look at the books in the Fair," Tom said. "Here's a hymn book called *Royal Favorites*. Andy wouldn't enjoy it for a joke, would he?"

"I doubt it, somehow. Can I ask you something?"

"What now?"

"Something quite different. Personal, if you don't mind. I was wondering what Christmas was like in the orphanage for you, that's all."

"It was all right," Tom answered. "A lot of praying and church, but we had treats – candy and some toys. Not much. Some had relatives to go to."

"But not you."

"No."

She put the potatoes in the pot and herded the discarded skins into a neat pile, not looking at him. "I've never heard you talk about your own family. But you do remember them, don't you? Your mother, your father?"

"Yes. I do."

"Tell me about them? If you don't mind," she said again. "I'm interested. I'd like to know."

So Tom told her. He told her about his father, who left Mayo for New York but ended up instead in the Pennsylvanian anthracite fields. Not a miner, a laborer, wheeling barrows of coal from the earth's black center to the base of the mine-shaft, ten or twelve hours every day. "I can't remember him. I was six when he died and I can't remember him; all I can do is remember the way he looked, so battered and dirty and thin, when he came home. I don't remember him talking. Maybe he didn't."

Facing the mine-shaft there was one long dirt-road of gray wooden shacks where the workers' families lived, and Tom played there with the other children, waiting until he was old enough to join the boys who picked coal from the slag-heaps for a living. There were three children, Tom and two younger brothers.

The winter Tom was six there was a strike that closed the mines for six months. "My brothers died; I don't know what killed them. First one and then the next day the other. There was no money to bury them and I remember my mother wrapped them up in canvas and my father took them somewhere into the hills and dug graves for them. And then he was killed, he and two other men, in a fire in the company store. They never knew what happened, but the truth must have been they were robbing it and had an accident with kerosene and the lantern. There was a terrible explosion."

They never found anything but charred limbs and stumps of the bodies, and after that Tom's mother took him and went to Baltimore. But none of those memories were very clear to him, Tom said. What he remembered, still in his dreams, and whenever he could not plunge it down into oblivion during the day, was the clawing hunger. "We often went into the fields and dug up whatever we could find to eat. Often. We ate where we stood, chewing herbs down to the roots and then getting sick afterward. Even the children would have killed for food, if we'd known where to get it."

His mother wanted to live in Baltimore because it was a Catholic city. She told Tom that America was a terrible and evil place, but that he would always be looked after among his own. "I think now that she knew from that time what she was going to do. I didn't realize it then, of course, but I saw it after. She got work in the basement of a big house, ironing linen and clothes, all day. Think of that, Liz, think of being so wealthy that you could hire a woman to stand and iron all day in the basement.

"Then one night she put on her hat and coat and went down and slipped into the Chesapeake Bay. I think she thought I'd be better off without her. But someone had seen her, and the police pulled her out. After that she went mad and they put her in the asylum, and the nuns took me away because she didn't know who I was any more."

Then Tom put his head on his arms and cried. Liz got up from where she sat and came around the table and put her arms around him, and comforted him as best she could.

He didn't see her again until the night of the verdict. He'd bought all his Christmas presents by then. Knight's *Shakespeare* for Andy with 400 illustrations, and five of the Windsor series of music and poetry books for Liz, fifty cents each; and the Charles Kingsley volumes, all eight, for the children. They were stowed in his room, tightly wrapped in a brown paper parcel, and every time he thought of how Mrs. Delaney must be tortured with curiosity he smiled.

On December 13th the jury retired. Everyone but Huntley predicted that the verdict would be speedy and the sentence fatal; Huntley held that the evidence just wasn't up to it. There would have to be some long talking and some bloodless compromising, he told Tom. Three days later, at two thirty in the afternoon, the jury brought in its conclusions.

Daniel Coughlan, Patrick O'Sullivan, Martin Burke, guilty of murder. John Kunze, guilty of manslaughter. John Beggs, not guilty.

And no one would hang. "Fellow who took it hardest a' all was John Devoy," Huntley said. "Told everyone who'd listen to him it was a travesty a' justice. How could they find three men guilty a' murder and then let 'em off with life imprisonment, he wanted to know. So," he looked at Tom slyly over his glasses, "seems he's a lot more bloodthirsty than the twelve respectable Protestants you was so het up about."

"All right. I was wrong." Tom said. "I apologize."

"Not to me you don't. He's got a point. For the sort a' murder it was, they got off light."

"You think they should have got the death sentence?"

"Jury couldn't be sure, in the end, or they would 'a swung, all right. But what did they know for certain? Dan Coughlan – hired a rig. Martin Burke – rented a cottage. Patrick O'Sullivan the ice-man – made arrangements with the doctor that he'd come when he was bid. Then this poor German fella, what'd they got on him? He's seen in various places, that's all. Longenecker knew he couldn't get more'n manslaughter for him. I s'pose they figured they'd only put him away for three years 'cause he didn't know what he'd got himself into. And they had nothin' at all on John Beggs. 'Cept that he was the presidin' officer at a meeting a' amnesia victims and patriots with poor hearin'. Can't hang men for a murder conspiracy on that kind a' evidence."

"John Devoy wanted hangings for his own victory, I think," Tom said. "And the papers. They wanted them, too. Percy's face fell a foot."

Huntley shook his head. "Papers wanna think they're fightin' wickedness and helpin' bringin' the guilty to justice.

226

Mighty fly swatters beatin' back a dust storm. But Devoy, he was hopin' if they got death, someone'd talk. Finger Alex Sullivan. That's what Devoy wanted. Half a' Chicago wanted that, too." He stopped talking abruptly and took off his glasses to polish them.

"You think that, too, don't you?" Tom said, watching him. "You think Sullivan was behind it all."

"Ain't got a whisker to connect him with it, I know that," Huntley said easily. He was at his pleasant best. "But who else had anythin' to lose if Cronin stayed alive? Anyway, it's over. They'll appeal, and that'll drag it on longer. Then it'll all die down, and they'll get out on parole someday, when it's all forgotten. Most likely nobody'll ever know what really happened."

To the grave with the secret, part of the oath, Tom thought. Well, it wasn't his business, in the end. He finished his beer and they went back to the paper.

It was coming up to midnight when he finally turned down Locust Street. It was colder; there was definitely snow in the air, you could smell it. Snow for Christmas. He had a week's leave before him and two weeks' pay in his wage packet, and was suddenly light-hearted, in spite of everything. Just as well. He didn't want to think about it any more. They could have a nice Christmas, anyway. He owed them that. He was exhausted, and looking forward now to his bed. The cottage door opened soundlessly as he drew near and Liz stepped out and ran down to him.

"Tom!" Her voice was miserable. "I've been watching for you."

"My God, Lizzie. What is it?"

"Andy. I don't know where he is. He hasn't been home in two days." She clutched his sleeve, her head bent. "I've tried all his friends. They say he hasn't been to Gleason's. I don't know if they're telling me the truth. But I know you've been other places with him, haven't you, Tom? I know you have. I wouldn't ask you this for the world, but I can't leave the children and I'm nearly out of my mind."

"I'll go now," Tom gasped. "Go inside and wait. I'll look everywhere I can think of."

He ran back to La Salle street and found a cab, thinking of the routes of the walks they'd taken in the fall, trying to place the strange saloons they'd paid their short, secretive visits to along the way. But in fact he found him easily, on the third stop, in a place on Wells Street, near the Chicago and North-western Station.

It was a railway bar, with a long front room occupied by a stand-up counter for hurrying passengers. Someone had stuck some tattered holly over the bar in a dismal tribute to the season. There was a back room with a stove, usually closed, but open in winter to accommodate the overflow of strangers stopping be-tween trains. But the last trains had fled into the night an hour ago, and there was no one there but Andy. He was sprawled on a bench against the wall with the evening paper over his face. He looked surrendered to sleep, deadweight. Tom went back out, paid the cabbie, and returned, prepared for a tussle waking him. But he removed the paper instantly when Tom called his name.

"Ah," he said. "The intrepid youth finds me out at last."

XXII

"**F**OR CHRIST'S SAKE, Andy. Liz is nearly out of her mind."

"Liz, Lizzie, Elizabeth, Lisa." Andy swung his legs down and sat up. "I wouldn't worry about Liz. Never. She's a resilient woman. As I'm sure you've noticed. Get the barman there to bring you a glass and we'll have a drink." He reached down on the floor and brought up a bottle of bourbon, nearly empty.

"I don't want one. Andy, come on home. For Christ's sake."

"She hates Liza, did you know that? Finds it affected. An unpretentious woman, is Liz. Where's your glass?"

"I don't want a drink. Andy, please."

"You don't want a drink. Well, I do. Don't worry, I'm coming home. Quietly. Lizzie knows I'll come home." His voice was clear but his eyes were bloodshot and wandering. He fished about on the floor and produced a shot glass, and began to pour carefully. There was only a trickle left.

"Where have you been? Where did you sleep?"

"Why, I had a selection of choice accommodation, Tom, thanks for asking. Every station in Chicago throws its hospitable doors open at midnight, you know that. I have spent my nights in the company of that class most honored by the father of Irish republicanism. The men of no property." He stopped and drank the shot. "That is not good bourbon," he added reflectively "I can't recommend it to you. You do know to whom I refer? The father of Irish republicanism, Tom? Wolfe Tone. You've heard of him, young narrowback?"

"Andy. Stop."

Andy dropped his eyes to his glass. "All right," he said after a moment. "I'll stop. You have been a friend to me. You walked the streets with me when I needed to walk the streets, and I won't forget that. So, fair enough," he added. "I've no call to be insulting."

"Andy," Tom said, hesitating. "I know you're upset."

"Up-set," he spoke in mechanical syllables. "I am up-set. Why, that is a very nice way to put it, very genteel, I think. I think I'll have another drink." He stood up and walked to the far side of the room, not too steadily, and rapped carefully at the small hatch opening to the bar. The bartender looked out at him and shook his head. "No more, buddy," he said. "You've had sufficient and I gotta close."

"Suff-ish-ent? Suff-ish-ent?" The bartender shut the window and Andy leaned against it, knocking lightly and rhythmically. "Not so wide as a church door," he recited, "nor so deep as a well, but t'will suffice. Mr. Shakespeare. My God!" He stopped knocking and stood upright, staring ahead. "That's just what I thought about Cronin, that very line. Isn't that strange. To think of that now."

"Andy," Tom began again. "Andy, it's all over now. You can forget about it. Whatever you decided to do in court, you had your reasons and it's over and done with." Whatever happened, Tom thought. And whatever you know.

"All over now. All over." Andy turned and focused with difficulty on Tom. Then he reached up and ran his fingers through his hair, dragging it down over his eyes. "Look at me, Tom," he said intently. "Look. Are you looking?" He lifted his voice to thin, pitiful pitch. "Chudge! Chudge! Mein Gott in Himmel, Chudge! Eet is oaffer, all oaffer!"

"Stop it, Andy! God Almighty." Tom looked away.

"Ein must go to chail for t'ree years. Mein Gott, vat haf I done?"

"Andy, sit down."

"I haff offended choo? But choo are not looking! Vat are you t'inking?"

Tom glanced at him, repelled, and looked away again. "I think it's in very poor taste to mock the poor devil, that's what I think. And I think we should go. Now. You're very drunk."

After a minute Andy spoke again. "You don't see, do you?" he said in a reasonable tone. "You don't see anything, Tom. Nothing at all. Look, Tom. You've got to look."

"Andy, I'm begging you to stop." But Tom felt something jump, a pulse somewhere in his throat. One small, sure jump, that was all; but suddenly he knew. It was right there staring at him; he had only to raise his eyes.

"Washing my feet," Andy said softly. "And talking to Dan Coughlan on the corner, Tom. And," he hissed, staggering over to him, "in Billy Niemann's saloon? Couldn't we be twins, poor Kunze and myself?"

There was no sound in the back room but the sputter of the gas-lamp. Tom could hear the smothered screams from the Chicago and Northwestern, the trains slotting into their sidings for the night, as he sat there, perfectly still. When he looked up Andy nodded, encouraging him, baiting him to speak. "You," Tom said. "It was you."

He started to stand but Andy cried "No!" sharply and seized him by the wrist, yanking him back into the chair. "No! Goddamn you. And I'm not drunk, not drunk at all, Tom. I haven't been drunk since. I cannot get drunk. I cannot, and I'm going to explain it to you, Tom. Because it seems senseless, but there were reasons; there's a reason for it, all of it. Are you listening, Tom? Listen now."

Andy began to talk swiftly in his light, rythmic way, leaping from one sentence to the next as if he was describing something he was watching. Tom sat with his wrist pinioned. It hurt. He could still feel the pulse, or perhaps it was his heart, throbbing and alert.

"There was supposed to be a gun. One shot from a pistol, straight through the heart. Or the eyes, if he didn't twist away too soon; straight through the eyes to the brain. That was the plan. We waited all day but the gun never came. So we had to use whatever there was.

"I had a chisel and the claw-hammer. From my tools; I had them because it had to look as if I was going to a job somewhere. And there was an ice-pick. Pat Cooney made O'Sullivan get it from the ice-house. I said why, for God's sake, and Pat said because it doesn't look like Coughlan's going to get here with the gun, does it? I knew then he was right, we'd have to do it any way we could. But even the ice-pick wasn't enough. He kept getting up. Every time he dropped to the ground he got up again. Once he dropped into the chair. The chair, sitting straight up in the chair; and he ripped the arm off it and got up again, as if he was going to fight back.

"There was so much blood he must have been dead, and he kept getting up, staring at us. Jesus God, he saw us perfectly, all three of us. But he never spoke. He said nothing. That was a lie, what the old woman said: he never cried out 'Jesus' or anything else. Nothing. And that's when I thought, it won't suffice. A little wound not so deep won't suffice."

He pulled Tom's wrist nearer to him, suddenly and deftly, and stopped speaking. When he spoke again his voice had dropped lower still. "We were drunk; yes, yes, we were very drunk. If we hadn't been kept to wait like that, all day, we would never have drunk so much. Coughlan let us down. He'll be done for that now, when they're inside. Martin Burke and O'Sullivan will have to make him pay for what's happened. Because it could have been right. He came just the way he was meant to, got in the buggy when Martin came for him on the emergency, just as he was meant to. But it was already too late. We'd waited so long. And we had to do it anyway, there was no way to go back then. And then we had no way to clean it up, there was so much blood. We found the paint and used that to try and cover it any way we could, and we got him into the wagon. But it took too long, it was too late to get to the boat. And there were cops out. Martin said he'd been noticed."

He stopped again. There was no sound at all in the little room now, and the lamp had all but flickered out. Tom held still, not daring to breath. Andy began once more in the same running monotone, each sentence complete but separate, falling into the well of silence.

"He was supposed to be dropped in the lake, out far; pushed over the side out far tied up with the weights. We forgot about the weights, though, it was too late and we had to leave him somewhere. We were watching for cops. Martin said they were out, he'd seen them earlier. They would have stopped us. Then we had to hide the clothes where we could go back for them. But there was no chance, not after the searching started. If we hadn't waited all day and drunk so much it would have been different. They would have found his clothes on a dead man in London with a note in the pocket to prove what he was, a rotten yellow spying bastard who was on the verge of destroying us."

Andy tightened his grip on Tom's wrist without warning and Tom cried out helplessly. "Are you listening, Tom? That's where he should have been, on the bottom of the lake where only the fishes would see him, and then in two weeks, or three weeks, there would be a man found dead in London who'd be him instead."

He released Tom's wrist. "But now there's Kunze being me instead of me." He closed his eyes and leaned back. "And now I can't get drunk."

Tom didn't move. He knew Andy was watching him. His hand was numb but there were sharp pains shooting up his arm to his shoulder; he thought wildly of the ice-pick.

"And Tom? Look at me, Tom," Andy said. Tom raised his eyes. "Liz knows, Tom." Andy smiled, a sad, malicious smile watching Tom's face, and then closed his eyes again. "Oh, yes, she knows. Liz knows everything."

After a long time Tom heard the door scrape open and the bartender came in, shuffling toward the table until he stopped behind him.

"Mister, you gonna get this stiff outta here, or what? It's starting to snow out there and I wanna get home."

Tom lifted his head. Andy had passed out. "Yes." He cleared his throat. "I wonder if I could ask you to try and hail a hack. I'm sorry for the trouble." He noted that his voice was fine. He moved his arm for the first time, carefully, and reached in his pocket for a fistful of coins which he spread pointedly out on the table. The bartender, mollified, disappeared, and Tom began to rub his wrist. He did sound fine, assured, someone else. It was how he had sounded that day, a long time ago now, when he chatted so easily to Nanda. He remembered her voice

233

too, light and sweet, and how warm and promising the day had been. What an extraordinarily pretty girl she had been. Or was, somewhere. At home with her family eating Greek sweets for Christmas. Tom imagined Nanda licking sticky fingers in a warm, stuffy little room over the shop, laughing up at someone. He might have had an entirely different life this year, Tom thought. He might be someone else now, someone quite different.

The bartender came back, announcing the hack, and Tom persuaded him to help haul Andy outside. The cabbie wasn't happy about taking them, but Tom promised him that Andy would not be sick, certainly not.

When they got to Locust Street, Tom handed the cabbie the rest of the coins in his pocket and between them they hauled Andy in and up the boxy little steps to the attic floor. Liz went ahead of them, her finger to her lips as they passed the sleeping children. Tom averted his eyes from the bed and the room and left her there while he went back down and saw the cabbie out. There was an empty roaring noise in his head.

He waited, standing in the doorway to the kitchen. It was dark; the lamp had been put out and the fire in the stove was nearly gone, only a few red coals like gashes in the grate. Liz came in and sat down but he didn't move. He wondered if she would ask where he had found Andy, in a woeful but grateful way, and what he would answer and how his voice would sound.

But in an even voice she asked whether he'd been asleep when Tom found him, or awake.

"He was awake," Tom said.

"And he talked for a while, did he?"

"Yes."

"What did he say?" She still sounded cool. But there was something else, too. Tom could barely see her, outlined in the light from the dying grate.

"He said you knew everything," he said finally.

She answered after a long time, her voice full of contempt. "I thought he might do that. He could have at least spared you that. But no."

"It's all true, then," Tom whispered. "All this time."

234

"Are you going to tell me what he told you?"

"You know," he said again, louder.

"I know he followed his orders. That's what I know."

"He's a murderer." Tom felt such a spurt of fear when he said it that he stepped backward. "You knew. You lied, about everything."

"There were no lies," Liz cried out, but her voice was low. "Some evasions, yes, all right. For your sake. What happened was something you didn't need to ever know."

There was no sound in the kitchen. Tom tried to see her face but it was too dark. "I will go to the police," he said.

"Will you? What will you say?" She sounded remote, only mildly curious. "Perhaps they would believe a drunken man's rantings. You will be the informer then. You won't live long. Will it do any good?"

"Yes."

"You would have to say he obeyed orders. He gave his allegiance and that meant he would be ready to take action when the time came. Only it didn't mean he would get to choose the action; it meant he'd be ordered what to do. Just like the card game the children play, that's the way it works. There isn't any other way, you can see that. So they think it's all going to mean doing something brave and important, and what it really means is doing things like savage animals in the darkness and being terrified and mad. You have to believe that it's all part of the cause, in the end, even if you can't understand it."

"You don't believe that," Tom said.

"No. I do not believe it," she said coldly. "But Andy believes it. Andy believes that there was a traitor, because they told him so. Because Alex Sullivan said so. Andy believes there's only one thing to do with a traitor. Andy believes he had to do what he had sworn to do, and I'm not sitting in judgment on him."

"I am," he said. His fear was gone. He kept his eyes away from her, on the angry little red coals in the grate, and he felt mute rage gathering. "I judge him. And I judge you."

"If it's any consolation to your judgment, the others have been judged. Two of them. Caught and judged. And found guilty."

"But what about the others, the planners? And what about Kunze? He's been judged guilty and he's innocent of everything, isn't he?"

"They say he'll be let off on appeal. I hope it's so."

"They say. They give orders and they say. But Kunze might not be let off, and he's already suffered, and that makes no difference to you."

"There is nothing I can do. Nothing, nothing at all. Some get away and some suffer for no reason. And the ones who give the orders, they never get caught. I can't change any of that. I condone nothing. And I leave judgment to God."

Tom took two steps toward her and stopped, unable to think. She hadn't moved since she sat down and she didn't move now. But the moon had risen, and he could see her quite clearly in the light reflected from the snow, which had begun to fall in thick and silent waves beyond the window. He knew his voice would crack if he spoke. She said nothing at all and looked at him with no expression.

He left her there and went out and up the street, battling through the snow. Inside his room he yanked the case out from under the bed, where he had pushed it just a year ago, the week before Christmas. He packed everything that he had, the row of books on the table and the shaving things on the window-ledge, his clothes. Then he waited by the window. The street below was coated with snow, brilliant under the moon.

When it was light Tom rose and put on his jacket and cap, and dragged the parcel full of Christmas presents for the Foy's out to look at it. He stood for a long time deliberating. Then he got out his pencil and notebook and wrote a note for Mrs. Delaney to say that he had been called away urgently, to see an aunt who was dying in Baltimore. He left that on the table with the money for his week's lodgings. He addressed an envelope then to Huntley, care of the *Tribune*, and wrote another note almost as brief: "I have had to leave suddenly. I am all right, and will write again. Thank you, for everything."

Then he started on a third sheet of paper.

"The great evasion is to invoke God or posterity," he wrote. "It means you can do what you want. The rest of us have a right to roast you on earth in case there's no God to do it later." He folded that several times and wrote "Mrs. Foy" on the outer flap and put it in his pocket.

He set out with the case in one hand and the parcel under his arm. The street was deserted, and the drifts of snow were up to his knees. When he got to Foy's he set the case down and felt for the note in his pocket, but he didn't take it out. He studied the door carefully for a minute and then picked the case up, dangerously sodden now on the bottom, and went on. On La Salle Street he found a lone, shivering cabby. Tom asked him to take him to Union Station, with some stops along the way. He asked him if he knew where there might be an orphanage and the cabby said there was the new place, Hull House, on the westside. Go there on your way, Tom told him, but first to the *Tribune*, where he could leave in a letter.

The cabby charged him a massive lot of money for the journey, with an extra charge for the snow. When he got to Union Station Tom compared the destinations of the day's trains and the amount he had left, and subtracted what it would take to stay alive somewhere for a week. He took the first train to Indianapolis, and before he left he threw the note for Mrs. Foy into the stove in the station waiting-room where it vanished in a curl of black smoke.

Epilogue
December, 1909

"TOM MARTIN. I knew it was you."

"Kate. It is Kate, isn't it?"

"Oh, I knew I was right, it is you!" She smiled broadly, almost childishly pleased with herself, before she recalled the circumstances and stepped forward. "You're very good to come," she said, and took his hands.

Tom fumbled for the phrase and said he was sorry for her trouble and they stood like that for a moment, caught in the convention, until he asked, "How in God's name did you recognize me?" and she released his hands.

"I saw your name in the book before mass began and I thought, no, it couldn't be, it must be someone else with the same name; and then on the way out I noticed you sitting there next to the pillar alone and I thought, well, who knows, perhaps it is. So I thought I'd just wait a little longer, just in case. My, it's so strange to see you. Mama will be so surprised. But you didn't come out to speak to her!"

"No," he said hurriedly. "I didn't think – well, it's been such a long time, I thought I'd just write my name and leave it at that."

"But you'll come to the house now! Won't you? I'm going ahead to get things ready at home for people coming back. That's why I could wait on a bit, satisfy my curiosity. I'd rather go to the grave myself. Later in the week, sometime when there's no one else there." She looked down, frowning, and Tom said quickly that he could understand that.

"You were great friends with my father, weren't you?" she asked.

"I was. Very."

"I knew that. He was a good father, in spite of everything," she said. "Oh, you were very good to come." She smiled at him again, so warmly that he looked away, out onto the church steps. "I'm sure Mama would be so pleased to see you."

"Let me walk with you," he said evasively. They went out together. No, Kate said, not Locust Street anymore, they'd left Locust Street long ago. They lived on Franklin now, nearer downtown. She and George were the only ones left at home. The rest were all married. He probably wouldn't remember George, she said. He was the youngest of the boys. Tom nodded and inserted questions as she talked. In spite of everything, he thought. But how much would she remember?

"And you live in South Bend now, I saw in the book? When did you leave Chicago?" She kept glancing at him sideways underneath the veil.

"It's twenty years now," Tom said. "I worked for a while at various things in Indianapolis and then I decided I wanted to teach and I went back and got a degree. So now I teach. At Notre Dame."

"And did you marry?"

"Oh, yes. My wife is from there. A native. We have two children, a boy and a girl."

"A native?" This time she turned around to face him, surprised.

"Yes. An Indiana girl, family there for generations."

She threw back her head and laughed and Tom thought with a small twist of pain how very like Liz she looked, just at that moment. "I thought you meant an Indian," she said gleefully. "I was thinking how exciting! Oh my, I hope I haven't offended you." He shook his head, smiling with her. So that expression had not gone in a generation. They walked on, up toward the river, and finally Tom asked how her mother was. Fine, Kate said; sad, of course, but fine. It must be hard on her, Tom said, probing warily. They had been together such a long time. Kate agreed, yes, it was hard, but he had died suddenly in the end without too much pain. Then she looked up at him again, shrewdly. She really looked more like Andy, Tom decided.

"I remember it all, you know," she said. "Everyone tries not to talk about it, but I was sixteen when she went into court and said everything. That's what you are thinking about, isn't it?"

Tom nodded. Yes, that was it. He had followed it all, every day, and kept the newspaper clippings in his cubbyhole in the university. They were probably still there somewhere, with other clippings.

There was one from January of 1890 on Kunze's release. Judge McConnell had ordered a new trial in a move that no one, on reflection, could really disagree with. McConnell said the evidence against Kunze was absurdly slight. Longenecker never attempted to try him again. "They" had been right about that.

The other clips came later. The Illinois Supreme Court had eventually agreed to an appeal on behalf of Coughlan, O'Sullivan and Burke, on the grounds that two of the jurors had been biased against them. It was January of 1893 by then, and too late for Burke and O'Sullivan. Both of them had died in the state penitentiary. Tuberculosis, the death certificates stated. Two young and healthy men, killed by unhealthy conditions in prison – or perhaps by other means. The reports were never clear about what happened.

So it was only Coughlan who was returned to Chicago for trial. This time the state produced a spectacular witness, the estranged wife of Andrew Foy. She was in the witness box for four days. She said Coughlan and her husband had met several times, that Coughlan had planned the murder on secret orders from the Clan, unknown to Camp 20 or its leader Johnny Beggs; orders which would have come directly from the leadership. But she broke down under cross-examination and wept, again and again, agreeing that her husband had left her for long periods of time in the four years since the murder, without any way to support her children.

She was desperate, she said; and she admitted that she had accepted help from Mrs. Conklin – clothes for the children, and a rug for her floor. The defense suggested that she was an unstable woman, driven by revenge and probably induced by bribes.

In the witness box Mrs. Foy said that she was tired of deceit and wanted only, finally, to tell the truth. But no fair-minded juror could send a man to the gallows on her evidence, and Coughlan was acquitted.

Tom decided that he might as well ask Kate what he wanted to know. "Why do you think she did it?"

They went on walking. Kate looked straight ahead. She was even more like her father in profile. "I remember that she said to me once that we have to prevent as much insane tragedy as we can, because it took all the strength there was to live with what we couldn't prevent. But I don't know if that means anything, because she didn't prevent anything, did she? I think she was a little crazy then. It was the same year that Marie died."

"Marie," Tom said. "The baby. She was always frail, and your mother worked so to keep her well."

Kate looked at him again, pleased that he remembered that. Yes, she said, and her mother had succeeded. Marie thrived and by the time she was four she was as sturdy a child as any. She was killed on the Fourth of July that year, 1893, when a cherry bomb exploded at her feet. The boy who'd flung it into their yard had turned the corner running. He never knew what happened, and they never knew who he was. At Marie's funeral, Kate said, her mother kept telling people how thankful she was that she didn't have to live knowing who had done it, and he didn't have to live knowing what he'd done. So she was a little crazy, Kate said. Everyone said so.

They walked on, and when they reached the next corner Tom stopped and held out his hand. "Kate," he said, "will you forgive me if I don't come back to the house? Maybe someday. But not today."

She took his hand slowly. "It isn't anything I've said?"

"No. Absolutely not. I can't tell you how glad I am that I met you."

"I wasn't sure. I will tell Mama we talked a bit, though."

"Whatever you think. Tell me this – were they estranged, as the papers said, your mother and father? I've always hoped that it was all right, afterward." He felt very weary.

242

"It was all right," Kate said simply. "That was just what it was. Papa was away a lot but he came back. He didn't work too much these last years but he didn't drink much either, which is what Mama hated most. She was always a little afraid of that. But he read and stayed home. And then he had the grandchildren, you know. To tell stories to and sing his songs. So it was all right. They did what people do. They just went on living."

He watched her until she was almost out of sight and then he turned left. Michigan Avenue lay ahead. It made him think of Huntley. Huntley was the only person in Chicago Tom had kept in touch with, from time to time. Huntley was killed in a freak accident, too. Not directly. He'd gone down to the Mexican border to write a piece about the military stationed there in the Spanish-American war and had been caught in a stampede of donkeys. The incident caused a lot of satirical comment at the time. Huntley was injured and mustn't have paid much attention to it, because he got complications weeks later, and they couldn't get medical attention in time to save him from the agony of slow death by gangrene.

But he and Liz would go on living, as people do. Dan Coughlan, too. After Coughlan was acquitted, he went to Michigan for a while and then came back to Chicago and opened a saloon. In 1899 he was arrested with six others on charge of running a jury bribing ring. He jumped bail. The newspapers said he was believed to be living since in Honduras.

And Alexander Sullivan. Tom had also followed Sullivan's path through the papers. In 1901 Sullivan was convicted of helping a jury briber to jump bail, but the case was thrown out on a technicality. The Chicago Bar Association eventually tried to disbar him because he was beginning to look a little too tarnished, but they were overruled by the Illinois Supreme Court. Peg died while that was going on. But Alex went on living. He'd been elected just the year before to the elite Irish Fellowship Club, in a tribute from prominent Irish nationalists for his long years of service to the cause of freedom in his native land.